M THAT ONE OMENT

THAT ONE MOMENT

TERESE LORAE SMAULDON

Urban soul

URBAN BOOKS

www.urbanbooks.net

URBAN SOUL is published by

Urban Books
1199 Straight Path
West Babylon, NY 11704

ISBN-13: 978-1-59983-101-5
ISBN-10: 1-59983-101-5

First Printing: June 2009
10 9 8 7 6 5 4 3 2 1

Printed in the United States of America

Acknowledgments

Toni Morrison once said, "If there's a book you really want to read, but it hasn't been written yet, then you must write it." That statement, in a nutshell, was the inspiration for creating this book. I wanted to write a story for women about self-discovery . . . about following your heart and finding yourself in the process. And throughout my own process of completing this project, there were some important people who really believed in my dream. Thank you to . . .

My agent, Sha Shana Critchon, for her fierce dedication to this project; my content editor, Nicole Peters, for helping me streamline my ideas; and Urban Soul Publishing for giving me the opportunity to share my vision of what a novel should be.

My wonderful parents, Barbara and Gerald Smauldon, who have supported everything I've ever done. And of course, my biggest fan and my biggest critic (in writing and in life), my beautiful sister and best friend, Helese.

I'd also like to thank the following people, new friends and old, for putting up with me through the years since I started writing this book in 2003. Whether it was giving much needed motivation, or simply sharing a few laughs over happy hour, I appreciate your presence in my life. Trust me, I know I'm not always the easiest person to love, like, and know.

Liselle, Kayla, Micah, Wan, LA, Jules, Akinfe, Dave, Crys, Khy, Marques, Christa, Jess, "the Nicoles", Tomekia, Nic, Kaye, and Jose.

You have all inspired me in ways you may never know.

Finally, to the readers: Thank you for letting me into your minds and, hopefully, into your hearts.

Chapter 1

Lia

Wow. I'm not one to brag, but looking this damn good should be illegal. My black Louis Vuitton stiletto boots are zipped up to right below my knees. My dark blue, low-rise mini jean skirt is hugging my ass just right. And my red blouse with a V-neck down to my belly button is ever so cleverly covering my 34-Bs. A simple ponytail and Chanel earrings seal the deal. I'm not really into makeup. I don't have to be with a face this perfect. Well, maybe not perfect, but as close as anyone will get. Sorry, but Halle Berry has nothin' on Lia Wells. Because my daddy is black and my mother is Korean, I was blessed with a graham cracker complexion, slanted black eyes (but not *too* slanted), full lips, very straight, jet-black hair (that doesn't curl up when I wash it), cheekbones from heaven, and, well . . . I guess you get the picture. I love my blackness, but I love it even

more because of my Asian-ness. That's a big issue I have
with some of my friends, but more about that later. Right
now I'm on my way to Janet Jackson's album release party.
I work for Virgin Records on their legal team and I'm
always getting into the hottest parties. Of course I invite
my three best friends every time, but the only one who has
ever come is Jas. The other two, Rena and Dee Dee (the
only white girl in our circle . . . well, something like that.
I'll explain later), are either (a) dealing with kids or (b)
dealing with husbands. Jas and I are the only true single
ones left, and as far as I can tell, it's going to stay that way
for a long time.

The phone rings and it's Jas telling me she's in front of
my building in a cab and to hurry my black ass up. I grab
my LV bag and rush toward the elevator. I live on the ninth
floor of a very chic condominium complex in SoHo. My
rent is about twenty-five hundred a month, but it's definitely worth it. After all, you get what you pay for, right?
Mostly businessmen and their young, blond trophy wives
live here. Very rarely you'll see a single, twenty-nine-year-
old "blasian" attorney such as me moving in, and honestly,
I haven't seen any others since I've been here. I love my job
and the work that I do for the company. It's gotten me
pretty wealthy in a short amount of time. I graduated from
NYU with a dual degree in East Asian studies and English
when I was twenty years old because of the fact that I graduated from high school when I was fifteen. Call me a
prodigy if you want; I just had a plan. From there I went on
to law school all the way across the country to UCLA.
Even though I was an army brat growing up, I had never
lived on the West Coast and wanted a change. And being
three thousand miles away from my parents was just icing.

That's when I made my Virgin connections. A guy I
dated for a few months introduced me to an intern who I
stayed in contact with. After I received my law degree

three years later, he was working for Virgin full-time as the head of the publishing department. Four interviews later I was working for the company. Six years later I'm practically the highest-ranking member of the team, VP of Legal Affairs. Of ten lawyers, only two of us are women and I am the only "ethnic" face in the bunch. It's really a big accomplishment. I'm proud of what I've done with my career . . . some might say a little too proud, but screw them. It was hard, but I earned every moment of it. No one in corporate America really wants to see a woman, especially a woman who's not white, in a position of power. But guess what? I'm here and I'm staying. I'm extremely good at what I do, and no, I've never had to have sex with anybody to move up in my career. Just so happens that I was more determined, ambitious, and, hell, I'll say it, smarter than my competition. Unfortunately, Jas doesn't seem to mind a little office sex here and there to get where she wants to be.

As I get to the lobby of my building, I see a tall, honey-colored man entering the double glass doors to the complex. His dark gray (obviously Armani) suit is tailored to fit his (obviously in-shape) body. His shoulders are wide . . . not linebacker wide, but just enough so you can tell he works out (or just has excellent genes). And his ass. Jesus! I know I shouldn't be staring, but I can feel my eyes lingering a few seconds too long on each part of his body. Even his hair is sexy. He has a low haircut that accentuates his dark eyebrows and even darker eyes so well. He glances up as he walks to the front desk and flashes the whitest, straightest set of teeth I have ever seen. I smile back, embarrassed that I had been caught staring, and dart outside the doors. Gorgeous. That's the word to describe him. And if I dated black guys I would definitely be interested. Yes, it's true. I don't deal with black guys. Sue me. I mean, I love my father, a black man, and all the other black men in my family, but . . . I don't want to be with one. I prefer white, Asian, Puerto Rican, or those "other" guys. At the very least, mixed, like myself. The truth is, I've never had a good experience with a black guy. There was always some hidden motive, some unsaid reason why they wanted to date me. It was as if I were some kind of prize. And they didn't consider themselves selling out because I'm not white, even though they secretly loved the fact that I'm not fully black. They would say some stupid things like, "Is that all your hair?" And for some reason they had this horribly wrong notion that I'm some submissive, head-giving geisha type of woman who just wants to please her man all day long. Me? I'd laugh if it wasn't so ridiculous. Honestly, it got annoying.

That's yet another issue I have with some of my friends, Rena mainly. I met Rena years ago at an alumni fundraiser for NYU. She's this mother earth type of woman who has long (and I have to admit, beautiful) dreadlocks, and attends a spoken word group on Wednesdays when her baby's daddy comes and takes Lion. Yes, her four-year-old son is named Lion Garvey (after Marcus Garvey, the slave revolutionist, for those not up on black history) Redding. Rena is an African-American studies professor at the Brooklyn campus of Long Island University. Her students always adore her. You know how some people teach just for the sake of teaching? Well, Rena really loves her subject and she feels a level of personal responsibility for every person who takes her class. She puts her all into her lectures and assignments. She truly wants all her students to do well. As a matter of fact, her baby's daddy is an ex student of hers. Tak (it's really Oluatakamen or something like that) is straight from Nigeria and about six years younger than Rena. And the rest of us applaud her for it. First of all, he's got a Tyson Beckford/Tyrese thing going on. He looks like what I'd think an African warrior would be. Six feet four inches of dark chocolate splendor, muscular . . . but with an innocent face and a mind-blowing smile. I mean, Tak probably could have had his pick of any woman in NYC. There are a lot of young, nice-looking ladies out here who would gladly beat the next woman with a bat to get a chance with Tak. But he chose Rena, older, settled, and sexy in an understated sort of way. For a young guy, he's got it together. He works with at-risk kids helping to implement programs in different communities that try to show them alternatives to the streets. I think Rena was telling me that he's trying to get into grad school, and hopefully get a few grants to start a scholarship program. So really, the two of them complement each other very well. Not to mention he has all the basics; a car, his own place, and the only baby he has is with Rena. The two of them standing next to each other is an "interesting" sight, to say the least . . . Rena with her light skin and five-foot, three-inch, hundred-and-twenty-pound frame. But they have a bond tighter than most married couples I know. If they ever do get married, though, only time will tell.

So I get to the cab and see Jas's face all twisted and annoyed. I don't care, though. Jas is never on time for anything but these parties, so why is she so frustrated that I'm a little behind schedule? That's probably why she can't keep a job now . . . that and the fact that she sleeps with almost every guy in the office. I love Jas like a sister, but the girl is a little bit slutty. Okay, she's a total slut. I try not to judge because we all have our personal demons, but I worry about her. She's always meeting some new guy, and sure, he spends his money to keep her around, but come on. That life can make you happy only for so long. Something has to be missing inside for her to be content with the way she's living.

Jasmine Lewis, small-town girl from some off-brand place called Aiken, South Carolina, made it to New York on a music scholarship to Marymount Manhattan College.

It was the first time she had ever been outside her little down South world, which remains ten years behind the rest of the country, and it showed in everything she did and said. She had never been on a subway or even seen a skyscraper. Poor thing is very lucky she was blessed with musical talent or else who knows where she would have ended up? Jas can play the hell out of almost any brass instrument you place in front of her. But her first love is the piano.

Now, at twenty-four, and the youngest of our group, she's bouncing from job to job every six months or so, trying to land some rich guy who will take care of her forever. I think that's a large part of why she comes to these parties with me. At first I thought it was to make connections, and maybe meet someone who could help her refine her skills and pursue music professionally. After all, I originally met her while she was interning at Virgin. But now I know better. I haven't heard Jas mention her music in months. After she graduated I thought she would go on to grad school or at least teach music theory, technique . . . something. But now it's all about meeting men and maybe enticing one for long enough to get a few hundred or, if she's lucky, a few thousand bucks to go shopping or pay a bill. If it were all about looks, she would have found someone already. But men don't want just a pretty face. Well, the men who are worth the time don't, at least. Jas is a very pretty brown-skinned girl with a beautiful smile, a flawless complexion, and a great figure, big hips, small waist, and big breasts. She reminds me of a taller, thicker Toni Braxton. She has that short, sleek pixie cut that Toni had back when she first came out in the nineties singing "Seven Whole Days," but unlike Toni, Jas's dresses are always too short, as short as her attention span. She has her eyebrow and tongue pierced (a way she rebelled against her small-town roots when she moved here) and she wears tiny silver jewelry in each.

But Jas is so hard to take seriously. A year ago I tried to get her a job working with a friend of mine at another record label. Homegirl didn't even show up for the interview. Yeah, and silly me also tried to hook her up with a guy who used to manage Lauryn Hill. They went on one date, had sex, and Jas refused to see him again because "he's not ambitious enough." All that really means is that he wasn't the actual president of the whole management company; therefore he couldn't afford her. I know she can date whom she wants, but the guy was really hurt. And she always does that. If he's not a Denzel clone (with a matching career and bank account), he's not good enough. Needless to say she'll be single for a long time. And after that, I vowed never to get involved with her career or love life.

"Tell the driver where we're goin', Lia. I've never heard of this club, Majestic," says Jas, her tone sounding rushed and ready to go.

"It's by Penn Station. Thirty-fourth and eighth," I tell the cabdriver while checking my bag to be sure I brought the invitations. This party is not a hundred percent exclusive, but not having an invite when you're not a recognizable celebrity means you'll be in the line, hoping to be let into the club.

The driver doesn't say a word as he takes off. I take a minute to check out Jas's outfit. A fly-ass black and white kimono-style dress by KLS and black, three-inch stiletto pumps that wrap around her ankles. Her hair is freshly done (I swear, the world could be on fire but you better believe she will not miss her weekly hair appointments) and she smells like Escada's Ibiza Hippie.

"Have you spoken to Dee recently?" she asks me as she reapplies her MAC lip gloss with a hint of pink for the third time. I think she's addicted to the stuff.

"She left me a message yesterday. Something about Deron, I think. But I haven't called her back yet."

Deanna "Dee Dee" Smalls (formerly Dee Dee Rodriguez) has been married to Deron for almost four years. In that time they have separated twice, gotten back together, and she has given birth to one chubby-cheeked, wide-eyed daughter named Deidre. Dee Dee, auburn-haired, tan, tall, and thin, looks like she just stepped out of a Lord & Taylor ad every day. Always classy and put together, and never one to follow trends. She grew up on Long Island with a trust fund and a silver spoon. She told me once that her family traced their roots back to a royal family in Spain. Her father was once affiliated with the Spanish ambassadorship to America, and her mother was (and still is if you ask her) a famous actress in Europe. She was the equivalent to America's Marilyn Monroe . . . sexy, but still respected. I don't think Dee Dee had ever worked a day in her life. Until, that is, she met and fell in love with a struggling writer turned police officer named Deron Smalls Jr. from Bushwick, Brooklyn. Deron's family is completely different from Dee's family. His father left Deron, his mom, and his three brothers alone when Deron was only five years old. And Deron is the only one of the siblings who has never been locked up or knocked anyone up. But he still had a hard time growing up, trying to be the man because his brothers were so immature. Deron couldn't catch a break to save his life. But he's a die-hard romantic with a very open mind for someone whose mother called white people (and anyone who looked the part) the Antichrist. Yes, folks, Deron is black. The two met at a literature seminar at NYU one evening and the rest is history. When Dee Dee brought Deron home to meet her parents, they were horrified. That's the word she always uses to describe it, *horrified.* They expected her to date some Yale graduate who came from old money and privilege. Not some black guy from the boroughs who rode the L train and attended a community college in

Queens. Her mother begged and her father bribed. He actually offered to pay Deron ten thousand dollars *not* to date Dee Dee. Some nerve, right? But of course, Deron refused.

On the flip side, Deron's family was also appalled. His older brother referred to Dee as "pale pussy" for the longest time and his mother didn't even acknowledge her existence. A lot of people think New Yorkers aren't racists. Not true. We just hide it better. So only friends were invited to the wedding, which was nice, yet understated. And I suppose it was for the best because no one wants bad vibes and possible drama on their wedding day. At first Dee Dee wanted her parents to attend, but once they realized that she was serious about the marriage, they turned their backs on her for a while. She didn't talk to them for months. She would cry to me about it sometimes, but Deron helped to keep her focused. His family reacted almost the same way. I think two of his brothers were going to go to the wedding, but their mother and oldest brother talked them out of it. It hurt him, but he was in love, so nothing else really mattered.

It wasn't until Deidre was born that the mothers on both sides opened up. Deidre is the one thing they have in common, and the glue that holds them together. The grandmothers met for the first time at the hospital a year ago when Dee Dee gave birth to the stunning little angel with light brown eyes and curly hair. They're far from best friends, but at least they're civil.

Now Dee Dee lives in Astoria and babysits a couple of kids in her home who attend a church in her neighborhood. She would volunteer whenever the church hosted a dinner for the homeless or a Christmas gift drive for needy children, and one day a woman, who I think is some sort of sales exec, asked if Dee would be interested in sitting for her two-year-old twins a few times a week.

Her regular nanny had started taking some college classes and wasn't always available. I think the woman offered, like a hundred and fifty a week and Dee agreed.

But that's nothing. She and Deron practically live off her trust fund, which also keeps her shopping at Macy's every month. Dee is one of those people who can buy almost whatever she wants without concerning herself with the price. And why should she? I mean, she never told me, and I never asked, but I think her trust fund is well over six digits, maybe pushing seven. And I'm pretty sure that since she's an only child she stands to inherit her parents' entire estate. Before Deron, she never gave money a second thought.

I think Deron resents that. He hates not making enough money to support the lifestyle Dee grew up in, and he hates depending on her parents' money. If it were up to him, he and Dee would only use his rookie salary from the NYPD (please!), the pocket change she makes babysitting, and that would be that. Silly pride. But Dee is not having that. She deserves to have a comfortable life.

I should call her, though. Sure, we speak on the regular, but I just have a bad feeling about this time. I hope nothing's wrong.

About half an hour later I tell the driver he can let us out half a block from the club. I'm feeling a little anxious and plus, I am just ready to get out of the car. Turns out a few streets are closed off anyway. Jas pays the fare and we begin to walk toward the club. It's a warm July evening, perfect weather for a party. There is a hint of a breeze that makes the short walk to the club a breeze itself. I love New York summers. They're not as humid as down South or as intense as the West Coast.

"I really wish you would get a damn car, Lia. You make all this money and still want to take a cab. And even worse, walk." Jas is a trip. She's been a New Yorker for at least five years and still isn't used to the way most of us get around.

"Why don't you wake up and realize we're not in South Hell anymore, Toto? New Yorkers don't have to drive. That's the beauty of the city. And anyway, if it's that important, get your own damn car."

"Please, I can barely afford my rent." She opens her tiny black Fendi bag and puts on more lip gloss.

"Well, if you'd stop tryin' to dress like J. Lo maybe you could," I say, rolling my eyes.

She shoots me a "shut the hell up" look and then glances up to see Beyoncé and Kelly from Destiny's Child entering the front doors of the club.

"See, if that child doesn't want Jay-Z I'll gladly take him off her hands. He's no supermodel, but damn . . . he got dough," she says a little too loudly while staring at the singer.

I laugh at what she says even though I know she's dead serious. I glance around too, wondering if I'll see any more celebs go inside or any fine-ass men as I pull out our passes and invites. The club is exquisite. A three-story, mirrored building with a red carpet and a crowded entrance. I can hear the DJ playing dance hall reggae . . . something by Sean Paul, I think (I heard its Janet's favorite music), as we finally get to the doors. First we have to get checked and checked again, which, by the way, really gets on my nerves. We have to get patted down by a Queen Latifah look-alike. And not the pretty Revlon commercial Queen Latifah, but the butch version like in the movie *Set It Off*. Then we have to open our purses and remove anything that is even remotely able to be used as a weapon, including my brand-new nail file. Jas complains under her breath that we're not a bunch of teenagers at a house party, but neither of us argues with the security. In the end, who cares? We're in.

Once inside, Jas and I begin to make our rounds. Immediately she is approached by some guy who looks no older than nineteen and is wearing a baby-blue Sean John button-up shirt over a wife beater, baggy-ass Enyce jeans, and every thug's favorite footwear, Timberlands. His shoulder-length hair is neatly cornrowed and in his hand is a Corona with lime.

"What's up, Ma? Yo, as soon as you walked in you had me hypnotized, no lie." He licks his lips L. L. Cool J style and grins at Jas.

"I'm going to get a drink, Jas. Catch up with you later." I slip away as quickly as I can. I don't want to be around for the dis, because I know Jas will waste no time telling this guy that she's not interested. Because of Jas's "around-the-way girl" style, a lot of younger, hip-hop heads try to get with her. She looks like the type of girl you'd see in one of those black men's magazine's like *King*, or *Smooth* . . . lots of ass and sass. The ideal arm candy for a rapper-to-be. She would never give anyone like that the time of day, though. She wants a man with assets in the bank now, not later. But the poor guys don't know it until it's too late.

As I make my way to the nearest bar, a fine, übersexy, tall, dark-haired man with green eyes and an olive complexion bumps into me. He smells like Curve and peppermint. It's an enticing scent because Curve isn't the most sophisticated cologne, but it smells so masculine, you know? And the peppermint means he's kiss-ready. He's dressed casually chic in black slacks, a white collared shirt with the collar up, and a black blazer over that.

"Excuse me, miss. I am so very sorry." He places his hand on my lower waist and continues to make his way through the crowd.

Damn. He looks so good. Italian. He has to be Italian. He reminds me of Al Pacino . . . if Al was, like, thirty years younger. He has an authentic "my parents came to Ellis

Island straight from Sicily" look. But why didn't he say more to me? As fly as I am . . . and he had the perfect opportunity. Damn. Well, my mission now is to find him before the night is over. He looks almost as fine as I do. How often does that happen?

I get to the bar and order a sex on the beach, all the while keeping an eye out for my mystery man, and I start to imagine Mr. Italy and me doing just that. Rolling around with him in the cool white sands under a Tuscan sunset . . . sigh. You just don't understand, he is that fine! He must be married. I didn't get a good look, but I don't think there was a ring on his finger. And you know how men are, they love to play single and take their rings off when they go out and think there's a possibility of getting some action. But how else do you explain him not trying to get with me? Someone at home? It's possible. Maybe he's gay. After all, in this city there is no shortage of gay men. But no. He can't be gay because I have big plans for him. Plans that include my sex on the beach fantasy. Maybe he's just shy. Well, if that's the case he doesn't have to worry because I'll make the first move . . . if I can just spot him again.

"Girl, why'd you leave me like that? See, you ain't right. I was going to tell him that you and I were together when you just bounced." Jas lightly pushes me on my shoulder, shaking me from my Italian dream.

"You should have let me know. I needed a drink. Besides, he was cute. Thought you might dig him."

"Cute my ass. He's a rapper, of course. Looking for a deal, blah, blah, blah. All that translates into is 'I'm broke as hell.' I'm so tired of that shit. Can a guy approach me who already has a damn deal?" She takes my drink from my hand and downs it in one gulp. "Girl, you always drinking these poodle drinks." She turns from me and orders two cocktails of Rémy Martin and Sprite, apparently for herself. "Do you want anything, Lia?" she asks as she tips the bartender.

"No, Jas. Um, I see a coworker of mine. I'll be back." Once again I slither away from her and into the busy crowd. I don't really see a coworker. I just want to find Mr. Italy. It's showtime.

The mixture of celebrities, industry people, and media always feels so right to me. Beautiful people make me feel comfortable. Rich people make me feel comfortable. I get called bougie so much it's like a second name. But I don't care. I have certain standards, and I don't compromise them for anyone. That's one of the reasons I was attracted to Mr. Italy. Yeah, he looks like he has money, but more than that, he looks like he knows how to get money, keep money, and spend money. At this point the DJ is playing songs from Janet's new album called "Slow Love." It has a jazzy type of vibe to it. Janet's sweet, yet erotic voice over the beat is telling someone to "take it to another level tonight." The song is hot. Definitely a hit. And definitely the perfect song to approach Mr. Italy to. And as if on cue, I see him. Sitting at an empty table, glancing down at his watch. I pull out my compact and check my face. Flawless. After popping in a Tic Tac just to be on the safe side, I maneuver my way through the dance floor and right up to his table.

"Do you mind?" I ask, glancing down at the empty chair next to him.

"Of course not," he replies, standing to pull the chair out for me. Fine *and* polite. Two for two.

I sit down and adjust my skirt so that I show just a little bit more leg. Now the easy part.

"Lia Wells, I work for Virgin's legal team." I extend my hand, signaling him to introduce himself. He reaches for my hand kisses it.

"So, you're a legal assistant? Nice." He sits back in his

chair and smiles at me as if I were a child who's bringing home her first A-plus. You know, that "good for you" smile.

"Um, no. I meant I'm an attorney myself. VP of Legal Affairs, actually." I'm totally thrown off by his assumption, but try not to let it get to me. He's just too fine.

"Oh, really? I'm sorry. I just thought . . . well, never mind. I'm Eric Amaretto, restaurateur."

"You own Amaretto's? That restaurant in Chelsea? I've been there. It's beautiful. The food is divine," I say while leaning in a little closer. Okay, maybe the food is not exactly divine, but stroking his ego can't hurt.

"There's also one in Park Slope. I have plans to open another one next summer." He gazes around the party as if he's looking for someone to come back to the table . . . either that or he's bored with the conversation.

"That's wonderful. So, did you come here alone, or did you bring a date?" I ask, hoping he says he came by himself so that this whole conversation is not in vain and I don't end up feeling like an idiot.

"Alone. How about yourself? I'm sure there's a man here looking for you as we speak," he says flatteringly.

"No, the only person looking for me is a girlfriend I came with. And anyway, I was looking for *you*. After you bumped into me I couldn't get your face out of my head." I fondle my earring a little bit and recross my legs. Hopefully he'll pick up on the fact that he has everything to gain right now so he needs to make a move.

Flirting is an art. You have to send subtle but very definite signals that you're interested. Easy does it.

"Is that so, Ms. Lia Wells?" He leans in closer and touches my nose. "You're rather cute yourself," he says as he leans back and looks around the club again.

What the hell is going on? That's it? And did he actually call me cute? Cute? No, no, no. This will not do. Time to just go in for the kill. I'm very much used to getting what

I want, and this situation is no different. I have to admit, though, that this is an odd case because most of the time, I don't have to put in so much work. And trust me, this is work. Beautiful women shouldn't have to come onto men. It destroys the balance between the two. However, there are always exceptions and I'm making an executive decision on behalf of beautiful women everywhere and claiming this one for me. I know he's trying to play it cool, but cool needs to take a backseat to this lust in the air.

"Listen, Eric, I would love to meet up with you again. Maybe later this week we can have lunch or something. I'm going to give you my card so you can call me and we'll see what happens." I reach into my bag and pull out my gold-embossed business card holder.

"You know what, Lia, I'll give you my card instead. Then you can call me, say, about Tuesday?" He reaches into his pocket and hands me his card. He then takes my other hand and kisses it as he gets up from his chair. "Nice meeting you," he says, and then walks away.

Yeah, he walks away and I'm left sitting here as if nothing even happened at all. I'm a little disappointed, but maybe he has a different plan of his own for me. I'll follow his lead . . .

But still I have to wonder . . . did that go well? I'm not sure. It wasn't normal, I'll tell you that. You know how many guys would kill to have me hand them my card? And he just kind of . . . rejected it in a way. Well, at least he wants me to hear from me again. I put his card in my purse and suddenly don't feel like being at the party anymore. I'm tired and really not interested in being in this crowd anymore tonight. Besides, I have Eric's number now, so I'm satisfied. Just when I'm about to get up and look for Jas, I see Eric chatting with a skinny blonde in a disgustingly short, yellow Versace dress. She reminds me of Heather Locklear . . . just trashier. She twirls her oily-looking hair around her finger and pulls a pen and a small piece of paper out of her purse. After jotting down what I assume to be her number, she hands the paper to Eric. Well, whatever. All that means is that he'll lose the number or just get too busy to call her. He doesn't want that *Playboy* pinup-looking chick. I didn't see him give her his number, so it must mean he doesn't really want her to call him. Right? Sure it does. I think. He was pretty quick to refuse my number . . . but I'm not going to stress over it. I'm clearly first-round pick and the fake Heather is just a bench player.

I get up and scan the crowd for Jas. Then I spot her on the dance floor with the same guy who tried to talk to her when we first came in. What's this all about? I mean, he is nowhere near her type. She was running away from him as soon as he stepped to her. I don't understand why she's still talking to him. She doesn't look annoyed, but something is not right. Maybe she needs me to save her. I get through the crowd and grab her arm.

"Are you cheating on me, woman?" I ask her while I glare at the young rapper. Every once in a while, when my friends and I get stuck with some loser guy in our face, another one of us will come to the rescue and pretend that we're a lesbian couple. Trust me, more often than not it works. Although we get the occasional "Can I watch?" or even nastier "Can I join?" She laughs. Okay, why is she laughing? I'm doing her a favor here.

"It's okay, Lia. And thank God I didn't really need you to save me. That was terrible acting."

The rapper puts his arms around Jas's waist and kisses her cheek.

"Your friend looks like she's ready to leave," he says, grinning at me. Um, did I miss something? This *is* the same guy from before, right?

"Yeah, I think she is. But I'm going to call you tonight,

okay? And we're still having brunch tomorrow." Jas kisses him on his cheek and says bye.

"Peace, *mami*," he replies.

Am I in another world or something? Brunch? Kisses? Is this really my friend Jas?

"Um, what was that all about?" I ask, totally confused.

"What?" Jas replies nonchalantly.

"Don't 'what' me, Jas. You're really feelin' the broke rapper?"

"His name is Asaji, Lia. And yeah, so what if I am? He's cool."

And by her firm tone I could tell that she didn't want to discuss it any further. Still, I was in shock. You don't understand. This is the same woman who vowed never to date anyone who wasn't making six figures. What is really going on?

"Okay. So, are you ready to leave? I know you need to get some rest so you can make it to your *brunch* on time," I say mockingly.

"Shut up, Lia. Yeah, we can go. But maybe we should take separate cabs. I want to make a quick stop before I go home," Jas says softly.

Uh-oh. I know what that's all about. Jas must need some cash. "Fine. But make sure you call me tomorrow. We still have some things to talk about." Actually, it makes more sense for us to take separate cabs anyway. Jas lives in the heart of Greenwich Village, the most eclectic part of the city. I like to walk around Greenwich sometimes; it always reminds me that everybody's not like me, and they don't have to be. Jas loves the Village because of all the different people it attracts. To be from Small Town, South Carolina, she totally believes in being an individual and not conforming just to make others feel comfortable. As a matter of fact, one of her good friends is a drag queen named Lamée, and Jas messed around with a girl in college once, but of course that didn't last. Her place is pretty nice for someone who can't keep a steady job. She pays a thousand dollars a month, even though the rent is really $1,850 (yep, she screwed the landlord for a discount. When I found out I was disappointed, but not surprised).

Once we make it outside we hug each other, say bye, and Jas hops into the nearest empty cab. I decide to stand outside a little bit longer before going home. The front of the club is still busy, mostly photographers trying to get shots of whichever celeb they can. I walk up the block, basking in the summer's cool heat. (I know, "cool heat" isn't possible, unless, of course, you're in New York. Anything's possible in New York.) I finally hail a cab and once inside the car, let down my ponytail and run my fingers through my hair. Tonight was somewhat eventful. I met my future husband and Jas met . . . well, I met my future husband. I tell the driver where to go and then turn my cell phone on to check my messages:

"Lia, this is Derrick. I tried to reach you earlier but you had already left the office. The meeting scheduled for Wednesday is now Monday at eight. I know you don't usually come in until ten. Please come on time. Thanks."

Great. I hate having these weekly meetings. My colleagues are cool, but one or two people can handle a lot of the stuff they want to discuss. Besides, eight in the morning? Sheesh! But oh, well. Next!

"Hey, Lia, it's Dee again. Are you that busy that you can't call me back? I need to talk to you. Deron is, well, he's been drinking and . . . I don't know. I'm getting concerned. Call me."

Whoa! She sounds bad. And what's this about Deron drinking? He's so sweet. I can't imagine it being anything too serious. But I have to remember to call her tomorrow.

"Li-Li, it's Mama. How you doing? You not call your mama for long time. Shame, girl. Your daddy say you have big head . . . think you too good for old parents. We come visit you any day now. I call you back later. Love you."

What is she talking about they'll come see me any day now? I don't have the time or patience to put up with my parents. My father, the army solider for life, and my mom, the quintessential Korean wife and mother. She's very demure and generous, but at the same time she expects so much from everyone. Especially from me, her only child. I love my parents to death, but I can do without a visit right now.

I turn my phone off again and close my eyes while I think about what I need to do tomorrow. It's a Saturday. Usually the girls and I have drinks at a martini bar called Twist in Midtown around seven, just to catch up. Lord knows there's a lot that we need to catch up on this week. I also go to the gym in my building to get a little workout in. Exercising is not something I look forward to, but I always feel stronger and that much closer to my six-pack when I'm done.

"This is it, miss," the driver says, not even turning around.

"Thanks." I hand him a twenty and get out of the cab. It's about 2:00 a.m. and the doorman is probably taking his break. I take my key card out of my purse and swipe it through the machine. The lobby doors open and I wave to Freddy, the guy at the front desk.

"Did you have a pleasant evening?" he asks, eying me up and down. Freddy has probably had a little thing for me since I moved in, but he's so damned professional he'd never ask me out. He always winks at me with his crystal-blue eyes when I see him, but nothing more. And that's fine by me. Freddy is decent looking, but decent isn't quite enough.

"It was fine, Freddy, thanks." I make my way to the elevators and press nine. Once it arrives, I step inside and begin to yearn for my bed. My feet hate me right about

now, but I know it was worth it. My outfit was bangin'
tonight. After I reach my floor and the door to my place, I
go inside and immediately begin taking off my boots and
unzipping my skirt. The off-white carpet feels soft under
my tired feet. As I look around the living room, I remember that Dinah, my housekeeper, will be arriving at nine.
Thank God. I'm not a slob or anything, but I'm far from
a neat freak. I'm also no decorator. I had to get Dee to help
me with that because I just don't have an eye for furniture
and stuff. She did a good job, though. My place has an
Asian feel. Simple lines, neutral colors, with a splash of
red here and there. Very modern, but something my
mother loves because it reminds her of home.

My bedroom is my favorite room. One entire wall is a
huge ceiling-to-floor mirror. I have two clear ceiling fans
and a walk-in closet that's big enough to double as a guest
room. My queen-size bed is covered with tan and red
sheets and, like, ten pillows. Just looking at it makes me
sleepy. But I'm in desperate need of a bath right now. The
one in my bedroom has these jets that massage the hell out
of your muscles. And if you position yourself just right
you get another type of massage, if you know what I mean.
I finish undressing and run the bathwater.

I stop to examine myself in the mirror. Maybe I should
get breast implants. I wouldn't mind being a C cup. I
squeeze my nipples and flinch a little at the sensation I get.
Pain is pleasure! Of course, I haven't had much of either
in a long time. Sex . . . it's almost like a foreign concept to
me. The last guy I slept with was determined to get me
pregnant, or give me a disease. He had me scared as hell.
I figured it out about the third time we did it. He kept
saying that condoms are not a hundred percent safe and
anything could happen. I didn't think much of it until I
caught him poking holes in one. I couldn't believe it. I
mean, the guy had to be crazy, right? Anyway, I threw him

out and blocked his number. I made an appointment to get tested the next day and luckily, was given a clean bill of health. That was three months ago and I'm still wary of men. I want it so badly, but sometimes I'm not sure it's worth it. Thank God for those vibrating, so-called neck massagers. I have yet to use mine on my neck . . . go figure.

After taking a relaxing bubble bath and rubbing myself with baby oil, I put on my deliciously comfortable, cherry-red terry cloth robe and walk to the kitchen for a glass of corn water. Yep, you heard me right. I was raised on corn water, crab legs, rice, and barbecued chicken, Korean style. It's an acquired taste, though, believe me. After I moved out of my parents' house I swore I would never drink it again. But here I am, still drinking it, even craving it sometimes. I go back to my room, drop my robe, and climb into bed. I'm so excited about Tuesday and talking to Eric that my mind wanders and I begin to fantasize. The two of us, kissing, touching . . . all the stuff that I haven't really thought about in months. I imagine him playing with my hair while I run my fingertips over his ripped abs. I reach into my nightstand, pull out my "neck massager," and buzz my way into a peaceful sleep.

Chapter 2

Lia

I wake up to the sound of Dinah vacuuming the living room. I lazily glance at my alarm clock. It's almost nine thirty in the morning. Damn, I'd usually be working out by this time. I get out of bed, throw on my robe, and head to the bathroom to pee and brush my teeth. After throwing on a pair of blue Nike running shorts, a sports bra, and tennis shoes, I put my hair in a bun, grab a towel, and head to the kitchen for a croissant. I can already smell the French roast coffee that Dinah has brewed.

"Hello, Dinah," I say as I enter the living room. Dinah reminds me of a Mrs. Claus . . . with a somewhat round shape and long, grayish hair that she keeps pulled back from her face. She's from Poland and her English isn't great. I try not to get into complicated conversations with her.

"Good morning," she replies in her thick, European

accent as she wipes down the coffee table. "The coffee is done and I brought some strawberries."

I love this woman! She's always looking out for me. Strawberries are my absolute favorite food in the world. I think the reason she babies me sometimes is that her own daughter is hundreds of miles away at some convent, and Dinah can't contact her. I feel bad for her about that, so I let her play mother to me as much as she wants.

"Look at the store list I made. Add what you need," Dinah says. She drags the vacuum cleaner into the hallway and begins cleaning again.

I glance down at the paper on the counter. Most of the time I never have to add anything to the grocery list. Dinah knows my house better than I do. I butter a croissant and grab a few strawberries from the bowl. Everything tastes so good. Hopefully it's a sign of what today will be. I finish my coffee and yell to Dinah that I'm going to the gym, although I doubt she can hear me over the obnoxious whirling of the vacuum.

As soon as I get to the gym I get a little cup of water from the watercooler. I really do not feel like working out, but I have no choice. I refuse to get out of shape. I do a few stretches and slowly make my way over to a bike. Damn it, I forgot my headset. Now I have to make do with the light rock station softly playing in the background. After about twenty minutes of nonstop cycling, I see the Armani guy from last night in the lobby enter the gym. He's wearing a black T-shirt, gray sweats, Jordans, and a do-rag. So, he actually lives here? Since when? He catches me looking, yet again, and smiles, yet again. I need to stop making eye contact before he gets the wrong idea. He hops onto a treadmill and begins running, hard. I can tell he does this all the time. He looks so at ease. Suddenly, I hear an annoying beeping sound from my machine and realize that I have twenty seconds to start cycling again. I didn't even notice that I stopped. I get distracted too easily. I swear I have ADD. I begin with the bike again and close my eyes while trying to block out the sounds of U2 coming from the speakers. Little beads of sweat form on my forehead, and my back feels wet. I open my eyes and Armani is on the bike next to me, pedaling away. It's been forty-five minutes. I'm ready to leave and he looks like he could go on forever. Since he's so close, I can look at him more carefully. His skin is perfect, young looking. And his hands . . . whoa. Quite large. His nails are impeccable, short and clean. I rarely see that in the guys I meet.

I get off my bike and go to the watercooler again. I think I have to call it a wrap for today. Just as I'm about to head to the sauna for my post-workout steam, Armani approaches me. That damn smile . . . stop it, please!

"Did you have a good workout?" he asks with the soulful, sexified voice of an R & B singer.

"Yeah, it was okay," I reply shortly. I swear he's looking me up and down. He takes the end of my towel that's hanging on my shoulder and dabs my forehead. Nice move, but who the hell does he think he is?

"I can tell," he says. I laugh a little bit. Yeah, right, if only he knew. I was quite slack in my workout today. But he doesn't need to know that. I hope he doesn't try to give me his number. I know how this works. He's setting it up. Next he'll introduce himself . . .

"I'm Ty, by the way. I just moved here last week from Chicago. Job transfer, you know how that goes," he says. I knew it.

"Lia," I say, not wanting to look at his eyes, those striking, dark brown eyes.

"Well, Lia, I don't know if you're seeing anyone, but if not, maybe we can go out tonight, if you don't already have plans."

"Sorry, Ty, but I do have plans. Some girlfriends and I are hanging out, so—"

"Oh, that's cool. I can just give you my number and we can do something later." He grabs a napkin and a pen from the watercooler table.

Ha. He's assuming that I actually want to go out with him. Like that would really happen. There's no way I'm going to call this guy; I don't want him to think I'm interested. At the most I'd take him to lunch, tell him a little about the city. But anything more serious is out of the question. Besides, I don't want to lead him on. He's really not my type. He's sexy and all, but still.

"Um, I'll give you my number instead, okay?" I take the pen out of his hand and scribble my office number on the napkin. "Call me Monday morning if you can. We'll do lunch." Monday, early in the week so we can get this over with. I hand him his pen and my number and head to the sauna. He really does look good, but he's no comparison to Eric, my Italian stallion. Damn, how corny am I?

After I get back to my apartment it looks like Dinah has already left. The house smells like ginger and peaches, a heavenly combination. I go to my bedroom and have kicked off my shoes when I notice a note on my bed: *Ladies don't leave toys all over the place. Love, Dinah.*

Oh my God! I must have forgotten to put my vibrator back in the nightstand. And then poor Dinah finds it lying in the sheets! I laugh as I envision her face after pulling back the covers and seeing my "man" covered in, well . . . how embarrassing.

I've begun to strip off my sweaty workout clothes when the phone rings.

"Hello," I answer.

"Hey, Lia, it's Rena."

"What's up, girl?"

"I don't think Dee Dee is going to make it tonight." Her

voice sounds empty. It's making me nervous. And I'm feeling really guilty about not calling Dee yet.

"Why not?" I ask, not really wanting to know.

"Well, she says she can't find a babysitter but . . ." She stops herself.

"But what? And anyway, doesn't Deron's mother take Deidre on Saturdays?" I don't mean to sound annoyed, but maybe I do because I don't want to sound scared.

"Look, Lia, all I know is that Dee is refusing to go out tonight and when I spoke to her she just didn't sound good. You need to call her. She confides in you more than anyone. And you've known her the longest."

"I will. I'll call you back later, okay?"

"Peace, sister."

We both hang up as I plop down onto my bed face-first. This is too much. All these awful thoughts are running through my mind. I don't really want to hear any bad news, but I suppose I have to. I'm no good when it comes to personal problems. Emotionally, I can't take much pressure or conflict. You might think that because I'm a lawyer and I deal with those types of issues on a regular basis at work, I'd be better equipped to handle them outside of work. But I freeze up. I get uncomfortable and I can't think straight. My number-one defense mechanism: avoidance. I'd rather run than try to figure out the problem and work on it. It's a huge character flaw that I'd rather not have. And now that my best friend is in some kind of trouble, my "flaw" is surfacing with a vengeance. I have to call her. I just hope she doesn't expect any kind of answers from me.

I turn around and lie on my back. After dialing Dee's number and letting it ring four times I breathe a sigh of relief and click the Off button. She's not home. I'll just have to call her later. I hop off my bed and have started to walk into my bathroom to run my bathwater when I hear it: the phone. I know it's Dee Dee. I thought I'd have more time before I'd have to talk to her. I sigh again, this time to calm myself, and answer the phone.

"Hi, Lia. You just called?" she asks. Has she been crying? Why does she sound so down?

"Dee, how have you been? I was just about to call you back." I shouldn't lie, but she sounds like she needs to hear something like that.

"Can I come to your place? You know, to talk?" she asks softly.

"You know we're all going to the bar tonight, right? It can't wait?" Not until after I say it does it sound so bad. God, I know I must sound incredibly insensitive. I try to soften my words. "I mean, everyone will be there and I'm sure we all have stories to tell." Okay, is that better? I don't know. I still feel like an ass.

"That's the thing. I'm not sure I want to tell Jas and Rena about this. Not yet anyway. Besides, I'm not going out tonight. I'm not feeling too well."

"Well, you should just stay home and get some rest. Have Deron be your personal nurse. You know he'll do it."

"Lia, if you don't want me to come over just say so." She begins to choke up; I can tell by her voice. "I don't want to bother you. You're only my closest friend." And then I hear it for sure . . . she's crying, sobbing actually. Why me?

"Dee, you know you can come over anytime. I'm sorry. I didn't realize it was that serious. Don't cry, girl." I feel myself stiffening. I'm at a loss for words. What the hell do I say now? "I have some of that tea you like, you know, the apple cinnamon one? I'll have some ready by the time you get here. It'll be all right, girl." I'm saying those last words more to convince myself than her.

"Okay. I'm leaving now," she says with a sniff between each word. I hang up the phone and go back to the bathroom to begin my bath. It will be a little while before she gets here, especially if she takes the train. I reach for my overly priced bath bubbles that I rarely use (a seventy-five-dollar gift courtesy of an AMEX that one of Jas's sex partners let her use for a day) and pour a few capfuls into my spalike tub. I need to feel completely refreshed when Dee gets here. It's going to be a long day.

An hour later I receive a ring from the front desk telling me I have a visitor. I tell them to let her up and then I pour two mugs of tea and put some strawberries on the coffee table. I hear Dee knocking at the door and go to open it for her.

"Dee Dee," I say as I hug her and let her in. That's all I can say, really. I'm stunned at how she looks. He face is still beautiful . . . her skin is actually glowing. But everything else about her looks tired. Her normally sleek and shiny hair is pulled back into a sloppy ponytail, and when I say sloppy, that's exactly what I mean. I can't even really tell if it's a ponytail, maybe it's more like a . . . knot, or something. She has on a tan, shapeless, flowered dress with beige flip-flops. This woman is normally the poster child for preppy-ness. Sweaters, loafers, Ralph Lauren everything. And now, well, she's a mess. I think she can sense my astonishment because she looks away and just takes a seat on the couch.

"So," I say sitting next to her, "what's going on?" She picks up a mug of tea and takes a couple of sips. Her eyes are puffy and red. I brace myself to hear the worst.

"I need you to just let me talk, okay? Save your questions and comments until I'm done."

I nod my head, tuck my feet under me, and grab a strawberry.

She sighs. "I know Deron loves me. I know he loves Deidre. We are his life." She takes another sip; I wait for the "but."

"But he is so stressed out . . . about work, his writing,

everything. And lately he's buying bottles of liquor. All kinds, all the time. He drinks every day. He goes to work drunk. He's already gotten written up for that, and one more time, he'll lose his job, I'm sure of it." She stops, drinks more tea, and looks around the living room, the living room she so expertly put together. It makes me think about how long the two of us have actually been friends. I met Dee Dee when I came back to New York after law school. She had just finished her business degree from Syracuse and came to the city to finally "live," as she put it. We were both twenty-three, had our lives ahead of us, and just so happened to end up at the same little café in Union Square at the same time. She commented that she liked my Chanel bag; I told her that I liked her Dior shoes and bam . . . instant friends. Even then she couldn't understand why I don't date black men. She adores them. At first I was thinking, *Oh, she's just another white chick who dates black guys to piss off Mom and Dad.* So I was really surprised when she told me she was Spanish. Dee totally shocked me. It doesn't look like there's an ethnic bone in her body. I don't think I've even heard her speak the language. She has assimilated herself so well that you can barely hear an accent. But she loves dark complexions and full lips and kinky hair. All the same things that I appreciate, but just can't get into.

"Lia, you're listening, right?" Her voice brings me back to the present.

"Yes, I'm listening. Go on." See, what'd I tell you? ADD.

"And now that I'm pregnant again, I just—"

"What? You're pregnant again? Congratulations, girl!" I'm sure I'm just beaming, looking like a complete dork. But then as I look at Dee's solemn expression, it all fades away.

"I just told you that Deron doesn't want another baby."

Oh, my bad. She looks at me like I'm the village idiot. How did I miss that part? "What do you mean? You haven't told him yet?"

"I can't. He's always saying how we can barely afford the baby we have now."

"But, Dee Dee, you have to tell him. How far are you?"

"Four months." She looks down at her empty mug and begins to cry. I put my arm around her and hug her tightly.

"Dee, please don't cry, girl. Everything is going to work out." Right?

"But that's not it." She suddenly sits up straight and looks at me dead in the eye. Are you kidding me? There's more? I sigh to myself instead of out loud, not wanting to make her feel like a burden. 'Cause really, she's not. It's just . . .

"Remember Manny?" she asks. Emanuel Velasquez.

Of course I remember. He's the starting pitcher for the Yankees. Well, he is now. When I was associated with him he was just a guy from the Bronx with a baseball and a dream. But he was recruited about four years ago and has been on a high ever since. The *Times* lists him as one of NYC's most eligible bachelors. He's been on MTV's *Cribs* and even *Oprah*. His story is timeless—parents moved to New York from the Dominican Republic in the seventies with him and his five sisters without a penny to their name. But Manny had talent. He put baseball over everything else, which meant he didn't get caught up in the drug game like a lot of young men in the projects. It paid off. Everyone knows Manny "The Arm" Velasquez.

"Manny V? Yeah, Dee, I remember him," I reply, wondering what he has to do with anything.

"What would you say if I told you he was back in my life?" She looks at me curiously.

"Back in your life? I mean, in what way? I thought you severed all ties with him when you met Deron," I say a little too loudly. Okay, let me give you all a little background info. Dee Dee and Manny met years ago before Deron and before the Yankees. He fell for her hard. She wasn't interested at first, but eventually he won her over. They dated off and on for about a year . . . and then he got signed to the team and everything changed. Groupies emerged. Fame and money clouded his head. He did Dee dirty and broke her heart. Shortly after, she met Deron and slowly etched Manny out of her life. Believe me when I tell you that Dee and I had many heated arguments over Manny and how he treated her. I hated when she would call me in tears because he stood her up (again) or he wasn't answering her calls. The whole thing was a mess.

"He, uh, has been calling me lately. I haven't met up with him yet, but—"

"Hell no, Dee Dee, don't even finish! Manny is a fuckin' dog. I don't know why he's trying to get close to you again, but don't let him get you wrapped up in his games!" I don't mean to yell at her, but I just can't believe that she would consider dealing with him again . . . on any level.

"Lia, I'm not getting wrapped up in anything. He's a friend," she says defensively.

"Look, don't try that friend crap with me, Dee. You haven't seen or heard from him in over four years. Deron is not going to go for that."

"This isn't about Deron," she says firmly. Well, damn.

"Excuse me, Dee. You're right. Deron is only the man you're married to," I say sarcastically. She looks at me with tears in her eyes. Uh-oh.

"I love Deron," she says. "But he's changing. And now Manny is back and I have another baby on the way. . . ." She wipes her eyes.

Sigh. I love Dee Dee to death but baby girl needs a serious reality check.

"I don't want to be harsh, but as your friend I suggest

you leave Manny alone and focus on your family. Deron will straighten out once you tell him," I say calmly, hoping that if I sound reasonable enough she will drop this whole issue.

"I just wanted to be able to figure things out, you know," she says.

"Well, in about five months your husband is going to have another mouth to feed. Shouldn't he know about it?"

"I know he should," she says.

"So you have to tell him. And you guys still have your trust fund money, right?"

"Well, not really. Deron gave it back. He told my father to close the account because we wouldn't be using it anymore."

"What? That was your money, Dee. He had no right. Besides, all you have to do is tell your dad the situation." Yeah, there ya go . . . sound advice. Maybe I'm not so bad after all.

"Perhaps when you get married you'll understand this more, but I can't just go behind my husband's back and beg my father for money, Lia."

She's right; it must be a married peoples' thing because I don't understand. "This isn't about Deron's ego. You have two kids to provide for."

"He'll leave me, Lia. If I go to my parents he'll say that I'm better off with them and leave me. That's the reason we were separated before." Okay, maybe there is no simple solution to this.

"So what are you going to do?" I have officially run out of suggestions.

"Maybe I shouldn't have the baby." She wipes her eyes with the back of her hand. Not have the baby? Is she for real?

"Dee Dee, don't say that. I know that you already love this child. How can you even consider having an abortion?"

"I've spoken to a doctor and he says I have until my fifth month to abort."

"You don't really want to do that, do you?" I ask. "Hey, let me tell you something . . . and this is something no one else knows," I start. "And I mean no one."

"What? What happened?" she asks.

"I had an abortion two years ago. It still haunts me to this day. I think about how she would have been a toddler now, walking around, getting into all my things. I think about how she would have cried when I left for work, and how she would have smiled and run to me when I came home. I imagine her little voice calling for me, her little body sitting on my lap when I read her stories." I stop talking because I know I can go on forever. My phantom child. The one I didn't let live because I allowed my career to run my life instead of my heart. I have never told anyone about this, not even the father. He wasn't someone I was dating seriously, and the thought of being a single mother scared the hell out of me. Plus, I knew that my position at Virgin would be compromised. I had come too far to give that up. I'm hesitant to talk about it now, but I feel that telling Dee would help not only her, but me as well.

"I'm sorry, Lia. I had no idea."

I can tell she's speechless. It's understandable. I mean, what do you say to a woman who appears to have it all, but then you find out she has a huge void in her soul?

"Just think about this, Dee. I'll support you no matter what, but think about it. You and Deron have been through so much. You'll get through this too. And I don't care if you want to hear this or not, but Manny has no place in your life. I mean, he's a cutie and all, but . . ." I stop and grin at her as she laughs. "Seriously, it sounds like trouble. And you really should tell Deron about the baby."

"I will. Thanks for listening. And don't tell Jas and Rena about this. I want to get things resolved first, okay?" She stands up and smoothes out her dress and I try to notice any sign of a bulge . . . but there's not much there.

I get up and walk her to the door. "What should I tell them tonight? Rena's already worried."

"Just tell them I need some alone time. But I'll be all right." She gives me a hug and a kiss on the cheek. "I love you, Lia."

"I love you too, girl." I shut the door and glance at my clock. It's nearly five. Time flies when you're spilling your guts. Pretty soon I have to get ready to meet the girls. I'm anxious to talk to Jas about Asaji and what the hell she sees in him. And Rena, with all her maturity, has been whining like a little kid about Tak and his aversion to marriage. Plus my own story of Eric "can't get him out of my mind" Amaretto. And oh yeah, Ty. The only thing is that I hate having to lie to them about Dee Dee.

I clean up the leftover tea and devour all of the remaining strawberries while I do it. Then I go to my room and into my closet to find something to wear. I'm thinking a pair of Miss Sixty jeans and little tee with these silver pumps that I haven't had a chance to wear yet. Sexy and cool . . . This is going to be one hell of a night.

Chapter 3

Rena

"Lion, come here, please! Your daddy is on his way and you need to get your face washed," I shout to my son.

"Okay, Mommy!" he yells back. I hear his little feet running toward me and hope that my downstairs neighbors aren't home. They always complain about the noise coming from my apartment.

"Lion, what did I tell you about running inside?"

He looks at me with his round, ebony eyes in a way that tells me he's sorry. He has a wet washcloth in his hand and gives it to me. I wipe his face and send him to his room to get his overnight bag.

"Don't forget to pack your allergy drops," I say as he goes down the hall.

Now, where is Tak? He's never late to pick up Lion, and in fifteen minutes it will be six. He knows I need to make it to Midtown by seven. I live in East Harlem, 116th Street. It's already going to take me some time to get there, and Lia is—I hate to say it but she's a bitch when it comes to being on time.

I'm going to my room to get a head wrap when I hear Tak at the front door.

"Rena, I'm here!"

Finally. I finish wrapping my locks and go to greet him.

"Hey, baby," I say as I hug him. He lifts me off my feet and kisses me lightly on the lips.

"Where's my little king?" he asks me, his sexy Nigerian accent rolling off his tongue. No sooner has he said the words than Lion runs up the hall. He must have seen me shake my head at him because he slows down as he gets closer to his daddy. My son is absolutely mad about his father. The two of them adore each other. And Lion looks just like him . . . dark brown, mahogany-colored skin, round expressive eyes that will forever look like they belong to a child, and those cute little ears that stick out just a little bit too much.

I remember when Lion was born. Tak was in the delivery room, crying worse than I was. He was only twenty years old then. Still in college and still new to this country. I met Tak originally when he was a freshman, eighteen, and taking a history course I was teaching. I could tell he had a serious crush on me the first day. And for the rest of the semester he made it clear that once he left my class he would pursue me romantically. I blew him off in the beginning. It wasn't until the start of the next year that I went out with him. And I don't like to use tired clichés and all that, but it really was love on that first date. I knew I would marry this man. Well, we're not married but you know. I *will* marry this man. I suppose he has to propose first, however. And I guess he would actually have to *want* to marry me for him to do that. I believe that he loves me; I know he does. But the man just won't take that extra step. It's been five years. I'm the mother of his child and everything, but yet . . . nothing. I'm not worried, though. It'll happen. It better happen.

"Shouldn't you be on your way to meet your friends? I'll lock up when I leave," he says.

"Well, Tak, you know we wouldn't have to worry about who's keeping Lion on the weekends or having to go home all the time if we just lived together." Logic. Pure logic. Men respond to that sort of thing, don't they?

"Come on, Rena. Don't start that again. We're not ready to live together. You know this."

God, he's so exasperating! And how dare he say we're not ready? He means *he's* not ready.

"Whatever." I grab my bag and say bye to Lion. Tak tries to give me a kiss, but I just walk past him and out the door. I don't know how much more of this I can take. I'm beginning to feel like it's never going to happen for me. I mean, if I were like Jas or Lia, marriage wouldn't matter half as much. Those two go through guys like it's nothing. And that's fine for them. I had my glory days of running the streets and sleeping around. Well, not really. I never slept around, but I dated a lot. But now I'm more settled, I have a son, and I want to make my family complete. I mean, what am I going to tell my son when he starts asking why his daddy won't marry his mommy? How does that make me look?

I walk up the block a little bit and hail a cab. I really should just hop on the 4, 5, or 6 trains, but I'm not in the mood to put up with a bunch of random people. I tell the driver where to go and start to think about all the sleazy tales I'm going to hear tonight from the crew, especially Jas. The sister is lost, to say the least. I don't understand how a woman as beautiful and talented as she is can just sell herself short like that. Her potential is infinite. And it's as if everyone can see that except her. We tell her all the time. Well, we used to anyway. But one night Lia made a big deal about Jas and how we should stay out of her career and personal life until she decided to make some changes first. She was really fed up, and the two of them didn't speak for two weeks after that. I see where Lia is coming from, though. Jas does need a reality check. I'd hate to see something bad happen to her because of the way she behaves. Not all men are mentally stable enough to handle her head games and gold digging. One day she's going to run into someone who's a little off and then who knows? It's always a shame to see young, black women with no idea of who they are. Wasting away on the inside, and showing it on the outside.

And then there's Dee Dee. She's one of my favorite people. She's so polite and cultured. Very intelligent with a nurturing side. I don't have many friends who aren't black. Okay, I have only one and it's Dee. But she's opened my eyes to the possibility of more someday. Lately, though, she seems aloof and upset. She's not even coming tonight. I wonder if Lia ever called her. I guess I'll find out at the bar.

"You want to get out here, miss?" the driver asks me with an Arabic accent.

"Yes, this is fine." I hand him the fare and get out of the cab. It's a warm July evening and the streets are busy with vendors, teens, and tourists. This spot is too close to Times Square for me. I would rather meet in Tribeca or down by Fulton Street, but Lia insists on being in the middle of things.

I walk to the front of the bar and see Jas and Lia sitting at an outside table.

"You barely made it, girl," Lia says in a less than pleased tone. She gets up from the chair and adjusts her outfit so that you can see a little bit more skin than necessary. Her long, straight hair is parted in the middle and hanging over her shoulders.

"It's good to see you too, Lia," I say ignoring her attitude. "Hey, Jas."

"Hi, Rena, what's up?" Jas says as she opens her purse and puts on some lip gloss.

We all head inside the bar and take a seat at the same table by the stage as we always do. I have to admit this place is really nice. Dim lights, bluesy tunes coming from the new talent that is playing for the night. And the crowd is very trendy. Of course Lia and Jas bask in this type of atmosphere. I glance over at Jas as she orders her first drink and an appetizer. She's wearing tight, faded blue jeans and a shimmery tank top. She has on about ten various silver bangles and necklaces, studded-out earrings that hang to her shoulders, and a black page boy hat.

"So, Jas. What's the deal with that guy, what's his name? You know, the rapper?" Lia looks at Jas in a condescending way, like she's really saying, *Tell us more about that loser you met even though he'll never compare to the man I'm talking to.* The two of them are like sisters . . . right down to the sibling rivalry. It's always funny to see them in action, describing how wonderfully they're being sexed, how many pairs of shoes they bought that week.

"A-sa-ji," Jas says slowly, glaring at Lia. "Get it right."

"Okay, fine. Asaji. So, tell us what's up. How was the sex?"

"We didn't have sex. It's not about that with him." Jas says that last part quietly, almost like she's embarrassed.

"With you, Jas, it's *always* about that." Lia laughs to herself while she takes a sip of her martini. I look at Jas's face and she's not smiling.

"Lia, that was wrong," I say. "Apparently this guy is different. He may even be the one."

"Be for real, Rena." She looks at Jas. "Is he the one,

Jas?" She sticks her finger in her drink, twirls it around, and puts it in her mouth.

"I just met him. Right now, we're getting to know each other. That's it. Besides, he has a studio Uptown and he is really interested in my music," Jas says.

"That's really good, Jas," I say. It's about time she focused on something other than clothes, money, and men.

"Jas, *you're* not even interested in your music. I'm pretty sure this guy only wants one thing," Lia says.

Damn, I hate to call my sisters out of their names, and Lia is my girl, but she really is a true bitch.

"Anyway, how's your love life, Lia?" I ask, trying to avoid a serious altercation.

"Well," she begins with a grin on her face, "I met this fine-ass guy. Eric Amaretto, owner of those restaurants, you know. And he wants me to call him. He's really feeling me." She's practically beaming.

"That's because he doesn't know you yet," Jas says. "Give him time. You'll scare him away like you do everyone else." Jas grins at me and I try not to smile back, but it's probably the truth.

"Don't hate because I met a rich, gorgeous, professional man, and you met . . . well, no one really."

"Damn, you two. Do you ever stop?" I ask. I'm really getting annoyed now.

"Rena, you know we're just talking shit. It's not serious," Jas says.

"Yeah, relax," Lia says, rolling her eyes. They are always playing around, but sometimes it's just over the top. Besides, no one has asked about me or Dee Dee. I'm mad Lia hasn't even brought her name up. "What's going on with Dee, Lia?" I ask, ready to move on to another topic.

Lia looks down at her second drink that the waiter just brought out. Her face isn't filled with the cocky silliness it just was. Now she looks uneasy.

"She's okay. Just going through some things with Deron. But she said she'd be fine. Just needs to be alone for a little while," she says quickly.

"What do you mean 'some things'?" I look at Jas and she has a concerned look on her face too.

"I don't know . . . things!" Lia's voice gets louder. "Don't question me like I'm her damn PR person. I'm done talking about it." She signals to the waiter that she wants to order another drink, even though she hasn't finished the one she has now. "Oh, I almost forgot. I met someone else. His name is Ty. He's from Chicago," she says.

I hate that she's changing the subject, but I doubt we're going to get any more information at this point.

"What's his story?" Jas asks, sounding far from interested.

"He's nice looking, his body is, like, whoa, but he's black, so . . ."

Jas and I both let out a disgusted sigh. Here we go again. Lia has some serious issues. The girl's head is warped, I swear. I just don't get her. She has this ridiculous thing against black men. And the sad thing is she can't really tell you why. She'll say something idiotic and stereotypical. It's hard to believe that someone as sharp and together as Lia would have such an ignorant point of view. Makes you wonder how together she really is.

"You know, Lia," I say, "your little issues with black men make you sound so stupid. It's fine to have preferences. If you're not attracted to someone, you're just not. But it's the reasons you're not attracted to black men that we all have a problem with."

Jas nods her head in agreement as she dips a tortilla chip in spinach dip.

"Well, guess what, Miss High and Mighty? I don't really give a damn if you have a problem with me. I mean, it's not like the two of you struck gold with your men. Jas can't get one to look at her as more than a lay and you've been with Tak since, like, 1950 and the man still won't give you a ring. So please, don't talk to me about the people I date." She sits back and tosses her hair off her shoulders.

I want to slap the hell out her and it looks like Jas is about to. That was really a low blow. But then Lia speaks again.

"I'm sorry, you guys. I'm just stressed about everything." She pauses and looks at us intently. "I want to tell you about Dee. I feel like it's too much for one person to keep inside. But she made me promise not to tell anyone."

"If Dee Dee doesn't want us to know, you shouldn't tell us. Simple as that," Jas says. I think she says this because she's too afraid to know what it is.

I'm not, though. "Lia, we're all friends here. We all care about each other. Maybe Dee doesn't realize that one of us could have the solution to whatever she's going through. Give us a chance to help."

She ponders this for a minute and gulps down the last of her third martini.

"Okay. She's pregnant with a baby that Deron doesn't want, hell, a baby he doesn't even know about. He's becoming an alcoholic, if he hasn't already surpassed that point. And Manny Velasquez, Dee's old boyfriend, is trying to get it on with her again." She looks at us through glazed-over eyes, which is the first sign of her having a little too much to drink. "Oh yeah, they're broke too."

Jas and I look at each other, then back at Lia. This whole thing seems unbelievable. All this time I've been envious of Dee and her perfect little family. Come to find out her situation is worse than the rest of ours. And what if Deron really is becoming an alcoholic? That in and of itself opens up a lot of dangerous doors for Dee and her daughter.

"What's she going to do?" Jas asks in a soft, timid voice.

Lia shrugs her shoulders. "I don't know. She doesn't know." She calls for the waiter to bring the tab. "You guys are ready to leave, right? I don't feel like talking anymore." She opens her little black and white Coach bag and pulls out a platinum card.

"I was kind of hoping to talk about Dee some more. And I wanted to get your opinions on Tak—"

"Rena, I'm just not in the mood. Maybe Jas will stay." She signs the credit card receipt with a quick flourish of her hand and gets up from her chair. "I'll call you tomorrow," she says as she walks away from the table and out of the bar. Jas and I are just sitting here, not saying anything.

"Lia is so rude," Jas finally says. I can't say I disagree with her. But that's not usually the way she is. Most of time when we get together, it's all laughs and jokes. Each of us brings a different dynamic to the group. Lia is somewhat the leader, I'd say. She's the one most of us talk to individually when something's going on. As a matter of fact, she introduced all of us to each other. She's the one who plans any type of event we all attend or a trip we all take, like when all of us went to Vegas last spring. She's the most outspoken, and probably the most self-centered. But I can't deny that she's a loyal friend. She has her mood swings; we all do. But when it comes down it, she'll have your back always. On the other hand, if you're an enemy . . . just don't get on her bad side, okay?

Jas is the young'n of the group. A little misguided, a little immature, and a total free spirit. She reminds us to lighten up and enjoy life, not just live it. She's a sweet girl, but sometimes it's like she needs a spanking (although according to some of her sexcapades I'm sure she wouldn't mind).

Dee Dee is the mothering type. If you need a shoulder to cry on, call her. She's constantly finding the silver lining in all situations, and quick to try to take your side no matter who may be at fault. She's always trying to please everyone, though. Sometimes at her own expense.

And then me, well . . . I guess I kind of balance everyone else out. I'm an educator. I like for people to understand themselves and their environments. I believe everything happens for a reason and so I try to get people to see the bigger picture.

Wait a minute. Everything happens for a reason. So I guess there's a reason why Tak and I haven't gotten married yet. Maybe it's not supposed to happen. Maybe there's someone else out there for me. Maybe Tak is just not the one. After all these years, maybe it's just not meant to be. I don't know how I feel about that revelation. It is quite possible that Tak is just in my life for a season and it's time for me to make a serious move in some direction. Especially since he can't seem to.

"Rena!" Jas is shaking my arm.

"Oh, sorry. Were you saying something?" Was I that deep in my thoughts?

"I was saying that I have plans to meet Asaji in a little while. Do you want to leave together? His studio is around where you live. We can share a cab."

"Um, how old is Asaji?"

"Twenty-two," she replies.

"Does he have any older friends? I feel like meeting someone tonight," I say casually.

Jas looks at me like I've lost my mind. I think I have.

"What about Tak?" she asks. Yeah, what about his non-committing ass?

"I just want to meet someone, not sleep with him," I say

to her. I guess I don't sound too convincing because she looks at me in an *I don't know about this'* kind of way.

"Well, I'm sure he does. There's always a bunch of niggas, I mean, guys hanging around the studio."

I laugh at her attempt to correct her slang. All my friends know I can't stand for our people to use that language when referring to ourselves. People can try to justify it all they want, but I know the history.

"Jas, you are a mess," I say, smiling. "Well, good. Let's go, then." We get up from the table and leave an extra ten-dollar tip even though Lia probably already put it on her card.

"And since when do you want an older man, cradle robber?" she asks me, laughing. I laugh too, but at the same time I really consider what she says. Maybe I should have wanted an older man all along.

"Let's go, smart-ass," I say as the two of us walk out of the bar.

We get back Uptown and arrive at Asaji's studio called "Streetz Is Talkin'. It's on the second floor of a six-story building maybe ten blocks from my house. I start to really think about what I'm doing and I begin to have second thoughts, but I'm curious to see the man who has Jas acting out of character. She calls him from her cell phone to tell him we're outside and then we wait for him to come downstairs to get us.

"He doesn't mind that I came, does he?" I ask her, almost hoping it is a problem so I can go home.

"Girl, no. It's cool," she says. Just then a tall, caramel-colored young man appears from inside. He's wearing a red, white, and blue Rocawear sweatsuit and all-white Nike Air Force Ones. On his head is a white do-rag and he's smoking a Black & Mild. Jas hugs him and says what's up?

"This is my homegirl, Rena. Rena, Asaji." She steps back so we can shake hands.

"Nice to meet you, Rena. Y'all ready to go upstairs?"

Jas nods her head and takes Asaji's hand. She turns and looks at me, wanting to know my opinion. I smile at her to let her know that I think he's cute. She smiles back and turns back around, squeezing his hand tighter.

Once we get upstairs, expensive-looking equipment, instruments, and what looks like thousands of records surround us. There's an old-looking couch in the corner and I take a seat, not wanting to interfere with whatever Jas and Asaji have in mind.

"So, where are your boys at?" Jas asks Asaji, picking up a piece of sheet music.

"Oh, my boy Lace will be here. He went up the block for a minute." He looks at me. "I think you'll like him. He's a dread too."

I nod my head and smile, wondering why people always think that all people with locks get along with each other. Like, just because we have our hair in the same style, our personalities must be similar. Please. Maybe this whole thing wasn't such a good idea. I decide to tell Jas I'm going to leave when I hear music playing from the speakers. It's a slow, intense beat. The melody is played by a piano, sounding smooth and sensual. I feel like I could get lost in the rhythm.

"I don't know, I think I want to redo the beginning," Jas says to Asaji. I snap out of my reverie.

"Jas, that's you?" I ask in awe. I always hear about Jas's talent, but I never actually *heard* her play, you know? "You sound incredible."

"You think so? I haven't played in months. I'm a little rusty," she say modestly, which is a rare emotion when it comes to Jas.

"No, baby, you hot," Asaji says, before looking at me.

"You know she writes too? She composed what you're listening to now."

"Really, Jas? You know you should really pursue this as a career. I knew you were good, but . . ." This whole thing is such a surprise to me.

"Yo, what's good, people?" A fairly tall, cinnamon-colored man with reddish brown dreads pulled back in a ponytail comes into the room. He daps up Asaji and hugs Jas. "How you doin', Ma?" he asks her.

"I'm fine, Lace." She walks over to me. "This is Rena."

Lace sits down next to me and holds out his hand.

"I'm Lace, sweetheart," he says. I shake his hand and smile.

"Good to meet you," I say. He smells so good, like a body oil that Tak sometimes wears . . . Egyptian Musk.

"Well, Jas and I are gonna go in the next room and work on some things. Holla if you need us," says Asaji. The two of them walk out and shut the door. Hmm, what now? It's been so long since I've had to talk with a man other than Tak, you know, on one of these levels.

"So, you're from Harlem?" Lace asks.

"Yes, I live not too far from here."

"True." He pauses. "You know you have some beautiful eyes." He reaches up and smoothes out my eyebrows. "They're the color of desert sand." God, I hope I'm not blushing. "Makes me wanna call you Sahara," he continues. Okay, I know I'm blushing. If this is how the young boys these days are doing it, then maybe I do need to get back in the game.

"You are too much," I say, looking away from him. I don't want him to see the huge grin I have on my face.

"Nah, I'm just telling the truth, Ma," he says nonchalantly while sitting back on the couch.

"How old are you anyway?" I ask.

"Old enough to know that age doesn't matter if two adults are feelin' each other."

"That sounds like a cop-out to me."

"Okay, I'm twenty-four," he says. Damn, I was hoping for at least a few more years. I already have a twenty-four-year-old. "Does that change anything? Does my age mean you'd rather not talk to me anymore?"

"No, not at all. I was just wondering."

"Well, how 'bout you wonder about this: the two of us, getting to know each other, seeing where this thing will lead? 'Cause seriously, I'm getting a vibe from you. And I wanna find out why," he says to me. Wow, I thought I was the only one who felt it.

"That sounds good. I feel like I'm getting a vibe from you too," I say, feeling like a schoolgirl.

He grins at me and adjusts the ankh necklace I have around my neck. I feel a tingling sensation as his hand briefly touches me. Not since I first started dating Tak have I felt such a strong connection with someone I just met. Like I know him from some place else.

"I feel like once I get to know you, it'll be like discovering something that was already there, ya know?" he says.

Damn, wasn't I just thinking that? This is so weird. "This is a trip, Lace. It's almost like you're reading my thoughts."

"Maybe you're sending them to me," he says.

Okay that's it. I'm starting to have feelings that I shouldn't be having when you just meet someone. Where the hell is Jas?

"I'm gonna give you my number, a'ight? Call me tomorrow. We can catch a flick maybe. And there's this West Indian spot on 145th I think you'll like."

"Is it called Caribe?" I ask.

"Yeah, you know it?"

"I've been there a few times with my . . ." I stop myself before I mention Tak's name. "Yeah, I've been there. I love their oxtails. Are you West Indian?

"Well, my grandparents were from Trinidad," he says.

"Really? My father is from Barbados," I say. "But yeah, I'd love to go."

"It's a plan, then." He takes a business card out of his pocket. It has all of his studio info and cell phone number on it. "Call me, Sahara," he says.

Just as he's standing up, Jas and Asaji emerge from the other room. Jas shoots me a look that says, *So, do you like him?* I grin at her and she laughs.

"You ready to go?" she asks.

"Yeah." I stand up and give Lace a hug. He squeezes me a little too tightly, but I don't mind.

"Don't forget, a'ight, Ma?"

"I won't," I say as Jas and Asaji say good-bye and the two of us leave the studio.

"It seems like you and Lace hit it off," Jas says, grinning.

"He's different. I'm anxious to know more about him. We're probably going out tomorrow." Jas doesn't say anything for a few minutes. I can tell she's feeling a little uncomfortable.

"This is just a friendship thing, right? You're still in love with Tak, right?" she asks, sounding really concerned. Although it was a question, it sounds like she's making a statement.

"Yes, I'm in love with him. I don't plan on leaving him." But as we all know, plans sometimes change.

"Well, that's good. The two of you are perfect for each other," she says.

I consider this as we walk down the steps to the subway. I can't deny that Tak and I are good together. We have a lot in common despite our age difference and we really do care for each other. But to think that we're "perfect" for each other? It's almost like the situation with Dee and Deron. From the outside looking in, all of us thought they were the ideal. It was true love, they were meant to be, all of that. But the reality is that they are suffering from problems none of us can begin to imagine. I think Jas is looking at Tak and me in that way. To anyone else, we're so right. But to me, there's just something wrong.

We walk through the turnstile and wait for the 6 to take Jas downtown and me back to 116th. It's about ten o'clock and the platform is filled with people on their way to begin their Saturday night. It makes me almost want to go to a club. But I haven't been out like that in a long time. Tak isn't too big on the club scene, so I try to stay away from it. But now that I think about it, why the hell shouldn't I go? I don't see any rings on my fingers. I glance over at Jas, who is being checked out by a couple of tomboyish females and enjoying every minute of it. She makes a big show of bending over to fix the bottom of her jeans and then applying some lip gloss. She's such a tease.

"Jas, what are you about to do now?" I ask her.

"I don't know. I have a cell phone bill that needs to be paid. I may have to visit a friend of mine," she says.

Oh, boy. "How about we go out? Take me to one of your spots . . . Bungalow or something." I really don't know where she hangs out, but at this point I'm just ready to go somewhere.

She looks at me in a funny way. "Girl, you are really showing out tonight. I'll take you to a club. But let's do it real easy for now . . . how about Webster Hall?"

"Webster Hall. What, you don't think I'm ready for anything else?"

"Girl, you ready. But you know . . ." She looks me up and down. ". . . maybe they ain't ready for you."

"What are you saying? You don't like my outfit?" Sure, I don't dress like Lia or Jas, but my style suits me. Right now I'm wearing a long purple wrap skirt, a lavender baby tee, and a gold-chain, belly-dancer-looking belt. My jewelry consists of an arm cuff, five gold bracelets on each arm, and the ankh choker that Tak gave me on our six-month anniversary. Of course my locks are wrapped and on my feet is a pair of thong sandals. It's not for everyone, but neither is that way-too-expensive Gucci stuff my friends wear.

"Hey, let's just go by my place and change. I know we're not the same size, but we can put something together." In other words, she's not taking me anywhere as long as I have this on. I sigh but give in.

"Fine, Jas," I say just as the train pulls up. As much as I loathe conformity, I do know that Jas is a fashion maven and if she has some ideas for me, I have nothing to lose by going along with them. As we board the train, I think about Tak and how disappointed he would be if he knew I was going to a club. But just as quickly as he enters my thoughts, he is replaced by Lace. I wonder if I should even tell Tak about him. I don't see what the point would be. Lace and I are just friends and nothing more. All we're going to do is hang out a little bit. He probably has a girl-friend anyway. And plus, he's, well, he's so attractive. And his complexion . . . yum. And I cannot get over our conversation. As short as it was, it still felt, I don't know, power-ful. Maybe I'm reading too much into it, though. I mean, look at me . . . thirty years old and acting like a teenager.

"Man, Rena, this is gonna be so fun. We haven't been out in, like, years. You're gonna forget all about Tak tonight, girl," Jas says.

Well, damn, maybe I already have.

Chapter 4

Jas

What a night. I just got back home from the club with Rena, and damn. It seems like she pulled more guys than I did. It was cool, though. I think she needed that. She's been wrapped up in Tak for so long I bet she forgot what it feels like to be wanted by other men. It's good that she has some-body, but I don't know. For me, I need lots of change and variety. Okay, maybe that sounds bad. I mean, it's not like I want to be with a lot of different guys, I just have to. I was sucked into this lifestyle and can't get out of it. That's one thing about me that my girls don't understand. They see me as this floozy, fucking my way through life without a care in the world. But the truth is, I don't enjoy it. I don't want to have to sleep with a man so I can go shopping or pay my electric bill. But I can't be a jazzy lawyer like Lia, or a super, soul-sister teacher like Rena. My talent is looking fly and meeting guys. Well, I suppose that's not entirely true. My music is pretty on point. I think that's why I like Asaji so much. He's the first man who focused on me and not my body, not the sex. It hasn't even come up, actually. It's new to me. And I need that.

The next morning I wake and hop into the shower. It's Sunday. Church day. None of my friends know that I attend church every week. I can't imagine telling Lia that I go to church. She'd look at me in that *I know better* kind of way and just talk shit. She'd ask me how someone with my background and way of living could possibly have the nerve to go to church on Sunday like I'm a good girl. I don't want to deal with that. Lia is my best friend, but she's also my worst critic. She thinks everyone should be like her. Well, my bad for not being some child genius/spoiled rich kid. Yeah, Lia was raised with money. She'd never admit it, though. If it were up to her, everyone would think that she made it happen all herself. Like she was born and raised in the ghetto and turned her life around to become this suave businesswoman. Not true. I mean, I give the girl credit. She did her thing in college and law school and has everything to show for it. But she didn't have a hard life. She didn't have to struggle for anything. If she weren't a lawyer she'd still be wearing Gucci because that's how she was raised. Her parents aren't millionaires like Dee's parents are or anything, but her mother is all about appearances, and any money that was made was put toward their wardrobes and luxury cars. I'm sure their finances suffered. I mean, how much dough does a military solider make anyway? But it didn't matter. As long as people *thought* they had unlimited funds, that was the main thing. Me, on the other hand . . . whoa. Totally different upbringing. I have two younger sisters and an older brother. My sisters and I shared a room in our three-bedroom home until I left for college. I mean, seriously. All three of us in one room. It was beyond hell. My dad was (and still is) a plumber and my mom was a seamstress. I never knew anything about new clothes because my mom made everything we wore. The only things we ever went shopping for were shoes. I guess at the time it didn't matter as much. The town I grew up in is really small, really country, and really quiet. Growing up, we didn't know there was anything more to life because everyone else was just like us. And I hate to think about it now, but if my high school music instructor hadn't encouraged me to apply to college in New York, I may still be in South Carolina, wasting my life. 'Cause trust me, SC is no place for black people.

After getting dressed (I decide on a cream-colored Calvin Klein pantsuit) I go outside to hail a cab. I'm not risking taking the train today. This outfit cost way too much. This guy I was dating for a little while bought it for me one day after we . . . Ya know what, never mind. We all know how the story ends. So anyway, I get in the cab, and it takes me over toward City Hall where my church is located. I pay the driver, get out of the cab, and make my way up the church steps.

Being here makes me feel so good. Like, no matter what I've done all week, at this point, I get to try again. I get another chance to make it better. I take my usual seat on the right-hand side of the sanctuary. The church isn't all that big. I think maybe there are about five hundred members. I've been to churches with thousands before. Although I make the decision to come every Sunday, if it hadn't been for the fact that I was brought up in the church, I probably wouldn't be here. My parents are very traditional, and very southern. They believe the church is the foundation of family, love, and life. I never really took to that point of view, but I appreciate that they gave me something to hold on to when I was younger. Something that gave me hope.

As the congregation fills the pews, the music begins

and the praise team starts a medley of call-and-response songs. Most people are standing, clapping, and singing along. All of this is cool. I mean, I like this part of the service, but I'm waiting for the pastor to preach. Pastor Theodore Gordon is one of the most charismatic, articulate people I've ever come in contact with. He's so real. He doesn't sugarcoat anything and his sermons are like a slap in the face sometimes. It's all good, though. The people need to hear the truth. We're New Yorkers, we can take it.

After all the choir hymns, announcements, and offering collections, Pastor Gordon takes the pulpit. He's about forty years old with a headful of gray hairs that don't add to his age at all. His skin is very dark, very shiny. He wears thin, wire-rimmed glasses and no wedding ring. I've always wondered why he's not married. He's handsome, for a preacher, that is, and I'm sure he has a lot to offer a woman. So anyway, he begins to speak and I'm totally captivated by what he's saying. The title of the sermon is "Letting Go and Giving It Up." I become lost in his words:

". . . and we all go through trials and tribulations, troubles and temptations. But you can't let the negative situations of your past keep you from living your present and preparing for your future. God does not want you to be a prisoner of the bad times you have encountered. 'No weapon formed against me shall prosper.' Nothing that has happened to you is stronger than what God has in store for you. Let go, my brother. Let go, my sister. God has a plan for your life. That thing that's keeping you down, that person who's keeping you down, that circumstance that's keeping you down . . . let it go, and give it up to God. He has started something in you and he's not finished yet. Many of us are holding on to the pain. Many of us have allowed the shackles of regret, guilt, and shame to keep us locked into a life that we know we don't deserve. Let it go, and give it up to God. . . ."

Tears fall from my eyes. I know people say this all the time, but I swear he's talking directly to me. I begin to have flashbacks. They take me back to a time that I don't want to go to. But in order to finally let it go, I have to go back.

It was a hot, sticky, May night. My dress was black. My mom made it for me. It fit my shape so well. My hair was long then, piled on top of my head with a sparkly head-band. The shoes I wore were the most expensive things I had on. Sixty-five dollars from Rich's. My sister polished my nails Platinum Princess. It was my prom night. My first date with Roderick Smith, shooting guard for the basket-ball team. He picked me up in his metallic-blue 1996 Mus-tang convertible . . . I shut down what I'm thinking. It scares me, ya know? I don't want to think about what happened. I don't want to have to remember. But I know in my heart that it's the reason my life is the way it is now. I've been a prisoner to my past, just like the pastor said. And as a result, I don't have the life I deserve. After the service is over, I make my way to the back of the church, hoping to get a meeting with the pastor. I don't have an appoint-ment, but I pray he can see me.

"You need to see Pastor Gordon, baby?" a slender, older woman with puffy white hair under one of those big church hats asks me.

"I really would like to speak with him," I reply, trying to hold back the tears.

"Well, have a seat in his office. He'll be down soon." She walks away as I sit in a chair opposite the pastor's desk. I'm nervous and scared . . . but more than that, I'm ready.

The prom was beautiful. We had a good time. Everyone loved my dress. I remember the punch . . . it was blue, with pineapples in it. Most of my friends went to the park after it was over. Rod and I went to the lake. We sat in the car for a while. I wanted him to kiss me. I wanted him to touch me. So he did. It felt good. Warm. But then he didn't pull away when I did. He continued to kiss and touch me, then much harder. I said stop. I yelled it. His hand pulled down my panties. I thought to myself, This is really happening. I'm really going to be raped. *I kept telling him to stop. He was all sweaty and his breath smelled like old Doublemint gum. He kind of grinned at me, like it was a game. I tried to push him off me, but he pinned my arms down with one hand as he unzipped his pants with the other. I cried. I begged him not to. But then, I was quiet. Once he entered me the tears still fell, but I was quiet. No matter what happened then it was too late. Even if the cops came knocking on the steamed-up car window or Rod suddenly decided he didn't want to anymore, it was too late. I had been raped as soon as his penis touched my body. I wasn't Jasmine Lewis anymore; I was the girl who had been raped. That's all I was.*

"How's everything today, miss?" Pastor Gordon asks ten minutes later when he walks in.

"Fine. I mean, not fine." I can't get my head straight. He takes a seat at his desk and hands me a tissue.

"You're here to talk, I'm here to listen. And if you want me to, I'll give you my perspective on what you tell me. You can start whenever you like." He's very in control. Very no-nonsense. I think his demeanor is going to make this a lot easier.

I take a deep breath and dab my eyes with the tissue. The pastor looks at me intently. Not in an impatient way, but rather in a way that's eager for me to confront what's bothering me.

"Your message touched me in a profound way. It made me come to terms with something that I've avoided for years. You said that I need to let go of the thing that's keeping me down. Well, I know what that thing is. And I need to tell someone so that I can finally put it to rest." I stop and think about all the other people I could have told this to. There's just something about the pastor that makes me feel stable enough to talk about it.

"Whenever you're ready."

"When I was eighteen, six years ago, I was raped. I have never told anyone. I barely admit it to myself." The tears fall again, angrily and steadily.

"Take your time," he says.

"No, I've taken too much time. That's the problem. I let what he did to me into every aspect of my life. I can't keep a job; I can't keep a relationship . . . I can't even start one. Not a real one anyway. I use men. I feel justified in it because somebody has to pay. Someone has to pay for what he did." I realize my voice has gotten higher and louder. I take another deep breath. "I don't want to hold on to the past anymore. I don't want to relive that night ever again. I want my life back. I want the control again." I listen to myself speak because I've never said these things before. I've never felt the way I feel now. It's all so clear to me.

"You came to me for insight, but I think you've gotten it from yourself. What you need to understand is that God did not want you to be raped. He did not want you to be taken advantage of. Don't confuse the devil's malice for God's plan."

"I know. I mean, shit happens." I think about what I just said. "Oh, sorry. Stuff happens." *Come on, Jas, get it together.*

The Pastor nods his head. "This rape doesn't define you. It doesn't make you any more or less of a person. It's how you deal with the aftermath that will add to or take away from your character. You said you use men, can't keep a job . . . it's because of the way you handled the rape. Or more accurately, didn't handle it. You told no one, you kept it all in. No wonder you feel like you've lost control. Your rapist still has the control. This is a first step, but it's not the only step." He reaches into his desk and pulls out a few pamphlets. "I want you to attend a rape survivors meeting. I also want you to practice looking in the mirror every day and saying, 'I have the control.' Because you do." He hands me the papers.

"You're right, Pastor. I do." I've stopped crying. But I'm not talking about external tears; I mean I've stopped crying on the inside. I stand and get ready to walk out.

"You never said your name. You don't have to . . ."

"Jasmine Lewis."

"Jasmine Lewis. I'm glad you came by. And if you ever need to talk again, about anything, just call." He stands to shake my hand.

"I will. Thank you, Pastor."

Once I get back to my apartment I begin to think of all the ways my life will change now that I'm moving on from my past. Just as I get comfortable on my couch, the phone rings. Sigh.

"Hello?"

"Jas, guess what!" It's Rena, sounding a little too giddy.

"Huh?"

"I just came back from the restaurant with Lace. We had such a good time. We're about to go to the movies in a minute. I just wanted to come home and grab a jacket."

"Wait a minute. You brought him back to your place?" I have to sit up for this. "What if Tak shows up? He does have a key, right?"

"Yeah, but he's not bringing Lion back until tonight. Anyway, it's not like that. We're just friends."

"Sure, Rena. If you're just friends why'd you feel the need to call and tell me about your date?" Silence.

"It's not a date. And we haven't done anything."

"I hope you know what you're doing. If Tak finds out . . ."

"There's nothing to find out. Besides, maybe if he did know it'd make him take this relationship more seriously."

I sigh and shake my head. Here we go. I'm not feeding into it, though. Rena can go on and on about this. I'm not going to scold her about Lace either. She can play this little affair game all she wants. I just hope she doesn't get caught up.

"Okay, Rena. Be careful, though. Some guys can be intoxicating. Lace may be one of them."

"I'm sure he is. But it's not about that. Anyway, I have to go. I'll call you later. Peace, sister."

We hang up and I go back to my original thoughts. I get so deep into them I don't even notice myself falling asleep.

The doorbell wakes me up four hours later. I'm not expecting company and I have no clue who it could be. I still have on my church clothes and everything. I go to the door and look through the peephole. It's Asaji. It looks like he has groceries in his hand. I open the door and he rushes past me.

"I'm making you dinner tonight, Ma. Damn, this shit is heavy," he says as puts the bags on the kitchen counter. This whole time I'm thinking, *Ummm* . . .

"You're cooking?" *Yeah, right,* I think.

"Yeah, I'm cooking. Mama taught me a lil' somethin' growin' up. I got all kinds of skills you don't know about." He walks over to me and kisses my forehead. "You, take a bath, change your clothes, and get comfortable."

I'm still in shock, but start to walk toward the bathroom.

"How do you like your steak, Ma?"

Steak? Damn, he's really serious. "Uh, medium-well."

"A'ight, cool." And that's it. He says nothing else and all I hear is sizzling and chopping.

About forty-five minutes later I've changed into a satin, pale pink Victoria's Secret shorts and tank top set and Asaji is putting the food on the table. It smells so good. I take a seat as he pours a glass of red wine for each of us. I've only known him for a few days, but he's doing things some of my exes never did. He really is different. He sits across from me and tells me to take the first bite. I cut a piece of steak and it's damn near orgasmic. It's perfect.

"Asaji, you are the shit, boy."

He smiles and begins to eat as well. "So, I've been talk-ing to a few people about you doing some things for other artists. Alicia Keys, Kelly Price . . . these are a few names that came up. I just want you to meet Alicia. You know, the whole piano thing is something you guys have in common. I think she could really put you on."

"Yeah," I say softly as I look down at my plate.

"You a'ight? You not feelin' that or something?"

"Of course I'm feelin' that. Everything you've done for me, I'm feelin'. It's just that . . . I really like you. I know it's soon, but I like you so much. This never happens to me," I tell him. And it's the truth. I never really like any guy in a way that makes me think about being with him.

"I like you too, Ma. I don't usually meet ladies as to-gether as you are."

As together as I am? Ha. It's only today that I accepted how triflin' I was living and why. I'm far from together. But Asaji doesn't have to know that.

"So, you're washing dishes too?" I ask, trying to get away from that subject.

"Oh, no doubt. But then I have to go. Got a few things I have to take care of." Aw, man. He's leaving?

"You sure you can't stay the night?" I ask as seductively as I can.

"Nah, Ma. I wish. Another time, fa sho."

"All right." Maybe it's for the best. I bet once we have sex it's all going straight to hell anyway. "But this," I say, gesturing toward the food, "was excellent. You better stop before I start expecting it."

"It's all good, Ma. I can handle it." And I'm thinking to myself, maybe I've been underestimating him all along. Maybe he really can handle it. And maybe he actually wants to.

Chapter 5

Dee Dee

Finally. Deidre is asleep. It took me forever to put her down for her midday nap. For some reason she was extra active today. Of course I'm the only one who has to deal with her when she's like that. Deron won't go near her anymore. When he's here he's either locked in his office, typing away, or drinking himself into a rage. Rage. That's really what it's become. He's never hit me. But I always feel like it's getting to that point. And then there are the people he brings to this house. People I don't trust. Always a lot of secrecy. Deron tells me to go into the bedroom when they come, but I still know. I still sense what's going on.

Tap, tap, tap, click, click, click. He's in there now, trying to finish the final chapter of his third novel. The sound of his computer used to comfort me. It used to make me feel like he was about something . . . like he was passionate about what he was doing. Now the sound just reminds me of the distance between us. We're no longer a part of each other's world. I hate that it's come to this. I love my husband with everything I have. But the way our lives have changed hurts. And I fear that it will only get worse.

I look down at my belly and rub my hand over it. It's a boy; I know it. I'll call him Donovan, or Devin. I shouldn't have named him, but he's my child. My son. After talking to Lia yesterday I realized I could never give him up. Now I just have to tell Deron. How do you tell a man you don't know that you're having his child, knowing he doesn't want it? Oh my. Did I just say that? Did I just say that I don't know my own husband? How in the world did this happen?

I remember the day we met. He was talking to a professor at Columbia after a seminar on the impact of twentieth-century writers on the literary movement. Okay, so it may not sound interesting, but that's what drew me to him; he's so sophisticated in that way. I must not have been too subtle while I was watching him, because the girl I was with, my cousin Gabriela, made a few less than kind remarks about him. See, I'm a New Yorker even though I spent the first ten or so years of my life in Spain, and when my family moved to New York, it wasn't to the city. There's a big difference. Long Island isn't too far, but it's a world away. Especially where I lived, in South Hampton. There are very few blacks there, except celebrities who vacation there and such. And even with them the white locals can be somewhat cliquish. It was never an issue with my family, however. Technically, we are Hispanic. But my parents didn't raise us with any pride in our heritage. Because we looked white, that's what we were. My father tried very hard to fit us in with white socialites and businessmen of New York. My parents never told me not to date a black man because they probably never considered the possibility. Where would I even meet one? They didn't use the "n word" in our house, not because they weren't racist, but because only lower-class individuals used that language. The only time I was allowed in the city (until I was about seventeen) was for shopping. So I didn't really grow up in the melting pot that is NYC. But I have to say, ever since I knew what it meant to want a boy, I've wanted black boys. And then I think about all those society, yacht club, and polo-playing guys my parents wanted me to date. Don't get me wrong; I met a few who were decent. But those guys just could not compare. Then there was the whole matter of culture. African-Americans, black people, they just have so much history . . . so much strength and beauty in their pasts. It intrigues me. Everything I learn about it makes me want to know more. That's why I'm so grateful to know Rena. She teaches me so much about where my child and husband come from. It's a beautiful thing.

Back to reality. This isn't four years ago. This is now. I have to tell him. I walk to the locked door of his office and stand there for a few minutes. I remember when I told him I was pregnant with Deidre. The love in his eyes and the smile on his face said more than any words he could have spoken. Maybe this time it'll be the same. Maybe . . .

"Dee, what the hell are you doing standing there?" Deron is six inches from my face, standing in the doorway.

"Nothing. I was on my way in. I was about to knock." I'm beginning to think this isn't a good time.

"You were listening to my phone conversation, weren't you?" He has his finger in my face. And is that brandy I smell on his breath?

"What? I didn't even know you were on the phone."

"Yeah, right. For some reason you've been really nosy lately. I don't know what your problem is, Dee, but what I do is my business. The next time I catch you spying on me, it's your ass." He walks past me, pushing me aside. This is the type of thing I've been putting up with for a while now. My marriage is a joke. But I refuse to continue to raise my child in this environment and I damn sure will not bring another one into it. We're going to fix this right now.

I follow him into the kitchen to see him pouring a glass of tea.

"What are you going to spike that with?" I ask sarcastically. He ignores me and opens the cabinet to get out a bottle of rum. He's too quiet. That can't be good.

"You received a call today," he says calmly. My heart starts racing. God, I hope it wasn't Manny.

"Who called?" I ask casually, not really wanting to know the answer.

"A loan company. They said you were approved for the ten thousand dollars you applied for. Now, why is it that I don't know anything about this loan, Dee?"

"I didn't think I would get it, first of all. And second—"

"Bullshit!" He slams the glass of rum and tea on the kitchen table. "You think I can't provide for us anymore? Are you wishing you would have married one of those white Wall Streeters like your daddy wanted you to? Fuck you, Dee! I don't need this shit!" He turns to walk away.

"Wait, Deron," I yell after him. "I'm pregnant again." The thickness in the air is unbearable. I have no idea what he'll do or say next.

"We can't afford another baby," he says emotionlessly. The expression on his face is uninterested. I'm flabbergasted at his reaction . . . or rather his lack of reaction. But even more so I'm pissed off.

"What the hell does that mean, Deron? We can't afford another baby? Well, guess what? Too fucking bad! We're having one! The question is, how are we going to handle it? *No le dejaré rasgar a esta familia aparte*!" I've never cursed at my husband before. I've never even raised my voice to him.

"Figure it out. You want to make all these decisions without me, then figure this one out. I'm outta here."

I jump as the door slams. Sigh. That did not go as I planned. I don't have any idea what to do next. Or maybe I do. I go to my bedroom and pull my address book out of my dresser drawer. I don't know exactly what I expect to happen, but whatever does happen can't possibly be any worse than what already has happened.

"Hello?"

"Manny? This is Dee Dee."

"Dee! I never expected to hear from you."

"I never expected to call. But I was wondering, if you're not busy, maybe we can have that dinner tonight." My heart is about to pound out of my chest.

"Tonight is good. But you had to know I wouldn't turn you down. You always had that effect on me," he says. I smile a little bit at his comment and think about where the two of us went wrong. What if I would have stuck it out with him? What would my life be like now? I'd be an athlete's wife. I wouldn't want for anything. And I'd be carrying his child instead of . . . sigh.

"How about seven, then?" I ask.

"Perfect. Should I come pick you up or do you want to meet?"

"I'll meet you." I'm bold but I'm not stupid. If Deron found out that I was even talking to Manny let alone meeting him, he'd . . . That's the thing, I have no clue what he'd do.

"I was thinking Ruth Chris down in Midtown. Is that okay?"

"Sounds good. I'll see you at seven, then. Wait, it's been four years. You won't recognize me," I say.

"Dee Dee, don't you know I could never forget you?"

"Okay, Manny. See you soon." Is it me or did I just arrange a date with my ex-boyfriend? I guess it's not that big of a deal. It's just an innocent dinner between old buddies. Old sex buddies.

I call Hannah, my neighbor and babysitter, to see if she can stay with Deidre for a few hours and she says she'll be over in thirty minutes. I take this time to hop in the shower and straighten my naturally wavy hair. I examine my naked body in the mirror. I'm so grateful that I always appear to be thin even when I'm pregnant. Not that I'm trying to hide anything. But I'm not ready to tell Manny my "situation" just yet. I put on a pair of slim black pants and a burgundy off-the-shoulder shirt. I'm not trying to look sexy, but I have to admit . . . I look sexy! I hear Hannah at the door and I let her in.

"Mrs. Smalls, you look so nice! Are you two having a date night?" Hannah asks naively.

Well, yes and no . . . "Actually I'm meeting a few friends. If Mr. Smalls comes home before I do, tell him to call my cell, okay? Deidre is in her playpen and her bottles are already made. She needs a bath too."

"No problem. Have fun," she says.

I smile and go outside to wait for the cab I called to arrive. Right now I'm feeling excited and extremely nervous about seeing Manny again. It's not like he's just another guy, you know? He's someone who once had my heart. And broke it.

After my cab arrives and I take my twenty-minute commute to Manhattan, I'm standing in front of the restaurant having second thoughts about the whole thing. I should just turn around and go home. I can't risk Deron finding out and I can't risk Manny thinking we can ever be more than friends again. I start to walk away from the entrance just as someone calls my name. I turn around and see Manny. He looks just as I remember him the last time we were face-to-face. I've seen him on TV and in the papers since then, but to see him in person. It's different . . . more real.

"Dee Dee! Baby, you are still so beautiful," he says as he embraces me in a tight hug. I step back and really take a long look at him. His crisp white button-up looks perfect against his pecan-colored skin. His smile is blinding.

"Thank you," I say. "You look great too. I guess the Yanks are treating you well."

"Can't complain. You want to go in now, or . . ."

"Sure," I say. He takes my hand and leads me past the hostess and into a private dining room. The server arrives shortly to offer us the wine selection.

"I'm not drinking tonight," I say.

"That makes two of us, then," Manny says. The server brings us water while we look over the menu. I can feel his eyes on me even though I'm not looking at him. "You seem a little nervous," he says.

"Nervous isn't the word."

"But it's something, right? Tell me because I want to make you feel as comfortable as possible. Whatever you need, let me know," he says.

"I'm fine, really," I say, trying not to focus on my discomfort. "So, four years. What have you been doing with yourself?" I ask teasingly.

"Well, remember that little sport I used to play all the time? I kind of made a career of it," he responds with a grin.

"Kind of? That's an understatement. I've been following you off and on and—"

"Off and on? You mean to tell me you weren't keeping track of my every move?" We laugh as the server comes back to take our orders. We both get the filet mignon and asparagus.

"Seriously, Manny. I'm proud of you. I never got to tell you that."

"That means everything coming from you. Look, Dee Dee, I, uh . . . I really feel the need to apologize for the way everything happened. I feel like I abandoned you and you know that's not the way I operate." He reaches out for my hand. "You can forgive me, right?"

I look into his midnight-colored eyes and see everything that I saw the first time he told me he loved me. "Of course I forgive you, Manny. That was a crazy time. I understand."

His fingers come to the one-carat diamond I'm wearing on my left hand. We both look at each other and a twinge of guilt shoots through my body. But I'm not sure if I feel guilty about being here with him, or guilty about moving on from him.

"Yeah," he says as he pulls away. "I really messed up." He sighs and leans back in his chair. I try to think of a way to change the subject.

"How are your sisters?" I ask.

"Rosa is doing well in high school, about to go to Rutgers in the fall. Eva and Christina are starting a jewelry business. Jessica just got married and Tina is pregnant. She's due in two months."

"Wow. I'm glad everyone is doing well."

"Look, Dee Dee. Can we cut the bullshit? We can do this small talk thing all night, but that's not why I've been calling you and asked you to meet me."

"So why did you, Manny? I mean, God. I've been racking my brain for the past few weeks trying to figure out why you decided to contact me after all these years. After I'm married with a child and another one on the way." I never get so dramatic, but I feel like I'm losing my mind. Thankfully the server comes back with our food and breaks the momentum. But not for long. . . .

"I'm sorry my timing is so bad. I knew you'd meet

someone else. I knew you'd get over me. But I never got over you."

"Damn it, Manny! What do you want me to do with this? You want me to leave my husband? Come running back to you?"

"I want to get the chance to fall in love again, Dee Dee. I love my life. I have all the cash and fame that I thought about having as a kid. And I thought that would be enough. I thought the girls who would do anything just to spend the night with me would be enough. But it's not. You were the only one who gave me everything. I fucked that up, I know. But I'll be fucking up even more if I don't try to make it right."

"Manny, you can't do this to me."

"I'm sorry, but I have to. We deserve another chance. We can take it as slow or as fast as you want, but I promise you . . . now that I have you back I'm holding on."

"But you don't have me back. And you can't hold on to what you don't have."

He lowers his eyes. The tension in the air is smothering me. Where is that damn server when you need him?

"I'm not giving up," he says solemnly.

"I'm married, Manny," I tell him in a way that's begging him to let go.

"But he doesn't love you the way I do. He can't," he says. And the sad thing is that he might be right.

After a very tense and difficult meal, Manny offers to take me back home, but I tell him no. He hails a cab for me after signing a few autographs for some tourists and gives me a good-bye hug.

"Interesting evening, right?" he asks with a smirk.

"Very. It was good to see you, though. I didn't realize how much I missed you." I lean over and kiss him on the cheek before getting into the cab. "And, um, I'll call *you*, okay?"

He gives me a half smile. "Okay, Dee Dee."

On the ride back I don't think about anything except the conversation I just had with Manny. I'm not thinking about how Deron will be when I get home or what kind of fight we'll have when I walk in the door. All I know is that Manny wants me back. And it seems like he's going to be pretty persistent about it. I'm debating on whether to tell Lia about this. I mean, she already told me her opinion. But if she could have seen Manny tonight she'd understand why I'm struggling with this. He was so genuine. I could feel what he was saying. He's not the same as he was back then.

When I get home Deron is already sleeping in bed. After I peek in on Deidre I change into a T-shirt and climb into bed. Deron rolls over and puts his arm around me.

"How was dinner?" he asks.

"Fine," I say shortly. I don't know why he's being so sweet, but I'm still upset about what happened earlier.

"Dee Dee, don't be mad, okay? I did some thinking and I was an asshole before."

"Go on," I say. He chuckles.

"I overreacted. I'm happy about the baby. And I got some good news." He reaches over to the nightstand and picks up an envelope. "Read this," he says as he hands it to me.

I turn on my lamp and take out the letter. I skim through the first few lines as I feel a smile forming on my face.

"Deron, oh my God! It finally happened! I knew someone would love it."

"I still don't believe I got a publisher now. I mean, this is my dream, baby."

"I know. It's our dream." I'm really excited about Deron's news. He's been writing forever. It's about time all his work is paying off.

"We should celebrate. Tomorrow I'm taking you wherever you want to go." He holds me tightly and kisses my cheek. "I think this is going to be the beginning of a new us."

"Yeah, I think so too," I say. I lie back in his arms and wonder, what if he's right? What if now everything is different and our family goes back to way we were? I fall asleep with thoughts of my new life with my husband . . . and none of Manny Velasquez.

Chapter 6

Lia

My alarm clock goes off at 6:00 a.m., scaring the hell out of me. I jump up and press a bunch of random buttons, hoping one of them will kill the sound. When it stops, I lie back down and try to prepare myself for the day ahead. After about fifteen minutes of being too lazy to get out of bed, I finally get up and go to the bathroom to begin my routine. I have that stupid meeting today. Oh yeah, that guy . . . um, Ty, is supposed to be calling me later. Maybe he'll forget. Yeah, right, like anyone could forget me. Well, I haven't seen him around the building, so that's a good sign. But I guess in the end it doesn't matter. It's just an hour or two of my time. I'll be all right. Besides, no matter what goes down today, what goes down tomorrow with Eric will make up for it. Sure, it's just lunch, but, and don't tell anyone this, my favorite time of the day to do the damn thing is the afternoon. You know, all your energy is up and you're ready for anything. I'm not saying I'm going to sleep with him, but then again, I'm not saying I'm not.

I decide to put on a black button-up collared shirt (of course with the first three buttons undone) and a black, tight-as-hell, knee-length skirt. I pair it with a skinny red belt and my red Prada sling-backs and matching handbag. I pull my hair back and check my watch at the same time. It's almost seven thirty. If I can catch a cab as soon as I get downstairs, I'll make it to my meeting on time. I rush to the elevator and press the Down button. After about twenty seconds it arrives. Good, I'm the only one on. With any luck I won't have to make any stops. I hit the lobby key and so far, so good . . . eight, seven, six . . . damn. It's stopping at five. Oh, great. It's Ty.

"How are you doing, Lia?" he asks as he steps inside the elevator.

Well, I was doing kind of okay until . . . "I'm fine. Running a little late."

"Really?" He glances at his watch. "I think I am too. I'm supposed to be meeting a client at his office at Eighty-six and Broadway. Do you know the best—"

The elevator doors pop open and I practically sprint out.

"Upper West Side, Ty. Just hop in a cab." I walk as quickly as I can out the lobby doors.

"I'll call you later, then!" he yells as a cab stops in front of me. I smile and wave and sigh all at the same time. I hope he's not one of those guys who can't take a hint. I'll just have to make it clear that I'm not available . . . not to him anyway.

Three hours later I'm sitting in my office looking over some contracts for a new artist we're about to sign. The meeting was pointless, as I knew it would be. It's now eleven o'clock. Ty hasn't called, but I know he will. Now that I think about it, no one has called me all day. Not Jas, not Rena, not even Dee. It's odd because normally my phone lines are blowing up.

"Ms. Wells, a Ty Jackson is on line one," my assistant buzzes through the intercom.

"I'll take it." I pick up the phone. "Hello, Ty." Here we go . . .

"Hey, Lia. You still feel like having lunch?"

"Sure. Where are you?"

"I'm in a cab now. I have to get back to the Wall Street area."

"Okay, there's a restaurant out there called Wall Street Kitchen and Bar. Have the driver take you to Broad Street . . . Seventy Broad Street at, um, Marketfield, I think. He'll find it. I'll meet you there."

"Okay, cool. See you in a minute."

"Hey, go ahead and order the grilled salmon for me." Anything to save time.

"All right," he says. We hang up and I tell my assistant to forward all social calls to my cell. Interruptions may help to cut this thing short.

I arrive at the restaurant and scan the crowd for Ty. He sees me and waves me over. Damn, I know I saw him earlier but I didn't really pay attention. He looks excellent. Crisp black suit, Stacy Adams shoes. And Gucci cuff links. Wow. The guy has style. Well, so what? A lot of men do. I take a seat across from him and notice his haircut is fresh. Really fresh, like he just left the barbershop.

"You look really nice, Lia," he says.

"Thanks, but they're just work clothes."

"Still, you look good. I didn't order a drink for you, what would you like?"

"I'll just take bottled water." He signals for the waiter and tells him what I want.

"So, Ty, what do you do?" *I already know you got dough, but . . .*

"I'm a financial consultant. I basically tell companies how they should invest their money."

Hmm . . . "Interesting."

"It is. But you know what, I'd much rather talk about you. I know you work for Virgin. You're a lawyer, right?"

"Yeah. I love my job."

"That's good."

The waiter brings our food at this point. I see that Ty has ordered the New York strip. The most expensive thing on the menu. Of course.

"I still can't get over that you're single. You're beautiful and smart . . . what's wrong with these New York guys?" he asks as he cuts into his steak.

"I ask myself the same thing. I really don't think most guys want to be with an extremely successful woman."

"That's crazy. That ambition, that confidence. It's a turn-on for me."

"You would think it's a good thing, but it's not working for me."

"Until now." He looks at me to see if I smile. I don't. *Hey, Ty, it's not that easy.*

He doesn't look swayed, though. "Seriously, I know we just met recently, but I like what I know. And I definitely like what I see. I'd like to take you out, on a real date."

"Ty, I really would like to but I can't."

"Well, we can do a night in, then. Rent a few movies, order a pizza . . . whatever you want."

"No, you don't understand. I can't date you. It wouldn't work out."

The waiter comes to check on us and I ask for the check.

"You're ready to leave?" he asks.

"I have to get back."

"So you really don't want to see me again?"

"I'm sure I'll see you. We live in the same building." I pull out one of my credit cards.

"No, I'm paying."

"It's okay, Ty. I got it."

He sighs. But I don't care. He'll have no reason to expect anything if I pay the tab.

"Lia, I'm not trying to give you a ring. I just think we could have a good time together. You don't have to run . . . I'm not chasing you."

Well, damn. This is awkward.

"I know you're not chasing me. I don't want you to anyway. I just don't want to lead you on."

"Trust me, Lia. You're not leading anything. Everything I do, I do because I want to, and not because of some signs you may or may not show me. I don't know what you're used to, but I'm not that guy, all right?" He tosses a fifty onto the table and walks out of the restaurant.

Hold up! Did he just walk out on me? Well, whatever. I don't want his ass anyway.

I get back to the office but can't concentrate. No, I don't give a damn about Ty. But . . . I don't know why he got so mad. Not that I care, but you know . . . just out of curiosity. And does he always have to look so good? That ain't even right.

At about four o'clock I decide to call it a day and go do a little shopping. It's a bright, warm day and I'm craving some La Perla. As I stroll down beautiful Madison Ave. I pick up a copy of the *Post* and thumb through the pages until I get to my favorite, Page Six. Page Six of the *New York Post* is one of the most popular gossip columns in NYC. You just never know whose picture you'll see once you . . . Oh no! I stop dead in my tracks. Right there in big, bold print read the headlines VELASQUEZ'S NEW HOBBY. And underneath is a picture of Dee Dee and Manny holding hands in front of a restaurant and another of her kissing him. This can't be right! I quickly read the article.

> *NYC's most sought after bachelor, Yankees pitcher Manny Velasquez, seems to have tossed his heart to an unknown young lady. The couple was seen last night having a romantic dinner at Ruth Chris Steakhouse in Midtown. Onlookers say Velasquez, 30, appeared to be totally smitten with the woman. The two shared an intimate rendezvous in a private room.*

I stop reading because I don't think I can take any more. Has Dee gone crazy? Why the hell would she set herself up like this? This is unbelievable. When Deron sees this it's over. I take a closer look at the photographs, hoping that maybe I'm mistaken and the woman in the picture is just a Dee Dee look-alike. Hell no . . . it's Dee. I told that girl not to see him! Sigh, see, this is what happens when people don't follow my advice . . . trouble!

I pull out my cell phone and dial Dee's number. After a few rings she answers sounding a little annoyed.

"Dee Dee, it's me. I have something you need to hear."

"Lia, can this wait? I have to feed the baby and—"

"No! You need to listen to what I'm about to say. This isn't a joke."

She sighs and tells me to hold on.

"Okay, Lia. What?" she asks gruffly.

See, normally I would warn her about her tone, but now is not the time for an argument. "First of all, why the hell did you go see Manny when I told you it would only cause problems?"

"I didn't see Manny," she lies.

"Really? You didn't see Manny? So I guess you weren't at Ruth Chris last night either?"

"What? Lia, what are you talking about?" Her voice is shaking.

"Dee Dee, cut the act! I'm looking at Page Six and guess whose happy little lips I see planted on Manny Velasquez's face?"

"Oh my God," she says softly.

"Hell yeah, 'oh your God'! Dee Dee, why would you do something like that? This article says you guys were on some hot date and just looked so in love. This shit is all over New York! If Deron hasn't found out by now, you can bet he will by the end of the day."

"He's here. He's off today. We're spending the day together to celebrate his book getting published."

"Damn, Dee. That man is about to get his heart broken. You better confess before someone else gets to him first."

"But it wasn't even the way they said! It was a friendly dinner. They twisted it to make it seem like something else."

"Don't tell me. I'm not your husband. Oh, what if his mom sees this? She'll be over in Queens so fast to whoop that ass," I say with a laugh. I know that the situation isn't something to joke about, but I feel no sympathy for her. She brought this on herself.

"Lia, qué clase de amigo es usted? Mi unión es una la línea y usted está haciendo bromas! Vete a la mierda!"

"Look, don't use that damn Spanish bullshit on me! This is not my problem. I was just letting you know." I hang up and toss the paper in the nearest trash can. Dee was getting mad at the wrong one. After all, I was doing her a favor!

When I get back home I see that I have a few messages on my phone. I press the button as I slide out of my clothes.

"Hey Lia. I need a huge favor. I have an important faculty meeting tonight and Tak has to work on a report for his job for a few hours. Can you please keep Lion? You're the best. Tak should be dropping him off at about six. Thanks, sister." I look at my watch . . . 6:10. Damn, damn, damn!

"I think I'm in love, girl. Asaji is it for me. Call me. I have some stories to tell you." Jas is a trip. She can't really be in love with that little boy. I need to talk some sense into her.

"Lia, it's Ty . . ." I press 3 to erase the message. I don't even want to hear the rest. And how did he get my home number anyway? Maybe my assistant forwarded the call.

I finish taking off my clothes and all of a sudden feel a little tingly. What do you expect? It's been three months. I really don't feel like going to the bedroom, so I grab a pillow from the couch and lie on the carpet . . . this soft, warm carpet. I run my fingers over my breasts slowly, slightly pulling at my nipples. I then put one of my fingers in my mouth and then rub it across my lips . . . my lower lips. I can feel my clit going crazy, so I place a few fingers inside me, increasing the speed of my movements as I get hotter. The feeling gets more and more intense as I use my other hand to massage the rest of my body. And then . . . I get a call that someone is here to see me. You've got to be kidding me. Sigh.

I send them up and go wash my hands and throw on a robe. I'm so pissed off. You just don't understand. I hear knocking at my door and go to answer it.

"Hey, Auntie Lia!" Lion gives me a hug, almost knocking me down.

"Hi, sweetie. I see you brought some movies with you."

"Yep. *Lion King One* and *Lion King Two*."

"Well, go put your stuff down and I'll put them on for you in a minute, okay?"

"Okay," he says as he runs off.

"Thanks for doing this. I know it's last minute," Tak says.

"It's fine. Lion is a sweetheart."

"Yeah, Rena suddenly had this meeting tonight. Usually they plan these things months in advance."

Is that the sound of suspicion I hear in his voice? He can't possibly think that Rena is doing dirt. "Well, things come up sometimes."

"Yeah." He focuses on my ensemble. "You look . . . nice."

"Are you trying to be funny?"

"No, seriously. That looks good on you." He stares at my chest. "Real good."

I look down and realize that my nipples are hard. Great. "Um, okay. What time is Rena picking him up?"

"Oh, I'll be picking him up around nine thirty or ten. Most of the time he falls asleep at about eight."

"Okay, Tak." I start to close the door.

"Do you always answer the door wearing that? I may have to come back a little early." He smiles and I laugh, trying to hide my discomfort. Something must be going through his mind for him to be so flirtatious.

"Bye, Tak." I shut the door and go to my room to put on something less revealing. Was he just coming on to me? No . . . he was just being silly, right? I don't doubt he's attracted to me, but not in that way. At least, I don't think so. And does he really think Rena is up to something? Hmm. I'm about to find out.

I get Lion some celery and peanut butter and start the DVD. Then I call Rena.

"Hello?"

"Rena, it's Lia."

"I know. Is Lion okay?"

"Yes . . ." I hear music in the background. "Are you okay?"

"I'm fine. Why?"

"Meeting going well?"

"Oh. Well, I'm not at a meeting. I'm with Lace."

"Lace?" Who the hell is that?

"Damn, Lia. I forgot I haven't told you about him. He's this guy I met. We're just hanging out."

"Oh, really? And Tak thinks you're doing work stuff?"

"So what? He needs to get it together. Lace and I are just friends anyway. But don't mention this to him."

"Yeah. But I have to tell you that when he was here he already seemed like he thought something was up."

"Whatever. He doesn't pay enough attention to me to notice anything. But I have to go. Peace, sister." And she hangs up. I don't believe she's doing this. Poor Tak. I mean, I see what she's trying to do, but she's going about it the wrong way.

I glance into the living room and see Lion trying to keep his eyes open. Now is the perfect time to take a bath. I go over to Lion and put him on the couch. After cleaning up his snack, I run my bathwater and pour a glass of wine. Yes, I have a champagne rack in my bathroom. Who wants to have to run to the kitchen to get a drink when you're trying to relax?

It's been a strange day. That whole thing with Ty just doesn't seem right. No man has ever spoken to me like that . . . you know, all assertively. Usually they're too scared to say anything. I guess it's a good thing, though. But whatever. All that matters now is my date with Eric tomorrow. I will be looking superfine and undeniably sexy. There's no way Mr. Italy will walk away from our lunch with anything but Lia Wells on his mind. Ahhh.

Forty-five minutes and three glasses of wine later, I'm out of the tub and into my baby-blue nightgown doing a horrible job of putting clear polish on my toenails. Maybe I should have stopped at two glasses. I peek into the living room and Lion is still knocked out. It's now almost nine o'clock. I'm actually getting tired myself. I decide to go ahead and plan out my outfit for tomorrow. I'm thinking something bright as I remember Eric flirting with that

blonde in the yellow dress. Just as I'm entering my closet,
I get a call that I have a visitor. It must be Tak.

I send him up and begin to collect Lion's things. He's
still sleeping peacefully on the sofa. I hear a knock and
open the door to see Tak holding a single, pink rose.

"Just to say thanks for watching Lion," he says as he
steps in. I take the rose but feel kind of weird about it.
Something just doesn't seem right.

"Did you talk to Rena?" I ask.

"Nope." He says it really short like he's done with that
subject. "You look nice . . . as usual."

"Anyway," I say, ignoring his comment, "I have a big
day tomorrow and I'm really tired."

"Yeah, me too," he says, taking a seat on the couch opposite Lion.

"Well, shouldn't you be leaving, then?"

"No, I'm cool. Come here, let's talk."

"What? No. We have nothing to discuss." *What the
hell . . .*

"Let's talk about why you're so damn fine."

"Tak, shut up. You play too much." *Please be playing.*

He gets up and walks over to me. I can see his muscles
bulging through his black Bob Marley T-shirt. His skin is
smooth and black. Like an onyx stone. He's so close I can
feel his minty breath on my forehead. But why is he so
close? What is he doing?

"Tak—" But I don't get to finish because he kisses me.
His tongue maneuvers its way into my mouth and the next
thing I know I'm kissing him back. There's a passion to
him. Like he's trying to make a point. If this is his way of
getting back at Rena for whatever he thinks she's up to,
then point well made. He wraps his arms around me, keeping his hands on my ass. I don't push him off. How come
I'm not pushing him off? He pulls away abruptly as if he
finally realized what was happening, leaving my lips (both

sets) throbbing. But I actually want more. I want this man to back me against the wall, lift my gown, and go to work. I want . . .

The phone rings.

"I have to go." He goes over to Lion and picks the little boy up. "I'll see you later." And he leaves, closing the door behind him. Did he just . . . did I just . . . ? It's got to be the wine. I am a little tipsy and . . . damn! I go to answer the phone.

"Hello?"

"Lia, what's up, girl?"

"Nothing, Jas." Wait, I can tell Jas about this. She's always into some kind of drama. Maybe she can help me figure out what to do. "Hey, listen. I just did something stupid. I mean, I know it was stupid even though at the time it didn't feel stupid. You following me?" I don't wait for her to answer. "So, Tak just left here . . . he was picking up Lion. And, girl, he kissed me." Silence.

"Um, Lia . . ." Jas says slowly.

"I know, I know. But like I said, it didn't feel wrong. In fact, it was hot. I was hot. I think if he wanted to do something else I would have. And I hate myself for that, but then I'm thinking, Rena is out running the streets with some random guy anyway. And I know I shouldn't think like that because it's none of my business, but damn. Tak was looking extra sexy tonight and I had already been drinking and—"

"Lia, shut the fuck up! Rena is on the fucking phone!"

"Oh my God . . . Rena," I say, my stomach turning. I hear a click.

"She hung up. Lia, what the hell? What did you do?" Jas asks disappointedly.

Tears form in my eyes. "Why didn't you tell me you guys were on three-way?"

"I was going to tell you. We were calling to talk to

you about Asaji and Lace . . . who, by the way, Rena is not sleeping with. But you just started running off at the mouth."

"I'm so sorry. I didn't mean . . ." I'm all choked up.

"Damn, Lia. I don't even know what else to say. You a foul bitch. Not to be trusted. I gotta go."

"No, Jas. I'm sorry. You know I'm not like that. Please, don't hang up. I need you now. Rena is probably—"

"On her way over there to knock your ass out. At least I would be. I really gotta go. I'll call you later." She hangs up.

I put the phone down and cry into my pillows. I'm such an idiot. How could I let this happen? Now shit will never be the same. Never.

Chapter 7

Rena

I drop the phone, not meaning to, but out of shock and anger. I just heard my best friend say she wanted my man to fuck her. I don't even know how to react. I mean, has she always wanted him like that? Has he always wanted her?

He should be bringing Lion back any minute. What do I say? Will he confess on his own? I don't really want to fight in front of my son. But I refuse not to confront him about this. I also refuse to cry. I didn't do anything wrong. Why should I be the one to cry? I hear the key in the door. He's here.

"Hey, baby. How was your meeting?" he asks as he walks in, carrying Lion.

"Put Lion is his room please," I say. I go to the kitchen to boil a pot of water. He walks to the back of the house to put Lion down, then comes into the kitchen with me.

"Sit," I tell him. He looks at me like he knows what I'm going to say.

"It was the first and last time, Rena." Is that his idea of an apology?

"What are you referring to?"

"Tonight. Don't play games. You know what happened with Lia."

"Tell me."

"We kissed. That's all."

"That's all? So, kissing is just an innocent thing? Kissing is just what friends do?"

"I don't mean it like that. We didn't have sex. I didn't let that happen."

"And I should be thankful? Tak, you cheated on me. You violated everything that I thought we had!"

"It was just a kiss. Nothing more."

"And nothing less. You will not make light of this. You will not minimize the severity of what you did."

"What does that mean?" The lack of remorse in his tone is amazing.

"It means get the hell out of my house. Don't call me, don't come see me. I'll let you know when you can see my son." I turn my back to him to prepare my tea.

"Fuck that, Rena. You can't keep me from my son!" He stands and knocks the chair over. "What I did wasn't right, but at least I'm man enough to own up to it. Your ass is out with some other guy and you're not even woman enough to tell me!"

"First of all, don't you dare raise your voice to me. I'm not your child. Secondly, I'm woman enough to be able to be around someone else and still respect the fact that I have a man. I'm woman enough to resist whatever urges I may get when I'm not with you. I'm woman enough to control myself when I'm with another guy. I'm woman enough to be faithful, Tak. That's the type of woman you had." I turn back around and finish making my tea.

"Had?" he asks. I finally hear the regret. He finally sounds sorry.

"Get out, Tak," I say with my back toward him.

"Rena—"

"Leave your key."

He doesn't move for a few minutes. Then he puts my house key on the table and leaves. It's over. But I don't feel mad. I feel disappointed. I feel like he threw everything away for a kiss. He messed up, though. I'm not going to be depressed and upset because of what he did. I pick up the phone and dial Lace's number.

"Hello?"

"Lace, it's Rena."

"Everything okay, Ma?"

"Yeah. Um, do you feel like coming over?"

"No doubt. I'll be over in twenty."

"Okay. Peace." All this time I've been looking at Lace as a friend. Just a friend. And he has respected that. But now . . . now I need more.

He arrives twenty minutes later as he said he would. His neatly twisted dreads are falling over his shoulders. He has on a cream-colored Akademiks sweatsuit and brown Timberlands. He looks lovely. He gives me a hug and a kiss on the cheek.

"So, what's up with the late-night call? Where's . . . ?" I know he's asking about Tak.

"Gone. And I mean really gone. Want some tea?"

"No, thanks. Gone? What you mean?"

"No need for you to concern yourself with it." I take his hand and lead him to my bedroom. Incense is burning and my blue light is on. One of my favorite albums, *Tweet's Southern Hummingbird*, is playing in the background.

"What's the deal with this, Serena?" he asks. I love it

when he calls me by my full name. No one else does, so
it feels kind of special.

"I want you, Lace. That's the deal." I kiss him, wondering
if I'm being too aggressive. This is very out of character
for me. But tonight, I'm just not feeling like myself. He
pulls back.

"I don't want you to regret anything that happens,"
he says.

"The only thing I'll regret is if nothing happens." I kiss
him again, this time putting all my weight into his body.
He kisses me back now . . . he kisses me like he's been
holding back for a long time and he's trying to make up for
it. I fall back on the bed, spreading my legs so he can lie
in between. He sits up and takes off his shirts while I slip
out of mine. Then he comes back down and puts his lips
against mine, this time with less urgency and more sweet-
ness. He goes from my mouth to my cheeks to my chin to
my neck. His lips are soft. I can already feel him grinding
on me through my jeans. His rhythm is smooth and con-
trolled. He unhooks my bra and puts his mouth on my
right breast, teasing my nipple with the fast movements of
his flickering tongue. I moan a little bit, letting him know
I'm feeling it, and he moves to the left one. I can feel the
juices inside me starting to seep out as his lips leave my
breasts and go down to my stomach. He traces the cave of
my belly button with his tongue as his dreads caress my
abs. I close my eyes and get lost in his touch to the sound
of Tweet singing, ". . . I'm nervous and trembling . . ." I
open my eyes when I feel him unbuttoning my jeans. He
looks up at me and I smile. He smiles back and comes up
to kiss me before finishing what he started. My jeans
come down and so do his pants. He's just there in his
Calvin Klein boxers, staring at my honey-colored body,
as if it were a work of art. He kisses my thighs while
pulling down my leopard-print bikini panties. My body is

shivering. Not because I'm cold, but in anticipation of what's about to happen.

He begins to lick his way up to my . . . damn it. I'm not usually as sexually expressive as Jas and them, but fuck it. Lace puts his face in my pussy and sucks my clit like a lollypop. This whole time I'm moaning and whispering his name like he's my savior. He starts to suck on my lips and lick his way around and around. I feel myself coming and grab his hair, pulling hard as my wetness comes spilling out. Oh my God. I pull him up to me and kiss him hard, enjoying the taste of me in his mouth. He kicks off his boxers, lifts my legs, and puts his big, beautiful dick inside me. He fills me up and gets so deep I swear I feel him in my stomach. He moves with such coolness. But it's powerful. A perfect combination. We switch from that position to me on top and him smacking my ass as I ride. Then I get on my knees and let him hit it from the back. That's something I've never done. But will definitely do again. I come from all of it, like, four times in all, but he holds out until the very end, when he's back on top of me and he's looking into my eyes. He calls me Sahara and Serena and goddess. And when it's over, he holds me. He kisses my hand. He lays his head on my chest and I play with his locks. Track twelve is on . . . "Heaven."

"You're not tired?" he asks.

"No, not really."

"I must not have done my job, then," he says.

"Please. Four times. That's all I have to say. Four times." We both laugh a little bit before we're quiet again for a little while.

"I'm sorry I didn't use a condom," he says.

Condoms? Oh, damn.

"I wasn't thinking about it either. Besides, I trust you. You wouldn't have slept with me if something were wrong, right?" I kiss him softly on the top of his head." He doesn't respond.

"Rena, maybe I should have told you this before, but I never thought it would be an issue with us 'cause you had a man."

"Tell me what?" I sit all the way up, forcing him to get off me. What now?

"I'm bisexual." And maybe he continues to speak, but I don't hear anything else. In fact, I can see his lips moving but my mind won't let me comprehend anything beyond his last words, "I'm bisexual."

"What?"

"I sleep with guys and ladies. I haven't been with a guy in a while, though. I haven't been with either actually, in a minute. Until you." He can't be serious. He can't be for real.

"Lace, you have sex with men and didn't think to tell me? Didn't you think to use protection? How could you do this?" I toss his stuff at him. "Put your shit on and go!"

"Serena, I have always used condoms before. And I get checked on a regular basis. I didn't give you anything." And he tells me this like that makes it better. Like now I'm supposed to just forget this conversation ever happened and go back to cuddling and having sex. He has lost his mind!

"Yeah, whatever. Just go!" God, twice in one night I'm throwing a man out. He puts on his clothes and heads for the door.

"No one knows. Not Asaji, not Jas. I would appreciate it if you kept this between us."

"I would have appreciated you telling me you're bi."

"Serena, please. I thought we were better than that. Besides, I'm really feeling you and I didn't want anything to fuck that up."

"Lace . . .

"Even if we can't have nothin' I still want to chill with you. We vibe together, ya know?"

He turns to leave and I just sit there. I feel like I've been getting betrayed all damn day. The people who I'm closest to just keep letting me down. Who can I trust? That's the question of my life.

I take a long, very hot shower and change the sheets on my bed. I lie down and my thoughts turn to Lia. I don't hate her. But how can I ever look at her the same way again? What do I say to her? How long will I feel this way? I don't know. This is that soap opera type of thing that I never thought I'd be dealing with. I wonder how long it's going to take for her to get enough guts to call me. And Lace. Sigh. The guy puts his penis inside the ass cracks of men. What can I do with that? How can I ever have sex with him again knowing that? I mean, his sexuality doesn't offend me. I pride myself on being open-minded and tolerant of others who are different from me. But the fact that he didn't tell me up front offends me. The fact that he didn't think I would accept him offends me. Perhaps I would not have had sex with him, but at least we could have maintained a friendship. Now I'm not so sure.

And Tak. The man I wanted to marry. The father of my child. The one who owned my heart. What a joke. He's not a real man. Real men have self-control. Real men don't do things out of spite. He's a boy. And I already have one of those. I damn sure don't need another.

I close my eyes and try to go to sleep. The sounds of bass from the passing SUVs and sirens from police cars are like my little Harlem lullaby. Tomorrow I'll feel better. Tomorrow I'll be okay.

Chapter 8

Dee Dee

I've been walking on pins and needles, just waiting for Deron to confront me about Manny. Somehow we managed to get through the day and most of the evening without any problems. Actually I'm really surprised because not one person besides Lia even seemed to see the *Post* today. No funny glances or shocked phone calls from anyone. It's almost as if last night didn't happen. And that's a good thing because Deron was on an absolute high today. He took me all around the city. We had lunch at a little French bistro downtown and went to a jazz lounge later in the evening. Everything was perfect until Lia called me with that horrible news. And now I don't know if I should even bring it up. After all, Deron has no clue about anything. And maybe he never will. . . .

I take a long shower when we get home and then call

Hannah to check on Deidre since she's staying overnight. After I get out I join Deron on the couch to watch a movie. His vibe is cool. Usually I can read him, but for some reason tonight I'm not picking up on anything.

"I had a really good time today, baby," I say as I snuggle up to him. "It reminded me of those days when we first started dating."

"Yeah, I know," he responds. "Because you had Manny Velasquez on your mind back then too. Right?"

I feel a chill run through my body. He knows. "Deron, I don't know what to say. . . ."

"Did you really think I wouldn't find out? Did you really think that this whole thing would blow over without me knowing about it?"

"No. I was going to tell you, but . . . it's not the way they made it seem. It wasn't a date. There wasn't anything romantic about it. I promise." I stop talking because at this point he either believes me or he doesn't. I can't plead my case anymore.

"I don't know why you went to see him, Dee. And I don't really care." He sits up and looks at me in my eyes. "I know you love me. I know that you want our marriage to work. That's all that matters."

"So, everything they said in the paper, and everything everyone is going to think . . . ?"

"Fuck all that. It's about us. Look, I got this book deal now. I'm not letting all this nonsense mess us up. I know I've been acting strange lately. I know I haven't been there for you or our daughter. But, baby, I'm different now. The drinking, it was just to help numb all the pressure of trying to get my career together. This has been five-plus years of trying to get my name out there and finally I'm getting that chance." He pauses for a few seconds. "And I didn't tell you this but I got passed over for a promotion twice in the past year. I was too ashamed to tell you. But it messed my head up. It hurt my pride. And I took it out on you. But I'm done with all that craziness from before. It's about you and me now."

For the first time in a long while I feel that passion from Deron that I used to feel. It's not strained or forced. It's natural and beautiful. I hate myself for even calling Manny in the first place. Well, never again.

"I love you so much," I say as I kiss him softly.

"I love you so much more," he says. He looks at his watch. "Damn, I have to get ready for work. I'm gonna hop in the shower."

"Okay, baby." As he goes into the bedroom the phone rings. It's late, so it could only be Deron's mom or one of my friends. Either way I don't want to answer, but I can't stand to hear the phone keep ringing.

"Hello?"

"Is this Dee Dee Smalls?"

"Yes, who is this?"

"How long have you and Manny Velasquez been together? Do you plan to leave your husband? Are you pregnant with Manny's child?"

"What? Who the hell is this? How did you get my number?" I ask angrily.

"Is the child you have now Manny Velasquez's child?"

I slam the phone down. What the hell just happened? Now I have reporters calling my house? What if Deron had answered? I mean, he said everything was fine, but . . . this is too much.

"Baby, who was that?" Deron asks, walking up behind me.

"Wrong number, I guess." I turn around and wrap my arms around him. "When is your shift over?"

"Eleven a.m. Are you okay? You look pale."

"No, I don't. I'm okay. Just tired. Look, baby, you better go."

He looks at me for a minute, studying my expression.

"I'll see you in the morning, then," he says after a long pause.

After he leaves I go into the bedroom and bury my head in the pillows. Why does there always have to be some drama going on? And damn, if these reporters are already calling my house, who knows what they'll do next? What if they approach Deron on the street? "How does it feel to know your wife is sleeping with Manny Velasquez?" I can't put him through this. This mess has to end right now. I dial Manny's number and wait patiently while the phone rings.

"This is Manny," he answers.

"Hi. It's Dee."

"Dee Dee. What's up? I was waiting for a call from you."

"Yeah. Listen, I know you saw Page Six today. Manny, I am married and all my family and friends live in New York. I can't be known as your secret lover."

"I'm really sorry about that. But I can't do anything about it. I didn't even notice any paparazzi that night."

"I'm not blaming you, but there's got to be something you can do." Even though I know the reality is that the situation is out of his control, I still feel he's responsible. Maybe it's unfair, but oh, well.

"I can get my publicist to make a rebuttal statement, but . . . Dee Dee, it's out there. People are going to believe what they want to believe regardless. The main thing is that you and your husband know the truth."

"The truth is that you want me back and this is just another way to weasel your way back into my life," I snap.

"That's bullshit! Yeah, maybe I'm not as concerned about the stupid article as you are. Maybe I couldn't care less if the city thinks you're my new girlfriend. But I don't have to manipulate anything to get you back, Dee Dee." He pauses. "You're considering it on your own."

"What? I'm not considering anything." Talk about bold

statements! I never had any intention to do anything with him. I really didn't even plan on seeing him . . . that just kind of happened.

"I felt you trying to fight it. But you can't fight it, Dee. It's bigger than you. Just go with it, *mi estrella*."

I feel a chill run up my spine. But I don't know why because he's not right. There is absolutely nothing between us anymore. Is there?

"Manny, let's not . . . I mean, don't do this."

"Okay. Then tell me that you don't love me. Tell me it's over for good."

His challenge is frightening to me because as much as I know in my mind that it has to be over with him, my heart refuses to give in. And that scares the hell out of me. Because if a part of me still loves Manny, what am I doing with Deron?

"I didn't think you could," he says. "So what are we going to do about this?"

"Nothing, Manny. We will both act like this conversation never happened."

"I can't do that," he says.

"You don't have much of a choice. I can't be with you." I'm sure I don't sound convincing at all, but I really believe in what I'm saying . . . for the most part. He sighs. So do I.

"Well, at least let me say good-bye . . . in person."

"Are you crazy? Look at what happened the last time we saw each other."

"It won't happen again. I'm going to be at the Hilton tonight. Room 1120. I hope you come."

He hopes I come? I'm not going anywhere near the Hilton or Manny.

The next few hours I spend in my bed, waking up every ten minutes. It's a little past midnight and even though most of my senses tell me to forget about Manny, I can't seem to get his offer out of my mind.

By 1:00 a.m. I'm on my way to the hotel. I didn't even call to let him know that I'm coming. The whole point of this visit is to say good-bye, so that's all that I'm going to do. When I arrive at the hotel I continually look over my shoulder for photographers, but I see none. Eleven floors later I'm standing in front of his door. I knock softly and a few seconds later I'm looking into his eyes.

"You didn't expect to see me, did you?" I ask as I slide past him and into the suite.

"But you're here." He pulls me close. "Go ahead. Say good-bye to me," he says with a grin. I pry his hands from my waist.

"Don't go there, Manny," I tell him sternly. But somehow he manages to get his arms around me again.

"Say good-bye, Dee Dee," he says again, this time in a whisper. And then . . . this not so unexpected kiss happens. I'm taken back to a place that was less complicated and a lot sweeter. Young love. Naive love. Pure love. Right now it's almost as if nothing else matters. Except that it does. I pull away abruptly.

"This cannot happen," I say. "This is wrong. This is . . ." He kisses me again, ignoring my protests. And all of my reservations and fears disappear along with my spotless record of fidelity.

"*Déjeme amarle, mi estrella*," he says while he runs his fingers over the curves of my shoulders. I can feel my nipples getting hard as my shirt gets lifted over my head and my bra straps slide down.

"*Soy listo*," I reply. I'm ready.

I find myself sneaking into my house even though I know that no one is home. I'm still shaking from my experience with Manny. Making love to him reawakened something inside me that . . . that I had forgotten was there. As I climb into bed I try to feel guilty about what happened. But I can't. It was good. No, it was great. God, I think I'm in love with Manny again. Oh God, what am I saying? Do I really want this? Do I want to be with him? Or just sleep with him? And Deron . . . I mean, do I leave him? Sigh. I am at a total loss. Either way it goes, someone is going to get hurt. I don't know if it will be Manny, or Deron . . . or me.

Chapter 9

Lia

I call in sick Tuesday morning. When my alarm goes off at eight I had been asleep for maybe three hours. My eyes are all red and puffy from crying all night. There's no way I'm going to be seen like this. So instead of the office, I make my way to a last-minute reservation at my favorite day spa, Oasis, on East Sixteenth. I have about five hours to get gorgeous again for Eric. Hey, I've mourned for Rena and what happened. I can't continue to dwell on it. And yes, I will call her and all that, but I think I should give her a few days to deal with it alone.

I'm not in a cab mood, so I have the front desk send a car service for me. I get to Oasis and indulge in massage therapy, seaweed and salt body treatment, facial, pedicure, and manicure, and I'm talked into getting some highlights in my hair. At about one thirty, I change into my date outfit (very Samantha from *Sex and the City*: a white blazer with a lacy yellow tank under it, a white skirt, and yellow Dolce & Gabbana pumps) and dial Eric's number from my cell.

"Amaretto Enterprises. This is Donna."

"I'm calling for Eric Amaretto. This is Lia Wells. He should be expecting my call." Silence. "Hello?"

"Did you say Eric Amaretto?"

"Yes." I hear laughing in the background along with Donna saying, "She actually thinks it's his name." More laughter.

"Uh, Miss Wells, is it? Amaretto is just the name of the company. You know, the restaurants, the lounges and bars. The CEO is Eric Discala."

"Oh. Um . . ." God, how embarrassing. I look at the business card he gave me and sure enough, it says Discala.

"I'll put you through," she says, sounding like she's sure he's going to reject my call. Now I'm kind of hoping he will.

"Discala here," Eric says.

"Hi, Eric. It's Lia . . . from the Janet party." Pause.

"Oh, okay. When my secretary said Miss Wells I didn't know who the hell she was talking about."

Um . . . I'm at a loss. He didn't remember?

"She says you called me Amaretto?" he asks. I can tell he's amused. "Well, honey, that's just the gimmick, you know. I should have explained that to you, but I assumed you would get it." In other words, *I didn't realize you were so stupid.* Quick, gotta change the subject.

"So, are we still on for lunch?" I ask.

"I suppose so. I'm in the mood for Chinese, so I'll meet you at, um . . . Dish of Salt. They have a great menu."

"What's the address?"

"I'm not sure, honey. You'll find it. Look in the Yellows or ask someone on the train."

"But I'm not taking the subway."

"Well, ask your cabbie. See you in half." He hangs up and I stand there looking and feeling dumb as hell. I get in my car and tell the chauffeur the name of the restaurant. Just by chance he knows where it is because two weeks ago he had to take someone else there. Truthfully, I'm not feeling Chinese right now. I was hoping we could go to a romantic little French spot, but he didn't even give me a chance to suggest it.

I get to the restaurant first and thankfully it's very nice. I order a Coke with a splash of grenadine and browse the menu. The prices start at about twenty bucks with the most expensive entrée being fifty-four. I'm not cheap at all, but I usually don't pay that much for lunch. But at least he didn't want to meet at McDonald's or something. About twenty-five minutes later, Eric shows up. I don't mind the wait because he looks just as tasty as I remember.

"Eric," I say, smiling. He walks over to the table and takes a seat.

"Did you already order the appetizer?" he asks.

"No, I didn't know you wanted one. We can just tell the waiter—"

"No, it'll just take longer. You should know what you want. You've had enough time," he says in a rushed tone.

"Yeah. I'm ordering the crazy drunk chicken. It sounds interesting."

"It's decent." The waiter comes over and Eric orders the steamed lobster with ginger and scallions. Since I already told him what I wanted I thought he would order for me. He doesn't. The waiter and Eric look at me with impatience.

"The crazy drunk chicken, please," I say to the annoyed waiter. Damn, my bad.

"So, how's your day been so far?" he asks me.

"Wonderful. I went to a spa and put some color in my hair. I never do that, but I thought it would be different."

"Well, obviously if you've never done it, it would be different, wouldn't it?"

Well, um . . . yeah, but . . .

"What I meant was—" I begin to say.

"Don't worry, honey, I know what you meant. So, this is some place, huh? I thought you might enjoy something like this."

"It is nice," I say, looking around.

"It doesn't compare to Amaretto's, though. We're doing really well this year. I'm thinking of expanding. My family owns some vineyards in France that I just found out about. I think we're going to do wines next."

"Really? That's impressive. My parents took a trip to France this past spring. I wanted to do something nice for their anniversary, so I sent them to Paris for a week."

"Is that so? That must have taken all your savings."

"No, not at all," I say. Eric really has no clue about my career. He does remember that I'm an actual lawyer, right? The stuck-up waiter returns with our food. The chicken is actually pretty good. But I'm not really focused on my meal. I think he wants me. I can feel it. But I don't think he'll make the first move. Maybe I should say something to let him know I'm down for whatever.

"Eric, I'm free for the rest of the day. If you can get away, I'd love to maybe go back to my place and cool out for a while." There's your bait, baby. Take a bite.

"Tempting offer, but I don't travel to the boroughs for pleasure. Only business." He takes a few bites of his lobster. He thinks I live in Brooklyn or the Bronx or something. Hey, nothing wrong with that except that . . . I don't! Why on earth would he think that anyway? Look at me! I'm practically screaming *Manhattan*.

"I live in SoHo," I say flatly. He looks surprised. I'm surprised by his surprise.

"Well, in that case, why not? I have a few hours to

spare." He asks the waiter for the check. I excuse myself
to go to the bathroom.

"You want me to just pay your half and you can give it
back to me later?" he asks. Okay, now it's getting bad. I
nod my head and keep walking. He wants me to pay my
half. And it's not really half 'cause his costs twenty-eight
dollars and mine is nineteen-fifty. Well, whatever. First
dates can be funny like that. He's still sexy.

I'm eager to get back home so I can show Eric I'm not
some ghettofied hood rat. He seems impressed by my
place, but there's another place I want him to be impressed
by, ya know? I take off my shoes and offer him a drink. He
declines. We sit on the couch and I lean in close to him.
He doesn't back away, but he doesn't respond to me either.

"You live alone?" he asks, eyeing my high-tech enter-
tainment system.

"Yes, I do. No roommates are going to pop up unexpect-
edly." I put my hand on his lap and kiss his neck. He's
wearing Curve again. Yummy.

"What are you doing?" He moves my hand away. I feel
my face getting hot from humiliation. He stands up. "I'm
sorry if I gave you the wrong impression, Lisa. But I'm not
interested in you in that way."

Oh, shit. Not the polite dis. I'd rather he just say I'm
ugly and leave. 'Cause if he said that, at least I'd know he
was crazy and forget about it. Now it's like he doesn't want
me because he just doesn't want me. Because I'm not
smart enough or classy enough or rich enough. And did he
just call me Lisa?

"I'm sorry, I thought you wanted to . . ."

"Have sex with you?" He rolls his eyes. "I don't even
know you. Look, honey, I'll give you a call."

Oh, hell no. His ass is not walking out on me like that.
I take off my blazer and pull down my top to reveal my
braless breasts. I stand there looking at him with my hand

on my hips. Just try to resist me now, Italy. He stares at me for a minute like I'm a damn fool. And you know maybe I am. But I am determined to bag this guy now more than ever. After all, I am going to be his wife. He walks over to me and pulls my shirt over my head and throws it on the floor. Yes!

"Yellow isn't your color," he says. And he walks out the door.

It takes me a minute to realize what just happened. I mean, I did all but gift-wrap my pussy and give it to him and he didn't even care. I must have been too forward for him. I was too dominating. I should have let him have all the control. That's all it was. Right? Too much, too soon. No problem. I'll know better next time. And there will be a next time. I could see it in his dark brown eyes.

After I change into some sweats and a baby tee, I watch a little TV and sip on a Smirnoff Ice. It's five o'clock and the rest of the day is mine. I need to call Dee Dee and see how she's doing. I also need to set the record straight about what went down with Tak before Jas or Rena talk to her.

I get halfway into a *Friends* rerun when I hear a knock on my door. I didn't send anyone up . . . I didn't even get a call. I look out the peephole and see Ty's big head outside my door. What does he think he's doing? I open the door.

"Yes?" I say with an attitude.

"I called your office today. They said you were sick, so I brought a few things, that's all." He has a bottle of cold medicine, an aromatherapy candle, a can of soup, and a *Cosmo* magazine. "Thought this might help."

Okay, I have to admit it's sweet, but it's Ty. I have my standards, ya know?

"Thank you, Ty." Should I invite him in or something?

"Well, I'll let you get some rest. I have some work to do anyway. But if you need anything . . ."

"Listen, you want to come in for a little while?" I ask casually.

"Sure," he says as I open the door wider.

"I'm just watching some TV. Do you want anything to drink?"

"No, I'm good," he says, sitting down on the couch. He spots my beer bottle and smiles. "So, you're sick, huh?"

I laugh and take another swig of the drink. "It's an old Korean cold remedy. Knocks it right out of you."

"I bet. So wait, your mom is Korean and your dad is black?"

"Yeah," I answer, taking a seat next to him. "Samuel married Chong and had little baby Lia."

"Chong?" he asks with a grin.

"Don't laugh," I say. "Chong is my middle name too."

"Aw, Lia Chong Wells. You gotta love that," he says, laughing.

"Shut up," I say half seriously. "Ty Jackson is so boring."

"It's Tysean Jackson."

"No middle name?"

"Uh . . ."

"Tell me," I say, turning toward him on the couch. "I told you mine."

"Nah, mine is horrible."

"Please," I beg with my signature puppy dog eyes.

"Rufus," he finally says with a straight face. But it doesn't help. We both burst out laughing.

"Rufus? Are you serious?" I take a deep breath and laugh all over again.

"It's my grandfather's name."

"Wow. That's . . . there are no words," I say before sipping on my drink.

"And that's why it will never be mentioned again."

"Trust me, it won't," I say, grinning. We sit in silence for a few minutes, watching the rest of my show. I feel strangely comfortable with him, as if this is something we do all the time. I glance over at him discreetly, examining his subtle movements. He does this thing where he'll bite his lip to hold back a smile. It's so damn cute . . . and sexy.

"What are you thinking?" he asks me.

"Umm," I say, scrambling for an answer. But his cell phones rings, thankfully. He looks at the caller ID and shakes his head and sighs.

"It's the office. I need to answer this. It was good to see you, though, Lia."

"Yeah, it was fun."

"And, um, your hair looks nice," he says before walking out the door. Hmm, he noticed.

After he leaves I light the candle (which seems to clear sinus problems I don't even have) and flip through the magazine. I guess Ty is okay. He actually seems like a genuinely nice guy. There has to be a catch. I'm not sure what it is, but I'm sure it will show soon enough.

The rest of the day I just chill out and reflect on the past week. I have a few missions to complete now. Get in good with Rena and Jas again. Make sure Dee isn't putting herself in deeper shit than she already has. And get Eric into my bed. Sure, we got off to a rocky start, but I mean, it is me we're talking about and I get what I want. Yep, this is going to be a great week.

Chapter 10

Jas

It's a rainy Wednesday morning. I'm sitting in my cubicle looking out of the window, thinking about this past weekend. I know what's going on with Rena and Lia really has nothing to do with me, but I can't help having an opinion. Lia is, well . . . she's not who I thought she was. And Rena is better than me. I would have hurt Lia . . . and Tak. If it would have been Asaji . . . Wait a minute. We're not even together like that. He's not my man. But still I don't want anybody else. I think I'm falling in love with him. I hate to say it. I hate to feel this way. But it's beyond my control. It's way too much, way too soon. And most of all, way too real.

My phone rings and I hesitate to answer it. I work at a mortgage company and the bulk of the calls I get are people wanting to have more time to pay up. And when the calls are transferred to me, it means there is no more time and they have to either come up with the dough or face losing their homes. I answer the phone dreading the voice on the other end.

"Source Mortgage. This is Miss Lewis."

"Hey, Jas." Oh, it's Rena.

"What's up, girl? How you feelin'?"

"I'm doing pretty well actually. The semester is starting soon and I'm ready to get back to work. I'm over here redoing some lesson plans now."

"It's good you're occupying your time. You been in contact with Tak or Lia?" Sorry, but I just have to know the dirt.

"No. Lia hasn't called. Neither has Tak. As far as I know they're doing each other as we speak."

"I doubt that, Rena."

"Yeah, I know. I called because I want to know if you would like to come to spoken word with me tonight."

"Oh, well . . . I can do that. Is Lace going?"

"I didn't ask him. I probably won't be hanging out with him too much anymore."

"Eww, why? I thought y'all were hitting it off."

"We did but . . . I'll tell you about it later."

Sounds bad, but I won't press the issue. "Do you mind if I bring Asaji?"

"No, bring him. You know where it is, right?"

"Yeah, we'll be there around eight."

"Okay, then. Peace, sister."

Okay, now I'm really curious. What's the deal with Lace? They really liked each other. And I was enjoying the whole friends dating friends thing. Oh, well. At five o'clock I leave my stinkin' job and head home. Once there I call Asaji and ask him if he wants to go out. He says yes and tells me he's on his way now. I hop in the shower and change into a jean skirt, an off-the-shoulder, long-sleeve, cream-colored shirt, and my cream-colored leather boots that tie up in the back that I ordered from the Victoria's Secret catalog. I wrap my hair and throw on a lime-green Kangol. Hey, I'm funky . . . what can I say? An hour later Asaji is knocking at my door with a notebook in his hand.

"Nice hat," he says with a grin.

"I know. What's up with that?" I ask, pointing at the notebook.

"Some rhymes. We goin' to a poetry reading, right?"

"Yeah. You recitin'?" He never told me he does that.

"Maybe. I wrote something last night. It's not great but I like it."

"Let me see," I say, reaching for it.

He pulls back. "No, Ma. Be cool."

I decide to leave him alone. Besides, I guess I'll hear what he's written later.

"A'ight. So, you ready? We don't have to go too far. It's a few blocks away. We can walk."

"Let's be out, then." We start our short stroll to the club hand in hand. There are a lot of couples out this evening. Rockers, skaters, preps, gays, interracial . . . you name it. It's an ideal picture. When we get to the club, a young man is onstage speaking about intolerance:

"There's nothing wrong with a kiss on the lips
a hug if you care
a hand on the thigh
a glance or a stare
or is there
not if you're
the 'norm'
or safe
I mean, stayin' in your place
not crossing lines
keeping within society's binds
maintaining closed minds

       don't make him uncomfortable
          don't make her squirm
        but see, people gotta learn
                 love
         can't be defined or confined
      there's as many ways as there are days
             and for you to say
              that's not right
    and try to fight to keep me from livin' my life
         all because you have short sight
           and refuse to see the light
            you see I don't judge you
          and all the things you may do
       you know . . . all those things you do
               my philosophy
            is to let a brotha be
        as long as he ain't hurting me
            I'm only fighting for
                equality."

The crowd starts clapping loudly as I search for Rena. I
see her sitting at the bar drinking a cocktail and . . . hold up.
Is she flirting with the man next to her? Damn. I think she is.

"There's Rena," Asaji says, leading me over to the bar.
Rena turns around and smiles at us.

"Jas, hey, sister. How're you doing, Asaji?"

"I'm good," Asaji says. "Have you been up yet?"

"I've done one. Think I may do another before we leave."
We?

"You and . . ." I glance at the guy she's sitting with. He
looks like he just came from the office. He is fine, though.
Pretty brown skin. And a bangin'-ass smile.

"Oh, I'm sorry. Jas, Asaji . . . this is Ty. Ty, my friends
Jas and Asaji."

"Nice to meet you," he says. "Do you guys want to move to a table?"

"No, that's okay. Rena, I'll be back over later." Asaji and I take a seat at a table near the back of the club. "Yo, what was up with that?"

"What?" Asaji asks, flipping through his notebook.

"Rena and that dude. He's not her style at all." I look over at Ty suspiciously. Why does that name sound familiar?

"Obviously he is, Jas. And why do you care so much?"

"Because, Asaji," I say in an exasperated tone, "Rena is on the rebound. I don't want her to get taken advantage of. He looks like a slick talker. And anyway, did you hear her say 'we' were leaving? She can't go home with him."

"Rena is grown, Ma. She knows what she's doing. Listen, I'm going to the bar. Want anything?"

"Get me a Hennessy and Coke."

He walks off and I look back over at Rena and Ty. Whatever he's saying is working. Rena is laughing and leaning in closer and closer. Maybe I'm being overprotective. But I know Rena. And what about Tak? Is he out of the picture for good? Sigh. Where is my drink? I glance around looking for Asaji. Where is he?

"This is dedicated to my beautiful Jasmine. Something I wrote called 'Prisoner.' It's my first time, so be easy on me, a'ight?" The crowd laughs a little and a woman yells, "Do ya thing, papi!"

I look up onstage and see Asaji sitting on a stool. The spotlight is on him and he's looking down at his papers. I take a quick look at Rena and she's grinning at me. I look back at Asaji and he's now facing the audience. Oh my God . . . what is he going to say? He takes a sip of something—probably my drink—and begins:

"Wasn't supposed to catch feelings
It was just casual dealings

And damn I really ain't willing
'Cause I know love is a villain
It claims your heart and your soul
It turns you outta control
Poison be takin its toll
It's like you out on parole
'Cause it will have you on lock
You think you free but you not
Can't really see with blind spots
Before you know it you're got
And now I'm in this damn mess
Consumed with tension and stress
I don't want more I want less
Don't wanna make no progress
Let's take it back a few weeks
To when I never would speak
The thought of love was too deep
Was never in this for keeps
But now you got me caught up
Poured so much into my cup
It's overflowing now but
I'm steady drinking it up
The more I hate it I love it
The more I push it I pull it
The more I shun it I want it
Like trying to stop getting blunted
But when you catch that contact
And don't know how to react
It's like you gotta go back
Emotions under attack
So I give in to this sin
Being the yang to your yin
'Cause ain't no way I can win
Your love has taken me in."

The crowd bursts into applause and some people stand up to clap. I'm sitting in my chair, though, still in shock from his flow. It was perfect. And it was for me. Asaji walks off the stage and people pat him on the back and give him dap. He comes over to our table and sits down as the next poet takes the stage.

"What you think?" he asks. He looks at me with seriousness in his eyes.

"It was, you were . . ." I search for the best word to use. ". . . phenomenal, Asaji. Why didn't you tell me you were doing that?"

He shrugs. "I don't know, Ma. I wanted to catch you off guard."

"Well, you did most definitely. It was good, though."

Neither of us says anything for a few minutes.

"I meant it."

"Huh?" I ask.

"The things I said in the poem. I meant it." He looks away. I can tell he's uncomfortable talking about feelings. Maybe that's why he did it in this way. You know, kind of indirectly.

"You mean, you feel that way about me?" My mind races to try to recall every word he said on that stage. It was deep. It was love. I want to ask him, but I don't want to make him feel uneasy. I wish he would just say it. I mean, do you love me, Asaji? Do you?

"I feel that way and more. This has never happened before, Ma. I don't even know what to do from here."

"Well, what do you want?"

"I want you to be my lady. I want us to be together. I leave my people alone, you leave yours alone. It's just us. That's what I want." Now he's looking at me eye to eye. Oh my God, y'all. I would love to be Asaji's girl. But . . . I have bills to pay. And a certain way that I pay them, ya know? I can't have a man and still maintain my lifestyle.

Who's gonna take me on shopping sprees and take care of my phone bills? Asaji deserves better than I can give him right now. I have to get myself right before I can get with anyone else.

"I feel the same way. I want to be with you exclusively . . ." I begin. He smiles, making this even harder. ". . . but I can't. We can't right now." I feel really bad, but I know I'm doing the right thing. Asaji looks down at the table. I want to say more, but I don't have the nerve.

"I understand, Ma," he says with a slight shrug. "I'm going to get another drink. I'll bring you one for real this time. Hen and Coke, right?" I nod. He walks away as Rena approaches.

"Asaji is something else, isn't he?" she asks.

"Yeah. He is," I say, trying not to sound too pitiful.

"Well, I'm leaving now. Going back to Ty's place for a little while. He's new in town, so he doesn't know too many people."

Um, wait a minute. Rena going home with a random man?

"Are you sure you want to do that, Rena?"

"Why not? He is so cute. And smart. And mature, Jas. That's the main thing right there."

"Well, call me if Mr. Maturity gets out of line. Where does he live anyway?"

"Actually, he lives in SoHo." She rolls her eyes as she says "SoHo".

I laugh at her and what I know she's thinking about. "Come on. What are the chances you'll see Lia?"

"True. I know I won't. But still. Too close, you know?"

"I feel you. Well, have fun. Be good."

She goes back to the bar and she and Ty leave the club. Asaji comes back with two drinks and says he'll have to leave in a few minutes.

"Aw. I thought we could go back to my place and chill.

Maybe we're not official, but I'm still your number one, right?" I ask, hoping to smooth over our earlier conversation.

"I can't tonight, Ma. Definitely another time, though."

Great, this is the second time he's passed up an evening with me. What's really going on? I sip on my drink and halfway listen to the girl onstage. She kinda looks like Lia, actually. Oh, wow! That's it! Ty . . . Lia! She mentioned she met a guy named Ty last Saturday when we went to the martini bar. Could it be the same one? I mean, they both live in SoHo. And I think she said he was from out of town. It may be a huge coincidence. But it may not be. Wouldn't it be a trip if it were the same guy, though? I laugh to myself just thinking about it.

"You ready, Ma?" Asaji asks after watching another poet and finishing his drink.

"Yeah, let's go." The two of us leave the bar and begin our walk back to my place. Once we get outside my door, he gives me a kiss and says bye.

"I'll call you tomorrow," I say as he walks away from me. He turns around briefly and nods. He's always running off to do something whenever I invite him to stay over. I don't get it. And I hope he's not mad at me for saying no earlier. But really, it's for the best. I go check the mail and sigh as I see my cell and cable bills in the stack of envelopes. Guess it's a good thing Asaji didn't stay. I think about the conversation I had with the pastor. Lord knows I want to stop. And I will. But it's like Asaji said in his poem, "The more I push it I pull it. The more I shun it I want it." Or in this case, need it. I'll get past it, I know. But it looks like I need to have some other company over tonight. . . .

Chapter 11

Lia

Damn. I'm practically sleepwalking my way through the lobby at 3:00 a.m. after a killer salt and vinegar potato chip craving. Sometimes I just don't understand myself. I wake up in the middle of the night and run to a convenience store, all for some damn chips! After I get inside the lobby, I drag myself over to the elevators and press UP. It pops open four seconds later and Rena and Ty come out, almost pushing me back.

"Oh . . . Lia. What's up?" Ty asks. I don't believe my eyes. He's wearing a wife beater and ball shorts, looking all . . . God, let me stop. "This is my friend, Rena—"

"We know each other." Rena looks at me with a grin. "How you doin', sister?" she asks, slurring her words a little. She must have been drinking. And wait a minute. It's three in the morning. What's she doing at Ty's at this hour?

"I'm fine. Can we talk for a second?" I ask. She looks at Ty, then back at me.

"Why not? Ty, can you get me a cab? I'll just be one minute."

"All right. I'll be outside." He turns from us and walks outside.

"Rena, first let me say I'm sorry about what happened. You know I never wanted to hurt you."

"You didn't hurt me, Lia. You hurt yourself. Because now you can't claim me as your friend anymore. You're the one who got played."

"Let's not hold grudges. We've been close for too long."

"Exactly." She steps up nearer to me. "That's what makes what you did so bad." She walks away. I don't call out after her. If she wants to cut me loose, it's her decision. I press the elevator button again and it opens just as Ty comes running up.

"I thought you were going to let it close on me," he says.

"I should have."

"Hold up, now. What's your problem?"

"How you gonna try to get with me since like day one of you being here and then the first chance you get you go sleep with my best friend?"

"What? Okay, I'm confused now," he says. I sigh.

"Never mind." The elevator stops at five. "This is you," I say.

"No, I wanna talk about this. Let me go up or you come with me."

"Ty, it's almost four in the morning."

"Well, hurry up and tell me what it's going to be. You can't just go off on me and not tell me why."

"Fine." We both get off on his floor and go to his place. I'm kind of dreading it because I'm sure the house smells like sex. We go in and fortunately I'm wrong about the smell. It doesn't even look like anyone has been here really.

"Sorry about the way this place looks. I haven't really had time to get settled yet." He sits on a black leather couch and offers me a seat. "So, what were you talking about before?"

"It's stupid."

"Yeah, probably, but still."

"Okay. Rena is, well, was my best friend. And it was just weird to see the two of you together. You know, considering . . ."

"Considering what? That I tried to date you and you weren't feeling me?"

"I never said I wasn't feeling you." Did I? At least not out loud.

"Lia, you said that. And as much as I liked you, I wasn't going to—"

"Chase me, I know."

"And not that it's any of your business, but I did not sleep with Rena. All we did really was talk about her 'young, dumb, and full of come' boyfriend and the ho he cheated with. Those were her exact words."

I laugh a little bit. Rena doesn't even speak like that. I can just imagine.

"I'm the ho," I say meekly.

"What? For real? Damn, Lia."

"No, he kissed me and I was a little tipsy. That's all it was. I swear."

"You don't have to convince me."

"Well, are you going to see her again?" I ask. *Please say no, please say no.*

"She's cool. I wouldn't mind hanging out with her. Unless . . . maybe you would rather I hang out with you."

Hmm . . . I don't want him with her, but I don't necessarily want him with me either.

"Ya know what. It has nothing to do with me." I get up and start to walk out toward the door, but Ty pulls my arm so I end up facing him again. He looks at me hard, as if to say I have a lot of nerve trying to leave in the middle of our conversation. I don't know why, but I let him hold on to me longer than I normally would in a situation like this.

"Are you going to respond?" he asks.

"Ty, come on. You're a grown man. You date who you want to date," I say as I finally shake away from his grip. "Why does it matter what I think?"

"You're right, it doesn't matter. But for some reason you're in my house for the first time ever, at four in the morning no less, and why? Because you saw me with your friend and you had to know what was up. It was eating you up inside to think about me with another woman." He smiles a little bit and shakes his head at me. "Just tell me what you want," he says, taking a few steps toward me. I can feel that he wants to kiss me. I can sense how badly he wants me right now. The question is, do I give in to my desires . . . I mean his desires? Damn, where is my head?

"I want," I say slowly, "to go home." We stand there for a second or two, like we need to digest what was just said. Like we need to make sure it really happened that way even though the thickness in the air makes it feel like it should have gone down differently. But it didn't.

"Okay, Lia," he says coolly as ever. "I'll see you later."

And with that phrase I walk out of his place into a world of mixed thoughts and emotions. Guess I was expecting more of a fight. Expecting . . . wanting, who knows? But I do know that I don't care if Rena is with Ty. They can do what they want. It's not like I want him anyway. Besides, I don't really have time to deal with anyone else except Eric, even though he's playing hard to get. But still . . . I have this sick feeling in the pit of my stomach when the thought of the two of them enters my mind.

I wake up early Thursday morning wondering what type of day I'll have. Lately it seems everything has been happening at once. After arriving at the office I check the messages that have already accumulated since eight this morning: I have to interview a new paralegal candidate on Friday. There's a company-wide meeting in two weeks. I have to redraft a contract for an artist who's getting higher royalties. And . . . oh no. Please no. I immediately buzz my assistant.

"Rhonda, when did this one message come in? The one from my parents."

"Your mom called as soon as I got here. She said to expect her at some point today."

"Are you serious? And that's all she said?" This can't be happening. Not now.

"Pretty much. She said don't make any plans for the rest of the week."

"Okay. Thanks." Great. She always does this. Pops up whenever she feels the need. It's invasive and inconsiderate and just plain rude. And the rest of the week? That's at least until Sunday. She can't do this. It's not fair! Besides, I was planning to invite Eric over for a romantic little dinner. Damn it, Mom!

When I get home around five thirty, I already know that my mom will be in the kitchen, making rice and drinking tea. Sure enough, after I open the door I'm hit with a strong whiff of eucalyptus.

"Li- Li. You finally come home." She rushes over to me and gives me a hug. She's wearing a sheer, gold-colored blouse with a silk camisole underneath and slim black pants. Her size 4, black Coach mules are side by side near my front door.

"Hey, Mom. I really wish you had told me you were coming. This isn't a good week."

She steps back with a solemn look on her face. She looks tired. Like she's been up for days. And she's much thinner than I remember.

"We need to sit," she says. We go over to my couch and she takes a seat, perfect posture intact. "Your daddy. He not well."

"What? What's wrong with him?"

"He have serious problem with prostate. Doctor not think they catch in time."

I feel like I've been punched in the stomach. What is she really saying to me? "How long has this been going on? And why are you just telling me, Mom?"

"We decide not to worry you. You have lot going on with job." She actually thinks that my job is more important than my family? Well, she actually thinks that *I* think that? Have I given them any impression that I feel that way?

"Mom, that's crazy! Of course I want to know what's going on with you guys."

"You never call us. We never know what's going on with you anymore." She begins to cry.

"Mom, I'm sorry. I didn't mean to . . . tell me more about Dad. Is he going to be okay?" My heart is beating so, so fast.

"They not give him long. Cancer too strong." She reaches over and holds me, her tears saturating my shirt.

I cry with her. I'm still trying to figure out if she just told me my father is dying. "I want to see him. I'll go back to Connecticut with you."

"No, Li-Li. He not want you to see him like that."

"I don't care, Mom. He's sick and I want to be with him . . . and you."

"No—" she whispers.

"To hell with his stupid pride. I'm his only child. He needs me."

She pulls back, wiping her eyes with the back of her hand. "He have another daughter."

"What?"

"When you were four and your daddy went away for three years . . . he meet another woman."

"Are you saying that he cheated on you? When he was in Taiwan?" I vaguely remember when my father was stationed there. We went to visit once. But I had no idea . . .

"He really only in Taiwan one year. Other two we were separated. He told me he had another baby but he still want to be with me. I needed time."

"Oh my God." This is too much. "So my whole life you two have been keeping this huge secret from me. Why?"

"Because. The woman marry another solider and move to United States with him. They raise the baby. We don't know nothing else about her."

"I bet Dad does."

"He have one picture. But nothing else."

I can tell this whole thing is upsetting my mom, so I decide to leave it alone for now. But it still lingers in my mind. "Okay, Mom. But I'm still going back home with you."

"Li-Li, please. Your daddy don't even know I come here. And I know you will ask about the baby. It will only make him worse."

"Well, what if I just go up on my own? He doesn't have to know that you told me anything. And I promise I won't mention the baby."

She thinks about this for a minute. "Fine. You make surprise visit."

"Okay. But in that case you should go back and be with him. I'll make my travel plans tomorrow."

She looks more comfortable now. "I go to bed now, Li-Li."

"Mom, it's only six o'clock."

"So what? There's no rules about what time I can sleep." I smile at her. "Okay, then. But you can take my bed."

"No. You taller than me. Couch more for my size."

"All right. I'll be in my room watching TV if you need anything. And, um, I was going to order something to eat. Want anything?"

"No. You need to eat the rice I made. You eat too many fatty foods." Okay, now there's the mom I know.

I go into my room to change out of my work clothes and can't help but think about the sister I have out there somewhere. Does she look like me? Act like me? What does she do? And my dad had an affair? It's the most far-fetched thing I ever heard. But it happened. It seems as though my mom has reconciled with the fact, so I guess I should too. But she's had nearly thirty years to accept it. I've had thirty minutes. He risked everything for one night. Or maybe it wasn't just one night. What if he was in love with her, but in the end he chose Mom and me because he already made that commitment? I know I promised that I wouldn't ask him about any of this, but that doesn't mean I can't find out on my own.

Chapter 12

Rena

I'm trying to straighten up a little before Ty comes over. I asked him if he would like to have dinner over my place tonight and he said yes. I'm not trying to make this into anything, though. He's a decent guy and we get along. That's it. But if he did ever wanted to take it to a sexual level, I think I would consider it. I set the table and am putting the finishing touches on my chicken Florentine when there's a knock on the door.

"Hey, Ty. Come in."

He has a bottle of wine in his hand. "I brought a little something I thought would complement the meal."

"Thank you," I say as I take the bottle and show him to the table.

"Your artwork is nice. Did you paint any of them?"

"No. I'm just a spectator. A lot of these paintings are

from Nigeria. My ex's family is very artistic." Damn. I was trying to make it a point not to mention Tak. We sit at the table quietly for a little while until . . .

"So, how long have you and Lia known each other?" Great. Is he actually asking me about her?

"A few years," I say curtly. Maybe he'll sense that I'd rather not discuss her.

"Oh. I've only known her a short time, but I can tell she's—"

"Ty, I'd really appreciate it if you wouldn't talk about Lia right now. I'm trying to enjoy myself."

"Sorry. I didn't know she was such a touchy subject. This chicken, by the way, is really good."

"Thanks. This is a recipe that Tak created." Damn!

"Okay, Rena. Obviously you have your ex on your mind and I have Lia on mine. I don't have a problem with you mentioning him or anything. So maybe you can be easy on me when it comes to Lia."

"It's not the same thing. I was in love with Tak for years. You don't know the first thing about Lia."

"Okay. But you do."

"Yes, I do. And there's nothing good about her."

"Come on, Rena. That's impossible."

"I'm serious. She's rude and condescending and materialistic and a slut."

He laughs. I don't.

"You're just upset with her."

"No. She's been like that since day one."

"So why waste your time being her friend all these years?"

"Don't talk about wasting time, Ty. You're doing just that by pursuing her. She will never give you a chance."

"Why is that?"

"I don't want to get into it." It's so stupid I can't even say it. "Anyway, what are you doing tomorrow night? There's a jazz concert in Central Park I want to attend."

"I have a lot of work I need to get a head start on for next week."

"Oh."

"Take your ex. Maybe if you spent time with him you wouldn't feel the need to talk about him all the time." He grins at me. "You still love him. And he is the father of your son." All of these things are true. But to take Tak back would mean forgiving him, and I'm not ready to let go of my anger.

"Okay, Dr. Phil," I say with a laugh. I've just gotten up to clear the table when I hear knocking again. "Ty, can you get that? It's the neighbor bringing Lion back." I begin to load the dishwasher and suddenly hear yelling. I run to the living room and see Tak with his hand in Ty's face.

"Tak, what the hell is wrong with you?"

He backs up and comes toward me. "Who the fuck is this cat and what is he doing here?"

"That's none of your business."

"It is my business, Rena. My son lives here, so everything that happens in this house is my business. Who is he?"

Is that jealousy I hear? I think I'm going to run with this one. "Good-bye, Tak."

"Rena, I'm not playin'."

"Neither am I. Do I need to get Ty to show you out?" I glance over at Ty. He's leaning against the wall expressionless.

"Oh, it's like that? Your new man is gonna put his hands on me? Fuck that." Tak goes over to Ty and pushes up on his shoulders. "You tryin' to get violent? Huh?"

"Look, this is between you and Rena. But seriously, man, keep your hands off me." Ty is calm but ready.

I step between them and push Tak back. "Ty, I'm so sorry. I'll call you, okay?"

"You sure you don't need me to stay?"

"Yo, man, she doesn't need your protection," Tak says.

"It's fine, really," I say. Ty grabs his jacket and leaves.

Tak looks at me with tears in his eyes. "So it's like that now, Rena? You're moving on?" He backs away from me.

"I'm not moving on, Tak." I'm getting choked up myself. "I still love you."

"Why are we doing this to each other, then?" He takes my hand. "You are my life. I am more than empty without you . . . I don't exist. You're so much a part of me that when you're gone . . ."

"I know, Tak. I feel the same way." The tears are rolling down my cheeks. He wipes them away. "But why did you come here? I don't understand."

"I missed you. I wanted to see you."

"But you didn't call or anything. It's not like I was on a date, but we have boundaries now."

"That's so bogus, Rena! Boundaries, are you kidding me?"

"I didn't mean it in a bad way. I mean, aren't we supposed to be broken up? Aren't we supposed to be using this time to think and reflect?"

"All I've been doing is thinking. Look, I am so sorry about what happened with Lia. My mind was a mess. I mean, I was paranoid that you might be messing around with another guy. I panicked and I acted out and I'm sorry. Hurting you, letting you down . . . I never want to do that to you again. I've made up my mind about a lot of things. That's why I came over here. I wanted to tell you what's been on my brain lately."

An apology. A sincere apology. I can feel the truth in his words. Maybe I should hear him out.

"Okay, that's fine. Let's sit and talk about it," I say, taking a seat at the table. "Come on, tell me everything you've been thinking about. He breathes in heavily and exhales just as strongly.

"Serena," he says as he kneels to one knee, "you are the

most phenomenal woman I have ever met. You bring such a brilliant light to everything and everyone who has the privilege of knowing you. I haven't been half as good to you as you've been to me, but I want to take the rest of my life trying to get there."

"Oh my God, Tak." That's all I can manage to say.

"Will you be my wife?" He reaches into his pocket and pulls out a ring with an emerald stone. It's beautiful . . . looks like something I would pick out for myself. I take the ring and put in on my finger. The light reflecting off the stone entrances me.

"Baby?" Tak says. I snap back to reality. I don't believe this is happening. All these years complaining and hoping and praying. And he's finally asking me to be his wife.

"Baby?" he asks again, his voice sounding a little shaky. After all that has happened . . . Lia and Lace and Ty. He now understands that nothing else matters but our bond . . . our family . . . our love.

"Rena, I know this probably isn't the way you thought it would happen. I mean, when I came here tonight I didn't expect you to have company. And, um, I want to apologize for acting like that. I was out of line. But don't let how I acted tonight or any other night affect all the nights I plan to spend with you as my wife." He glances around the room, unsure of what to say next.

I don't know why I'm not answering. I know I want to marry him. But as I open my mouth to say yes . . .

"I'm sorry, Tak." I take the ring off my finger and put it back in his hand.

He looks at me with disappointment, but not surprise in his eyes. He stands up and wipes the sweat off his face. "Why, Rena? Are you in love with someone else?"

"No. I'm not in love with anyone."

He starts to say something, but then I see the realization of what I said sinking in.

"I see. I understand. Well, I should go, then." He walks to the door.

"Tak, I'm sorry. I didn't want it to be this way. I wanted you to be the one for so long."

He turns to me.

"So what happened?" he asks. I shrug my shoulders slightly.

"You're not," I reply. He walks out the door without saying good-bye.

For the past four years I've wanted him to make a real commitment to me, and now that he has . . . I don't want it. And if I do, I don't want it now. But please don't ask me why . . . because truthfully, I don't know. Life is just a barrage of experiences that you can let either push you back or push you forward. You have to decide which way the current will take you. And this current is taking me on a journey through what's really in my heart. I'm waiting to find out what that is.

Chapter 13

Dee Dee

"Deron, I'm leaving now. I'll be back late this evening," I yell as I step outside the front door. I'm on my way to Long Island for my cousin's baby shower. At least, that's my story. I am going to Long Island, but not for my cousin. I'm meeting Manny. This is the third time since I met him at the hotel that I've lied about what I was doing so that we could see each other.

"Have fun, baby. Call me when you get to your parents' house," Deron says before the door closes. Yeah, I will definitely have fun.

Once I get to Penn Station and on the train, I pull out my cell phone and dial Lia's number. I haven't really told her the extent of my affair with Manny yet. It's not that I'm ashamed. I mean, if it were just a sexual fling, then maybe

I would be. But Manny and I have legitimate feelings for each other. This isn't a game. I'm really in love.

"Hello," Lia answers.

"Hi. Are you busy?"

"Not really. What's up?"

"I'm on the train. Going to the Hamptons," I say carefully. I'm not really sure how to lead into what I want to say.

"Okay . . . that's nice," she says, sounding uninterested. "What's going on there?"

"I'm meeting Manny. I've been meeting up with him for weeks."

"Well, have a good time," she says. Okay, I didn't want her to yell at me, but I didn't want her to be so flippant either.

"So you think this is a good idea?" I ask.

"Dee Dee, if you want someone to reprimand you, then you called the wrong one. You know that this shit is wrong. But you are a grown woman. I'm not going to scold you."

"Maybe it is wrong because of Deron. But the way we feel about each other makes it right."

"Well, I guess you have it all figured out, then," she says.

But that's just it. I don't. And I'm about to tell her this when I get another call.

"I'll call you later, Lia." After I switch lines I hear a lot of noise on the other end. "Hello?" I ask. No one says anything, but the noise continues. It sounds like a woman talking, but I can't make out what she's saying. "Hello?" I ask again, more forcefully. And then a man says, "You know it's all about you, baby." I click the Off button on my cell and shake my head in confusion. It was Manny. I'd recognize his voice anywhere. But who was the woman and what was he talking about? I would call him back, but I'll be seeing him soon, so there's no point. I lean back in my seat and try to catch a short nap, but all I can think about is what I just heard on my phone. "You know it's all about you, baby." I can't imagine why he would say that to anyone. But I'm definitely going to ask him.

It feels like an eternity before I get to Long Island, but once I do I quickly scan the crowd at the train station for Manny. He told me he'd be wearing sunglasses and a cowboy hat. Go figure. Five minutes later I see him leaning against the wall with a big grin on his face. I run over to him and give him a tight hug. He kisses me briefly before pulling back. He looks down at my stomach, which is steadily growing, and smiles.

"How safe is it to keep doing what we do with that baby inside you?" he asks.

"Very safe. Now can we go? That hat is giving me a headache," I say. He laughs and smacks my butt as we walk to his car.

"Manny, I think you accidentally dialed my number earlier," I say as he opens the passenger door of his Benz for me.

"What do you mean?" he asks before he walks over to the other side and gets in.

"I heard a woman talking to you. And then you said something odd."

"What'd I say?" he asks. He doesn't sound too concerned about the whole thing. I was thinking I'd hear a hint of "Damn, I've been caught" in his voice.

"You said 'it's all about you, baby.'" I look at him, but he keeps his eyes on the road.

"I think you got it wrong, Dee Dee," he says calmly.

"No, Manny. I don't think I do. I almost called you back but—"

"Dee! You got it wrong," he snaps. "Now can we just enjoy this time we have together?" He picks up my hand and kisses it. "Are you hungry? What do you want to eat?" His total dismissal of the issue pisses me off. I know what I heard and he knows what he said. But he's right. I didn't come all this way to argue. Besides, whoever he was talking to then is gone. He's with me now.

"Pasta. With tons of garlic," I say.

"Pasta it is, then," he says. We take rest of the ride in silence. The whole time I'm trying to push the whole incident out of my mind, but I can't. Something just doesn't make sense. I don't think Manny is seeing anyone else. After all, he loves me. He wants to be with me again. It's not like I'm pursuing him . . . he came to me. Maybe I am blowing it out of proportion. In any case, it's over now. And I only have a few hours to spend with him, so I'm not going to waste them stressing over that call.

After we eat we head to his hotel room and of course have sex. We have sex an hour after that and then another three hours after that. It's great. I mean, it's okay. Even if I don't have an orgasm every time, it still feels good . . . for the most part. Sigh. I don't know what it is. It seems like when we make love it's less passionate than before. I don't want to say Manny is going through the motions, but it really feels that way. I just don't feel the love.

"What's wrong, Dee Dee?" he asks as we lie in bed.

"It's nothing. I mean, I was just thinking that—" Just as I'm about to tell him my thoughts, his cell phone rings. I know for a fact that he won't answer it. But then he does. Sigh.

"Yeah," he answers. "Oh, um, no. That can't happen today. I'm sorry. My plans changed." He rambles on to the person on the phone for about three more minutes before he finally hangs up.

"Who was that?" I ask. He looks at me with a confused look on his face, like he can't believe I'm asking him this question. I do have a right to ask. Don't I?

"Uh, Dee Dee," he says with a chuckle. "*That* was none of your business." He gets out of bed and heads to the kitchen area of the suite. "Want anything to drink?"

"Wait," I say, sitting up. "It is my business. You're my . . ." I stop because I realize that he's my nothing.

"I'm not your husband. I'm not even your fucking boyfriend. At best I'm your 'secret lover,' but damn . . . you're carrying someone else's kid! Don't question who I'm talking to on the phone. I have no real claim to you, so you have no claim to me."

I don't know if it's the overall tone of the conversation, the fact that he's being so defensive, or my pregnant hormones, but something makes me burst into tears. I didn't know that any of that stuff mattered to Manny. The only thing I thought he cared about was the fact that we were together. Fuck titles and circumstances. We're in love.

"Okay. I'm sorry," I say through sobs. "But then why am I here? What's the whole point of us seeing each other?"

He comes over to me and sits on the bed.

"Because I love you. But I have to tell you the truth," he says.

Oh God. The truth? I can't handle the truth! "What, Manny?"

"The truth is, I can't be your little secret anymore. I want to be with you and I want the world to know. No more sneaking around and meeting away from home."

"You want me to leave Deron?" Even though I knew that my marriage would be a constant issue for myself, I never fully came to terms with how much of an issue it would be for him. I didn't think that I'd ever be pressured into making a real decision.

"How much longer do you want to play this game, Dee Dee? I'm thirty years old and I've never been married, don't have any kids . . . I'm ready for that life. I never signed up to be anyone's man on the side."

"Manny, I can't just up and leave my husband and my family. I'm about to have another one of his kids. I can't—"

"Can't or won't? Look, this isn't really up for debate, Dee Dee. As long as you're still married, I'm still dating."

"Manny, that's crazy. You can't compare my marriage to your stupid little flings with your stupid little whores!"

"You're one of them, Dee Dee," he shouts. It seems like everything is happening in slow motion at this point. If what he said is a slap in the face, then this moment is like the burning sensation after his hand leaves my cheek. That's what I am to him? A simple whore? What happened to *mi estrella* and being his true love? I look at him and I can see the regret of what he said in his eyes, but I'm not sure any apologies can lessen the pain.

"I didn't mean to say that," he says. "I was angry and I shouldn't have said it."

"You shouldn't have said it, but you still believe it," I say. He sighs. I guess that's my answer.

"I want us to be together. For real. In front of everyone with no shame. Can you do that for me? For us?" He sounds so sincere.

"I—I think so," I say hesitantly. "But, Manny, I have to do it my way, in my time."

"I understand. But don't keep me waiting, *mi estrella.*"

When I get home late that evening, Deron is at the computer, typing away at his newest book venture.

"Baby, how was the shower?" he asks as he gives me a hug.

"Nice. Very nice," I say distractedly.

"Is something wrong?"

I snap out of my trance and focus on Deron. The father of my children, the man I promised my life to. Things have gotten so much better for us. It's so selfish of Manny to expect me to give up everything after it took so long to get to this place with Deron. Or am I the selfish one for wanting to hold on to the life I have as well as the life I want to have?

"Everything is fine, baby. Did Deidre give you any trouble today?"

"She was perfect. I missed you so much. You didn't even call me. And I kept getting the voice mail," he says.

"No signal in that area for some reason. I couldn't really make any calls." It gets easier to lie to him with every day that passes. It's kind of scary to think about the person I've become since reuniting with Manny.

"Oh. Well, you're safe, so that's all that matters. I'm tired, though. You ready to go to bed?"

"Let me take a quick shower first."

"Okay," he says before going into the bedroom.

While I wash away any hint of Manny, I feel more and more dirty. So far I've managed to avoid the mandatory guilt you should feel when you're cheating on your husband. But the more I think about the betrayal, the deceit, and the disregard I'm showing toward my wedding vows, the nastier I feel. The harder I scrub. The more it hurts. I tilt my head toward the running water of the shower and let the flow mix with my tears. I can't deny my feelings for Deron, but my feelings for Manny just keep growing.

Chapter 14

Jas

It's been about a week since I've talked to any of my friends and that's a good thing 'cause I've needed that time to collect my thoughts. Today is the first time I'm attending the meeting Pastor Gordon suggested I look into. I'm a little bit nervous but very anxious to see what it's all about. The meeting is held in a building about fifteen blocks up from where I live, so I decide to walk. The sun is setting and the sky is a pretty orangeish color. It kinda puts me in a good mood considering where I'm about to be. I try to imagine what it will be like. Probably a bunch of crying, sad women sitting in a circle and holding hands. Well, I'm not sad, and I'm definitely not gonna cry.

I arrive at the address and take a deep breath as I walk inside. I'm shocked to see about twenty women, all different races and ages, laughing and talking among each other.

This can't be it. I am almost turning to leave when a short, green-eyed, fair-skinned woman with very long dark brown hair approaches me.

"It's okay. You don't have to leave."

"Uh, I think I'm in the wrong place. I'm looking for the rape survivors meeting," I whisper.

She grins at me. "This is it. I'm Joelle."

"Jas."

"Okay, Jas, nice to meet you. We're going to be starting in a few minutes, so make yourself comfortable. There are refreshments over there and tissues, if you think you'll need them." She smiles again and walks away as I go to the snack table and get some punch and settle into a chair.

"Okay, ladies, we're going to begin now. For our first-time visitors, welcome. Please don't feel obligated to speak, but also feel free to. This is an open discussion. All questions and comments are okay. Everyone is here for everyone." Joelle is standing up speaking to the group, but it feels like her eyes are on me. As she sits, a blond woman stands. She looks frail, her eyes sunken in. She's shaking a little as she speaks.

"My name is Katherine. I was raped a year ago by a coworker. I never reported it and he soon was promoted and moved to another department. Three months later I started bingeing and throwing up my food. At first I did it to lose weight. I thought if the only guy who wanted me turned out to be a rapist loser, something must be wrong with me. But then it became an escape . . . a way to control something in my life. Now I'm seeking treatment, but it's so hard. I see him sometimes. The bastard has the nerve to smile at me. It takes everything in me not to get a gun and . . ." She stops talking and begins to cry. The woman next to her hugs her and hands her a tissue.

"We all have been there, Katherine. Does anyone have any suggestions?" Joelle asks us.

"Well, my therapist told me to start a journal. An anger journal. Be as explicit or violent as you want. Every time you feel the need to lash out, write what you want to do. Then reread it and write all the negative consequences of actually doing what you wrote. You'll see how much better you are than that, and that your life is too precious to throw away for a 'rapist loser,'" a woman about my age says.

"That sounds great," Joelle says.

"Maybe she should get another job," I say. "I mean, part of what helped me forget what happened to me was to move away from where it took place."

"But is that forgetting, or repressing? And will we ever really forget?" Joelle asks.

"No, I guess not. Sorry." I feel so dumb right now.

"Don't apologize. This is what we're here for."

Yeah, I hear what she's saying, but I still feel bad. I listen to the rest of the meeting and when it's over, I try to slip out unnoticed.

"Hey, can't say bye?" Joelle asks when I'm two feet from the exit.

"Oh, you were busy and I didn't want . . ."

"Jas, you don't have to feel tense or out of place. No one is going to judge you. We're all in the same boat here, okay?"

Her smile makes me feel at ease. "Okay. But this is so new to me."

"That's fine. I was new once, too. Move at your own pace. We're not going anywhere."

"Thanks."

"So, you'll be back, right?"

"Um, yes, I'll be back."

"Great. We meet every Monday. Same time and place."

"Okay, I'll see you next Monday, then," I say.

She hugs me. "I think this group is really going to help you. And I'm sure your story will help us." She smiles and walks away as I leave the room.

On my walk home I reflect on the meeting and think about whether it will make a difference. I mean, how much can it really help? I guess I feel a little better actually talking about it, but like Joelle said, I'll never forget. Speaking of Joelle, something's up with her. I can't pinpoint it right now. But have you ever just had a feeling about someone . . . like they're hiding something? Don't misunderstand; she's cool, very nice. But maybe too nice. Then again, it's her job to make people feel comfortable. I guess only time will tell.

As soon as I get home my cell rings and it's one of my "contacts" (that's what I like to call them now). I press the Ignore button. I'm not really in the mood for any of that nonsense right now. Wow, a week ago I would never have called a free meal or a paid bill nonsense. But today I see that it is. I don't need that. I don't need them. I'm really going to try to get away from the way I've been living for the past few years. After all, I do have a pretty good job, my music, and most importantly, Asaji. Maybe being with him can be the first step to my new life. Yeah, I think it's time. I've never had this connection with anyone else. I've never wanted to be someone's girl. And Asaji just makes everything right. He does everything right. I would be crazy not to be with him.

I decide to call him and invite him over for a drink. After he says he's on his way, I change into some sweats and a T-shirt and wait. Half an hour later he's knocking at my door.

"Hey, sweetie," I say as I give him a hug.

"'Sup, mami?" he says with a smile. "How ya day been?"

"It was nice," I tell him. "You want a drink?"

"Yeah, you got a Corona?" He takes a seat on the couch. "Yo, I found out some ill shit today."

"Oh yeah? What happened?" I bring his beer and my rum and Coke over to the couch and sit next to him.

"You know Lace, right? Well, homeboy is gay. Last night at the studio one of my boys caught him and another dude laid out, naked and shit." He laughs as he brings the bottle to his lips.

"Oh my God! That's crazy!" My thoughts go straight to Rena. I wonder if she knows. Damn . . . I hope she didn't do anything with him. "So, what happened?"

"Well, he starts cryin' and shit. Talkin' 'bout he bi and he only be using the guys for head. I mean, I don't give a damn who he's fuckin'. But in my damn studio? That's why I'm trippin'."

"Yeah, that's wrong."

"He don't want us to tell no one. You know, he tryin' to drop an album soon. This can destroy his career." He stops talking to finish off the bottle and turns to me. "Enough about that though. I feel like we haven't talked for a while. What's up with you?"

"Not much. A lot of nothing. Thinkin' about you." I run my finger along his face and kiss him. It feels so good, like . . . oh, damn. But then he pulls back. "What's wrong?" I ask.

"Nothin'. I was supposed to go holla at my boy . . . he got something for me and—"

"Asaji, no. That bullshit you be pullin' with me all the time, it's not happening tonight." I kiss him again, and this time I straddle his lap. This man ain't goin' anywhere.

"Ma, chill. I promise I'll make it up to you," he says.

I just don't get it. I don't understand what he's running from. But shit, if he wants to run, I'm not gonna make it easy for him. I start to kiss on his neck and ears, while putting his hands under my shirt and on my breasts. It seems like it's working. He fondles me a little bit, very gently. I slide out of my shirt and try taking off his, but he holds my arms down.

"Be easy," he says.

Okay, the frustration has officially set in. "Look, Asaji. I can't play these games with you. You need to tell me what the fuck is your problem. What? I don't turn you on? Oh my God . . . do you have someone else? Is it a guy?"

"Yo, Jas, you buggin'. It's none of that. Of course you turn me on."

"So why won't you make love to me?" I don't think I've ever said those words in my life.

"I will. We'll get there."

"But, Asaji, I'm ready now. I thought we meant something to each other." Whoa. Talk about role reversal.

"Jas . . ." He looks away from me, almost in an embarrassed way.

"What is it? Tell me please."

"It's some dumb shit."

"Tell me, Asaji." At this point I can't imagine what he's going to say. There's an awkward silence before he takes a deep breath.

"I just . . . never did this before."

"Sweetie, I've never done it either. I mean, I've had sex and fucked and all that . . . but making love is new to me too."

"No, Ma. I never did any of it before."

"You mean you're a . . . " He gotta be lyin'! Asaji is a virgin?

"I understand if you don't wanna kick with me like that anymore."

"No, I mean yes. I mean, of course we can still kick it. I'm just surprised. I mean, you're so . . ." I don't know what I'm trying to say.

"You don't think I'm some kinda lame or punk?"

"No. Not at all." But now I feel like a sleaze for pressuring him so much. Maybe he really is too good for me. This man has been saving himself for the right girl and I've been giving it up to every wrong guy.

"I was gonna tell you before, ya know . . . but I couldn't say the words."

I can tell he's loosening up and feeling more at ease.

"I should have known you'd be cool, though. You're not like one of those triflin' chicks."

"Uh, yeah." I get off his lap and put my shirt back on.

"I mean, it's gonna go down, Ma. That's my word. And I definitely want you to be the one, feel me? You special. And I'm gonna make it special for you."

"Uh-huh," I say. But I'm not special. And I shouldn't be the one. If he knew about what I've been doing, why I couldn't be his girl . . . he'd realize just how unspecial I really am.

"You a'ight? You seem a little distracted."

"No, I'm okay. I just . . . I have a long day tomorrow. I should go to bed."

"Oh. That's cool. I'll call you later, then." He sounds disappointed.

"Yeah, do that." I walk him to the door and he tries to kiss me, but I turn my head. "Bye," I say while closing the door. Just when I think that everything is gonna be all right, I remember that my life is garbage. I'm falling in love with a guy who shouldn't be with me. I was planning on telling him everything. I was gonna be totally honest, totally real. And then I was gonna tell him that all of that is over and I'm ready to commit to him. But now . . . he'd laugh in my face. I know he's not saving himself for a slut. So I should just do both of us a favor and end it before it starts. That way, neither of us will get hurt.

Chapter 15

Lia

It's about 10:00 p.m. and I'm just getting home from my trip to Connecticut. It was very painful to see my father like that . . . so sick and, well . . . dying. But even though he was weak and hurting, he still tried to be the stoic and strong man that he always has been. We laughed about the good times and joked about funny times. I cried a lot. So did he. I guess you never really know what to say to someone when you know that it'll probably be the last time you see him. I didn't want to leave, but he insisted. A few hours before I was to leave to catch my train, he told me to sit next to him for a minute. . . .

"Lia, I love you. You have been the one thing in my life that I have been the most proud of."

"I love you too, Daddy."

"I'm ashamed that I didn't tell you this before." He

reaches under his pillow and pulls out a picture. "This is your sister, Maya-Lin. I never met her. Her mother sent me her picture about twenty-five years ago."

"Daddy . . ."

"I'm sorry I kept this from you. You deserved to know. She is your blood. I just didn't want to upset your mother. Please understand." Tears begin to fall from his eyes.

"It's okay. You don't have to explain." I take the picture from his hand. Maya-Lin. My little sister. Looks just like the pictures I've seen of myself as a baby.

"You should find her. Her mother's name is June. But she married, so I don't know her last name. Look in the bottom drawer of my desk. That's all the information I have about where I was stationed."

"Daddy, are you sure? I'm fine with not knowing. You and Mom are the only family I need."

"But soon you won't have me." This is the first time either of us actually mentions the fact that all of this is real. "I want my daughters to be together, finally. Even if I can't be here to see it." He takes my hand in his. "Tell her about me. Tell her that I have always loved her and that I thought of her every day." He dabs his wet eyes with the back of his other hand.

I kiss him on the forehead. "Get some rest now. I have to go to the train station soon." I tuck him into his bed and try to give the picture back to him.

"Keep it, Lia."

"All right, Daddy." I turn to leave the room, but then I think of something. "Daddy, what if I find her before you . . . I mean, would you want to meet her?" I ask. He shakes his head.

"Tell her I'm gone," he says. And I knew he would say that. He doesn't want the first impression his daughter has of him to be . . . this.

"Bye, Daddy. I love you always."

When I first found out about my sister, I really wanted to meet her. But now I don't know. She may not know a damn thing about my dad. Who knows what her mother has told her, if anything? It's a scary thought. What if I find her and she wants to have nothing to do with me? Sigh. Enough of this heavy stuff for now. I run some bathwater and pour a glass of wine. Wow, I haven't really talked to anyone in a while. I didn't even tell anyone I was going out of town. Although I doubt they would care. As far as I know, Rena is still pissed and Jas is still busy with that guy she's dating. And Dee Dee, I never know what's going on with her. She's actually cheating on her husband with some dog ass guy. But then again, I guess all of us are a little screwed up.

The next morning I get to work tired and frazzled.

"Good morning, Ms. Wells. There's a surprise for you in your office," my assistant says as she hands me my mail.

"If it's not a trip to Jamaica I'm not interested." I walk into the office and there's a big bouquet of flowers on my desk. I smile as I open the card, thinking Eric must have sent them along with an invitation to dinner or something.

from one friend to another
—Ty

Great. I really wasn't expecting this. He's good, though. Now I have to call him and say thanks. I pick up the phone but realize I don't have his number. Damn, now I have to go to his place after work. He's damn good.

Once the clock says five I practically run for the elevators. Today has just been rough. I had to fire one of the associates. I've never had a problem with that before, but for some reason today I had a hard time with it. At home, I change out of my heels and into some slippers. I turn on the TV and watch a few shows before I finally go downstairs to see Ty. I knock on the door and he answers it shirtless. Good God Almighty!

"Lia, what's up?" he asks with that smile of his.

"Ty . . . hey. I just wanted to come by and say thanks for sending the flowers. I had a long week and I needed that."

"No problem." He looks over his shoulder and laughs. Is someone there?

"Um, are you busy?" I ask.

"Huh? Oh, nah."

"Okay . . . it's just that you haven't invited me in."

"Actually, I guess I am a little bit busy right now. Can I call you later, though?"

I hear some giggling coming from behind him. He's busier than I thought, I guess.

"Sure. Later," I say. He smiles and closes the door. Well, I did my part. It doesn't matter if he didn't ask me in. It doesn't matter if he has company. Wait . . . what if it's Rena? Didn't he say he was gonna leave her alone? Ya know what, never mind. I don't care.

I go back to my place and give Eric a call. Maybe he'd like to come over and, um, help me out.

"Hello?"

"Eric, hi. It's Lia."

"*Who* is this?"

"Lia. Lia Wells. We had lunch a couple of weeks ago."

"Lia? Oh yeah. The Chinese chick," he says.

Okay, usually I'd go to someone's ass for a comment like that, but now's not the time. I am too horny. "Okay . . . um, how about you stop by tonight?"

"Sorry, hon. I'm gonna have to pass."

"Oh, well . . . another time, then."

"Sure," he says, and hangs up. I don't believe this. He barely remembered me. This is crazy. He's treating me like I'm nothing. I mean, I'm Lia Wells, damn it! Ya know, maybe Eric's not all that I made him out to be.

I plop down on my bed right after I turn on my CD player. The sounds of Teddy Pendergrass fill my eardrums. Right about now I'm wishing I had someone to turn off my damn lights. But before I can sulk for too long I start to think about Maya-Lin and my dad. Tomorrow I'm going to begin my search for her. If I don't get anywhere within a week, I'll hire a private investigator. Either way, I will find her. And hopefully, she wants to be found.

Dee Dee calls me the next day and asks me to meet her at a coffee shop. I know it's some news about Manny, and truthfully, I don't really care to know. I mean, not in that way. But if she's going to tell me how they're so in love and all that crap, I don't want to hear it. I leave my job early and meet Dee around three. She's sitting at a table drinking chocolate milk.

"Dee, hi. How are you?" I ask as I sit next to her. She looks up at me with a gleam in her eyes.

"Hello, Lia. I'm so glad you could come. After our last conversation I wasn't too sure."

"Of course I would. So, what's up?"

"Well, I've decided that I'm not going to keep up this affair with Manny anymore." She takes a sip of her milk.

"About time you came to your damn senses, Dee Dee. Deron may not be perfect, but he deserves better than that," I say.

"Yeah, well . . . I'm not going to continue the affair with Manny because I'm leaving Deron, and Manny and I are going to be together officially," she says somewhat quickly. Okay, this girl is just traveling deeper and deeper into Dumb-ass-ville.

"You're actually going to leave your marriage for a man who treated you like shit only a few years ago? Wake the fuck up, Dee Dee! Manny is not good enough for you."

"Manny is the true love of my life. He's always loved me. He just didn't know how to deal with the pressures of—"

"Oh my God, am I in the fucking twilight zone? Do you hear yourself?"

"Like you said before, I don't need a lecture. I wanted to discuss my legal options. I want full custody of Deidre and the baby. He can have the house and everything else. I just want my kids."

"That probably won't happen. You're the one leaving the marriage to be with your lover. Deron's lawyer will run with that. Besides, what's wrong with joint custody?"

"I want my kids, Lia."

"Do you realize that this will get nasty? Every detail of your life will be put before a judge. Imagine what this will do to your daughter." This is too much. Dee Dee is really trippin' right now.

"Will you be on my side? That's all I want to know," she says.

"I love you to death, but I think you're making a huge mistake."

"Will you be on my side?" she asks again.

Sigh. This is bad business. I can feel it. But she's my girl. I have to have her back. "I'm always on your side, Dee."

"That's all I needed to hear. Can you recommend any divorce lawyers?"

"Yeah. I know a few. Hey, have you told Deron yet?"

"No. I will soon. I just . . . need to find the right words."

"The right words, huh? Good luck with that," I say as I stand up.

"I'm going to call you for those names," she says. I nod and walk out of the café. I don't know what to say about Dee Dee. Sometimes she seems so . . . out there.

Wednesday at work I go online to continue looking up information on Maya-Lin. So far I've come up with nothing. After going through my dad's paperwork, I try to look up all women by the name of June who lived in the area he was stationed in. That proves to be futile. Without a last name or an address it's way too hard. So now I'm doing a search on births in the year that Maya-Lin was born. Oh my God. There's, like, a million results. As much as I want to do this alone, I see now that I really need a professional. I pull out my phone book and dial the number of the PI that has the biggest, most colorful ad. After I've spoken with a secretary for ten minutes, Mr. Rick Roman picks up. I once again explain my situation and we schedule a meeting for the following day. He practically guarantees that he can find my sister, so I hang up feeling quite confident about everything.

"Miss Wells," my assistant says through the intercom, "you have a visitor. Mr. Burgess." My heart drops. Mr. Burgess is one of my parents' closest friends. Never has he come to my office in person.

"Send him in, please, Rhonda," I tell her, almost in a whisper. I stand up from my desk to greet him. He enters slowly, taking calculated steps.

"Lia, how are you?" he asks.

"Not so good anymore, Mr. Burgess. You came about my father, right?"

"I'm sorry." He stiffens to keep from breaking down.

"When did it happen?" I ask through tears.

"Around eleven o'clock this morning. I caught the first flight I could."

"Who was there? What did he say?" I sit back down because I feel faint.

"Your mother and I were there. It was peaceful, Lia. He was prepared." He pauses. "Before he left us, he said that he loved you and what you're doing for him."

I smile a little bit. He walks over to me and hugs me. "Your father was my best friend. And you have always been like a daughter to me. If you need anything I'm here."

I hug him back tightly.

"Thank you. Thank you so much," I say. I let go and

grab a tissue from my desk. "Um, do you have a returning flight already?"

"No, I don't."

"Well, I'm about to book the next one, so I'll go ahead and get yours too. I'm going to have to go home to get some things. I'll put you in a cab and meet you at the airport. . . . You have my cell number, right?"

"Yes. Mine is the same as well."

"So I'll see you in about an hour at the Delta terminal."

"Okay, Lia."

"And thank you again for being there for me and my mother. My dad loved you very much."

"I loved him too," he says. I have Rhonda get a cab for Mr. Burgess and book two flights to Bridgeport, Connecticut. Then I call Rich Roman back and tell him I have to cancel tomorrow but I'll fax all the information I have.

Surprisingly, what I thought this experience would be like, it's not. My visit to go see my dad is a beautiful ending to our beautiful relationship. I'm upset that he's gone, of course, but the way he passed makes me feel good. He was surrounded by people who love him and the thought of his two daughters finally knowing each other. He was happy. I know it. And so now I am too.

Chapter 16

Rena

These past few days have been hell. I haven't seen or heard from Tak since the night he proposed. I still don't know why I couldn't say yes. I don't think it had anything to do with Lia, but maybe I'm kidding myself. That whole incident hurt me, perhaps more than I'd like to admit. Maybe I'm just not in love with him anymore. Or maybe I'm too scared to be. I call Lion into my bedroom and tell him to sit down so I can rebraid his hair. I turn on the TV and flip through the channels, hoping to catch a good Lifetime movie. Just as I begin to settle into one of those teen dramas, I get some drama of my own when my phone rings and it's Lia. I almost don't answer, but what the hell? It can't get any worse than it already is.

"Yes, Lia," I answer.

"Rena, are you busy?"

"I'm braiding."

"Oh. Well, I'll make this quick."

"Would you please?" I say.

"Um, I've been doing some thinking. And, Rena, life's too short. I've seen that firsthand. My father passed a few days ago, and when something like that happens it really puts everything in perspective. I love you. You're my best friend. I really want to put everything behind us and move on." She gets quiet and waits for a response.

Oh my God. I had no idea. I feel like an ass now. "Lia, I'm sorry."

"I'm okay. He was ready. But I meant what I just said. Can we get past this bullshit we put ourselves in?"

Even though a part of me wants to be angry indefinitely, she's right. Life really is too short to harbor animosity and ill will. People mess up. It doesn't make them evil. I know Lia loves me and would do anything for me. It really is time to forgive.

"I'm over it. It was silly of me to get so upset anyway," I say.

"No, don't say that. You were justified in everything you said. But it's over and done with."

"Yeah. It's over."

"So, I was thinking we should all meet in a couple of days. We need to catch up. Besides, I miss your stankin' ass," she says laughingly. "And Jas and . . . Lawd, Dee Dee."

"What? What's wrong with Dee Dee?"

"Everything! She is out of her mind. But I'll let her tell you. Anyway, I'll let you get back to braiding. Bye."

I feel like a huge burden has been lifted. Holding grudges and being angry only weigh you down. It hurts your spirit more than the person you're upset with. So, now one major issue of my life is resolved. Now if I could only get the rest of it together.

The next day I wake up to the sun shining brightly in my

face. I pull the covers over my eyes, hoping my body will remain in sleep mode. It doesn't work. I know I need to be waking up early anyway. Today I have a lot of meetings at the university. Tak and I planned for him to watch Lion today way before everything happened, so I'm still expecting him to come, even though he hasn't called.

After bathing Lion and feeding him breakfast, I let him watch a few cartoons while I get in the shower. Not too long after that, Tak shows up.

"I came early so we could talk," he says while I'm ironing my skirt.

"So talk, then."

"I just need to know what went wrong, Rena. When you said no, did you just mean 'not yet'? Or 'no' forever?"

"Tak, I just said what I felt," I tell him.

"But I don't understand. Is this supposed to be payback for all those years I didn't ask? Because that's some childish shit."

"Look, I never said that. I'm not paying you back or getting revenge." He really had the nerve to say that to me! At least the man has balls.

"Okay, then. But you still didn't answer my question. Is this the way you want it forever? Is this the end?" At this point he's standing next to me, his arms around my waist. I don't know if I want to kiss him or push him away.

"All I know is that now is not the time. I'm not ready," I say. His arms drop and he takes a few steps back.

"I can respect that. But in the meantime, we're still together, right?" he asks.

A million and one thoughts rush through my mind. I still care about him. I still love him dearly. He's the only man I've ever loved. But I've lost that passionate, kinetic feeling that you have when you're a hundred percent sure it's right. I don't feel the powerful connection and the beautiful bond I felt months ago. I'm not in love anymore.

"It wouldn't be fair to you or me if I say yes," I respond. "Can we both just live for now, and take it day by day?"

"I guess I have no choice," he says.

I hate seeing him hurt, but I'd be hurting myself more by getting back with him at this point. If being with him is not a cure for my loneliness, why be with him and be lonely still?

When I get home I find Tak and Lion napping on my couch. Lion is lying on top of his father, holding on to him tightly. They look so perfect together. So peaceful. Looking at them almost makes me forget the events of the day . . . and the events of my life. Watching Tak sleep as he embraces our son almost makes me forget how strained our relationship is. I almost forget how much we've both changed over the past month. I run my fingers over Tak's face and he opens his eyes and tries to focus.

"You can go back to sleep. I didn't mean to wake you up."

"It's cool. I need to get up anyway. Can you get him?" he asks.

"Sure." I scoop Lion up and carry him to his bed. When I return, Tak is getting ready to leave.

"How was your day?" he asks.

"Okay. I'm ready for classes to start."

"Me too. Oh, did I tell you I got into grad school? I got the letter yesterday."

"Congratulations. I'm really happy for you."

"Yeah. Thanks," he says as he heads for the door.

"You're leaving now?" I ask.

"Well, yeah. Why? You need me to do something?"

"No. Not really. I just didn't expect you to leave so soon." I can't even look him in the eye.

"Okay. What's up?" He puts his keys down and looks at me, trying to read my mind. I rack my brain, struggling to think of something to say. I come up with nothing. "Rena?"

"I guess you can leave after all," I say. Of all of the possible responses . . .

"Fine. See you later." He walks out without another word.

I wish I knew what I'm supposed to do. How long will we remain in this purgatory-like state? Do we need closure so we can move on? Or do we need to get back together and make it work? My heart isn't pulling me toward either direction. I'm at a total standstill.

A few hours after Tak leaves, Lion goes to a friend's house to play, and I do a little cleaning and start twisting my hair. I have a lot of new growth, so I really need to get it done. Unfortunately, my phone rings just as I'm getting into the groove. I wipe the beeswax from my fingers and answer.

"Yes?"

"Serena? This is Lace."

Lace? I haven't heard from him since the night he came over. "How are you? It's been a while."

"I know. Listen, Serena. I'm going to get straight to the point. I got a call from the department of health yesterday. They said that someone I slept with is HIV-positive. I got tested today, so I don't know my results yet. But I needed to let you know. I know you have a son."

I feel a lump in my throat. My eyes are watering, but I don't know why because I don't believe him. "Why would you even joke like that, Lace? Look, I don't have time for games."

"Serena, listen to me. You have to get tested. This is not a game. I wish it wasn't true, but it is. I'm sorry."

I feel like my heart has exploded. How is this possible?

"Good-bye, Lace," I say, and hang up. Logic tells me not to be scared. Besides, Lace told me that he always used condoms before me. Aren't they 99.9 percent effective? Isn't it almost impossible to contract an STD when one is used? Yeah, I think so . . . but of course, he didn't tell me he was bi either. Can I really trust him about the condoms, then? In any case, nowadays there are plenty of meds for HIV patients. People are living for ten-plus years with the disease. I know it's not the end of the world. So why am I crying so hard? Why when I go to the bathroom to wipe my face am I afraid to look in the mirror? Because I don't want to see the reflection of a dying woman. I don't want to see a potential victim of AIDS. And I don't want to see the woman who will leave her son motherless all because of one stupid night. If I end up being positive I don't think I could ever forgive myself.

Chapter 17

Jas

Right now I'm at another survivors' meeting, a little early actually. I think maybe today I'll share my own story with the group. Step by step, right?

"How're you doing, Jas? It's good to see you again." It's Joelle, leaning down to give me a hug.

"Good to see you too, Joelle. I know I'm early. I just wanted to get out of the house."

"It's not a problem." She glances around for a second. She seems a little nervous.

I try to break the uncomfortable pause with a random question. "So, what do you do?"

"Oh, I'm an artist. A painter actually. I also teach a few art classes at CUNY."

"That's cool. Do you do portraits? Think you could paint me?" I ask with a laugh.

"Definitely. You'd make a beautiful subject."

"Really? Well, I'll think about it, then. I wouldn't mind having a painting of myself hanging in my bedroom or somethin'."

"What side of town do you live on?" she asks.

"I live in the West Village."

"I love it there. That's where I hang out most of the time."

"Is that so? Well, maybe one day you can swing by and say what's up. I'll give you my number after the meeting."

"Cool. Well, I should go get things started," she says as she walks away.

About an hour later the session is over and everyone is saying their good-byes. I walk over to Joelle, who is talking to a young girl, and signal that I'll be waiting outside the door. A few minutes later Joelle approaches me with a pen in her hand.

"Sorry for making you wait," she says.

"It's cool. I'm not in a hurry."

"So, you're writing your number down, right?" she asks, handing me the pen.

"Yeah. Do you have any paper?"

"Oh, damn. Well, you can write it on my hand," she says with a grin.

I laugh. "Okay, if you say so." She holds out her hand and I scribble the digits on her skin. "Just give me a call whenever."

"Cool. See you later, Jas."

I wave good-bye and begin my long stroll back home. Joelle seems like a really nice person. And the way things have been lately, I need as many friends in my life as possible. I have no Asaji . . . I miss him so much, y'all. But we haven't spoken since that night he told me he was a virgin. I wanted to call him, really I did. But I didn't know what to say . . . still don't. He revealed something to me that he had been holding back out of fear of rejection. And I'm doing the same thing, except I don't think I'm strong enough to come clean. Man, I'm sure he thinks I'm some kinda jerk, or somethin'. I mean, who breaks it off with someone because he's never had sex? How much of an asshole does that make me? He could be the one guy for me. But do I deserve him? Can I match up to his idea of the ideal woman? The woman he's been saving himself for? I love him, y'all. I really do. I just don't know what to do.

The next day I get a call from Lia saying that she would like to meet me, Rena, and Dee at our usual spot. This will be the first time the four of us have been together in, like, a month. As I'm rambling through my closet and dresser drawers for something to wear, I come across the piece of paper that Asaji gave me with his number on it the very first night we met. I smile to myself remembering my first impression of him. I would never have guessed it'd go this far this quickly. Thing is, he stepped up to the plate in such a major way, proving himself from the start. Asaji taught me the truth about relationships. He showed me the way a man treats a woman he really cares about. He wasn't afraid to let me into his heart. How could I not fall in love? But what do I have to show for it now? Sigh.

After finally deciding to put on a mildly conservative (but very clingy) gray sweater dress and black boots, I leave my house and head to the nearest subway entrance. Almost an hour later I'm walking into the bar and see Lia at our table, sipping a margarita.

"'Sup, Lia?"

She gets up and gives me a long hug. "Hey, girl. How are you?"

"Doing well. Doing all right," I say, taking a seat.

"Are you sure? You sound upset."

I know Lia is a good person deep down, but I rarely hear

her speak with so much concern. "I'm not talking to Asaji anymore."

"Damn, Jas. I thought you really liked him."

"I do. I mean, I love him. But, Lia, he's a virgin."

"So?"

"So, I can't be his first. If he knew about everything I've been doing—"

"Jas, come on. I bet you are one of the few women he knows who can actually speak in complete sentences." We both laugh a little bit at her comment. "I don't understand why you can't see what he sees."

Just then Rena walks up to the table. We all hug each other and Lia orders two more drinks for us.

"What are we talking about?" Rena asks.

"Jas won't be with Asaji because he's a virgin."

"Asaji's a virgin?"

"Yeah. But you guys don't understand," I begin. "I've been dealing with a lot lately."

"We all have. And now's not the time to push people away. Especially the good ones," says Rena, her voice fading to almost a whisper.

"Hi, everyone," Dee Dee says as she approaches the table. She's unusually upbeat.

"Hey, Dee," I say as she takes a seat next to me. "Whoa, that belly is out of control, girl!"

"I know. I'm only five months. He's going to be a big one." She orders a glass of orange juice when the waitress comes back around. "I didn't mean to interrupt. Go ahead, you guys."

Well, I guess it's now or never.

"I have somethin' to tell y'all," I say.

"Me too," Rena and Lia say at the same time. We all look at each other like, *You go first.* Finally Lia speaks.

"Well, as you know my father passed a little while ago. But before he died, I went to see him. And he told me that

I have a half sister somewhere. Apparently, he had an affair when I was little and the woman got pregnant, married someone else, and moved away."

"Seriously, Lia?" I ask.

"Seriously. And his dying wish was for me to find her. So that's what I'm trying to do. Even though she may not have a clue about my father."

"Wow. That's amazing. You actually have a little sister out there," says Rena.

"That's the story," Lia says. "Tomorrow I'm speaking with the detective to see if he's made any progress. And the next step is to contact her."

"Well, I hope it works out for you," Dee tells her.

"Thanks. But enough about that. Who's next?" Lia looks at Rena and me.

"Okay, well," Rena starts, "Tak proposed to me."

"Girl! Did he really?" I ask excitedly. Rena nods her head.

"Hold out that hand, Rena. I need to make an assessment," Lia says jokingly.

"I told him no." Rena looks away from us before taking a long sip of her drink.

"No? You told that man no?" Lia seems totally appalled. "I hope it wasn't because of, you know . . ."

"No, it wasn't."

"Rena, you've been waitin' to marry Tak for, like, four years now. Why the hell did you say no?" I ask.

"She's crazy. Maybe once in a lifetime will a man come along that loves you the way Tak loves you. I mean, he may not be perfect. But hell, neither are you, Rena," says Lia.

"I just wouldn't have felt right saying yes," Rena says.

"Why? Do you have feelings for someone else?" I ask her. Lia sits up straight, waiting anxiously for Rena to answer.

"No. I don't think I do."

"What about Ty? You guys seemed to be hitting it off," Lia says.

Wait a minute. Is that a little jealousy I hear? This is too funny, y'all.

"Lia, you want to know the truth about Ty? That man is completely infatuated with you. Don't ask me why. I'm sure you treat him like crap."

"Hey, that may be his thing," I say with a smirk.

"I don't treat him like crap. I don't treat him any kind of way. We don't even spend a lot of time together," Lia says, trying to defend herself.

"Listen, Lia," Rena says with an attitude, "you talk the talk, but you damn sure don't walk the walk. It astounds me how you can tell me how much I should be with Tak because he treats me so well and loves me so much—"

"And you just said the same about Asaji a minute ago," I add, interrupting.

"But when you finally meet a guy who actually wants to do right by you, you dismiss him. And why, because he's black? Lia, *you're* black! How much of an idiot are you?"

I've never heard Rena speak to Lia, or anyone for that matter, in such a harsh way. I look at Lia and wait for the counterattack. But it doesn't happen. The waitress comes over and asks if we need more drinks. We all shake our heads no.

"You have no idea, Rena, what it was like for me." Are those tears in Lia's eyes? Real tears?

"What are you talking about?"

"On second thought, never mind. I'm done with this conversation." Lia reverts to her normal bitch mode and turns to me. "Jas, what did you have to tell us?"

"Lia, don't change the subject," Rena says. Lia ignores her.

"Go ahead Jas," she says.

I feel like I'm being put on the spot. Like what I have to

say is going to save the rest of the night. If only they knew.
Luckily, Dee steps in and saves me.

"Well, I already told Lia this, but I guess that it's no
secret. I'm divorcing Deron."

We all sit in shock for a minute.

"Divorce? Aren't you about to have his baby?" I ask.

"No, no, no, Dee Dee. Tell them the *whole* story," Lia
says, staring her down.

"Okay, fine. I'm not ashamed. I'm in love with someone else," Dee Dee says defiantly.

"Not just somebody . . . Emanuel Velasquez. The dog
with a baseball."

"Say it ain't so, Dee," I say in a semiserious tone. I don't
know Manny personally but I've heard plenty of stories.

"Come on! Didn't you guys hear the part about me
being in love? This isn't a game to me."

"But what about your family?" Rena asks.

"My family will change a little, but—"

"Dee Dee, cut the crap! Somehow Manny managed to
sweep you up into his little world all over again. And now
you think it's love. It's manipulation, girl," Lia says.

"And it's my choice! You said you were on my side, Lia."

"But that doesn't mean I have to agree."

"I understand your feelings, Dee, but I don't think
you're doing the right thing either," Rena says.

"Don't waste your breath, Rena. She's going to do what
she wants anyway," Lia says before turning to me. "Go
ahead, Jas. Tell us what you wanted to say before."

"No, that's cool," I say.

"Jas, come on."

"Another time, I promise." I really want to tell them
about what happened to me and the survivors' meetings
I'm going to. But there are just too many bad vibes and too
much bad news going around. I'm not tryin' to bring
anyone down. We all sit quietly for a minute, playing with

what's left of our drinks. This being bummed out shit is just not gonna work. At that moment a thought pops into my mind outta the blue.

"Hey, remember when we all slept over at Lia's house and Dee told us about the first time she had sex?"

"Oh my God, yes!" Lia laughs. "The guy kept trying to talk dirty to her and she just had a look on her face like, 'Huh? What?.'" The three of us start crackin' up.

"Whose pussy is this? These are my fuckin' titties, right? Right?" I almost choke on my drink as I try to mock the guy. Dee Dee turns bright red and puts her hands over her face.

"Stop, you guys," she says.

"And those faces she said he made! Teeth hanging out; face all tight," Rena says. We all laugh uncontrollably. Okay, now this is much better. This is how the end of the convo should be.

Lia takes out her platinum card and calls the waitress over. "Well, I'll call you guys tomorrow."

"All right, girl. Be safe," I tell her. She signs the receipt and leaves the bar. Just as Rena, Dee, and I prepare to leave, my cell phone rings. I don't recognize the number, so I tell Rena to answer.

"Hello? Hold on." She hands me the phone.

"It's a guy, right? Who is it?"

She shrugs. "Some girl. Hey, I'm going to catch a cab back. I'll call you."

"Be good, Jas," Dee says before she walks out. She kisses my cheek and walks away.

"Hello," I say cautiously. This isn't the first time some guy's girlfriend or somethin' has called me lookin' for beef."

"What's up, Jas? It's Joelle."

"Oh, hey, girl. What you up to?"

"Nothing really. I'm in your area with a friend of mine and thought maybe you'd want to grab a drink with us."

"Well, I'm not at home right now, but you and your friend can stop by after you're done. I should be there by then."

"Cool. I'll call you back then." It was nice of her to invite me along. But what do I look like being the third wheel?

After I get home I change into a pair of hot-pink mini shorts and a white tank top. My ass cheeks are hanging out a little, but I don't care. I hope Joelle isn't expecting a perfect hostess. I make myself a Hen and Coke and pop in one of my favorite movies, *Love and Basketball*. About forty-five minutes later at ten thirty, my cell rings. It's Joelle asking if I'm still up for company. I say yeah and give her directions. She's not too far away so she gets to my house in, like, fifteen minutes.

"Hey, Jas. You have a nice place," she says as she walks in.

"Thanks."

"This is my friend Terrence. Terrence, this is Jas." It's obvious that Terrence is gay. He's kinda tall, but very thin with a bunch of blond curls on top of his head. His brows are arched and his manicure is better than mine.

"Hello, Jas. Girl, you are lookin' too cute. I'm lovin' the booty shorts, honey. Go 'head, now," Terrence says. I laugh and say thanks and offer them a drink. They both want Coronas, so I go into the kitchen to get them.

"I love this movie. Sanaa looks so good," I hear Joelle say. Okay, um, maybe she's right. But to actually make a point to say it is a little weird. Unless . . .

"So, Jas, what have you been up to?" she asks as I hand them the beers.

I take a seat on the couch and stretch my legs out onto the coffee table. "Just work. Not much else. How was the bar?"

"Not worth my time," says Terrence. "These boys need to get it together. I can't do nothin' with a pretty boy. I need me a thug." Joelle and I laugh as Terrence sucks his teeth in disgust.

"It wasn't that bad, TT," Joelle says.

"Honey, you can say that because you had about three or four young ladies approach you. And all of them were cute. Except that one with the nose. She looked a mess."

"You guys went to a gay bar?" I ask.

"It's not really a gay bar, but it has a mixed crowd."

"Oh, okay." I really want to ask her if she's gay, but I don't want to assume anything. I used to go to gay bars. I've flirted with women. Hell, I even dated one for a few weeks. And I'm not gay.

"So, Miss Jas. Are you dating anyone? Or are you a happy bachelorette, like myself?" Terrence asks. This guy is funny as hell.

"Neither, I guess. I'm not really dating anyone anymore, but I'm damn sure not happy about it."

"Mm-hmm. Sounds like someone else I know," he says, glancing at Joelle.

"Shut up, TT." Joelle looks a little embarrassed.

"It's the truth. Girl, let me tell you," Terrence says, turning to me. "This one right here is what you call a true romantic. She falls hard and fast. But always for the wrong ones."

"TT, damn! Why are you blasting me like that?" Joelle looks like she's blushing.

"Now, Miss Jas, I don't know if you swim with the fishes, but if you do, I think you and Miss Thing right here would look cute together." Terrence sits back, satisfied with his suggestion.

Okay, this is a little bit awkward. I guess I got my question answered, though. Joelle is gay. How did I miss that? I guess looking back at our conversations I can see it. But at the time I just didn't think about it. So wait a minute. Does she have a crush on me or somethin'?

"Jas, don't pay him any attention," Joelle says.

"Jas and Joelle. The two Js. I'm lovin' it, honey," Terrence says jokingly.

"That's why I don't take you anywhere," Joelle says to Terrence. "I'm really sorry about him," she says to me.

"No, it's cool. I'm not offended or anything," I tell her. "Come on, I live in the Village. I'm comfortable around just about anyone."

"If I would have known he was going to show out I wouldn't have brought him," she says to me while looking at him.

"No! You know I had to finally meet the young lady you've been goin' on and on about. Oh! Oops! My bad, Joey, honey."

Wow. Guess I have the answer to question two now.

"Oh my God," Joelle says. She falls back into the couch and pulls a pillow over her face. I really don't know what to say at this point. Should I just laugh it off or what?

"Terrence, stop messin' with her," I say, trying to keep things light. "You guys want another beer?"

"Oh no, honey. I think me and Miss Thing need to get goin'. Come on, Joey. Let's go." Terrence pulls Joelle by her arm.

"Thanks for having us over, Jas," she says.

"Anytime."

"Have you thought about that portrait yet?"

"Oh yeah. I think it'd be a good idea. I need some new art around here."

"Cool. I'll call you later this week."

"Okay. Bye, y'all," I say as they're walking out."

Hmm. That was . . . interesting. Joelle has a thing for me. I mean, it doesn't change anything. She's still cool. We can still hang out. But Terrence was dead wrong bringin' her out like that. I don't know. Even if I was dating women I'm not sure Joelle would be my type. She's pretty enough. Maybe mixed with black and something else because she's

very light. She has black features, though, like her lips.
Her eyes are beautiful. Greenish with long-ass lashes.
There's nothing wrong with her. I just think that if I were
going to date a female, she'd have to be a tomboy. One
diva in the relationship is enough.

    Anyway, it's late and I'm very tired. I think I'll go to
sleep and try to dream about Asaji. I wonder what he's up
to. And I wonder if he's dreaming about me.

Chapter 18

Dee Dee

Today I'm going to tell Deron that it's over. I'm going to tell him that I'm in love with someone else. And I'm going to tell him that I want custody of the kids. I'm scared to death but it's time. When he comes home from work I'm sitting in the living room, staring at a blank screen on the TV.

"Baby, looks like you forgot to turn the TV on," he says, smiling. He kisses my cheek and sits next to me. "Where's Deidre?"

"Hannah's. I needed to get some housework done, so I asked her to babysit for a few hours. Are you hungry? I made fish. You like my fish, don't you? And string beans and brown rice. Is that okay? Because if not I can—"

"Baby, stop. Yes, fish is fine. What's up with you? You seem nervous." Nervous doesn't begin to describe how

I'm feeling. I look at him and I can see all the love in his eyes. Lately he's been so sweet and into the family. And he's been meeting with editors about his book; it's possible it could be in publication by the end of the year. These are, like, the happiest days of his life. Until now.

"Deron, we have to talk about something," I say.

"First I have tell you something. I've been shopping around for a bigger place."

"What? A house? But, Deron—"

"Listen, baby, it's perfect. I wanted to be sure I could afford it before I told you, but I got a call from the Realtor today and it's a done deal, if you like it. And, baby, you'll love it. Now the kids won't have to share a room and we'll have a yard. We can go tomorrow and you can check it out yourself. I just have to call—"

"Deron, no," I say quietly. "No yard, no extra room, no new house. I don't want any of it."

"Well . . . we can stay here. I just thought that with the baby we'd need more space and—"

"No. You don't understand, Deron." I stand up and take a few steps back. "I—I can't be in this marriage anymore."

"You're joking, right," he asks. His eyes dart back and forth between the floor and the empty space next to him on the couch.

"I'm sorry. I'm in love with someone . . . someone from my past. And I can't keep living life this way."

"Manny," he says, tears slowly rolling down his face. "So what I saw in the paper was true?"

"No, not at the time . . . things just developed. I didn't expect to feel this way. I didn't want to feel this way." The more I say, the more I want to say. "I've been seeing him here and there for the past few weeks and I love him, Deron. I want to start a life with him."

"A few fucking weeks, Dee Dee? We've had four years of marriage!" He's standing now, looking me up and down with a horrible snarl on his face . . . like someone forgot to take out the trash.

"I'm sorry," I say again. "I can be out by the end of the week."

"Two days," he says.

"Two days, then."

"And Deidre stays. You will not take my daughter to another man's house."

"What? My baby goes where I go!"

"Fuck you, Dee Dee! You're not taking the one good thing that has come of this bullshit marriage away from me! If you want to take her, then you're gonna have to go through the courts."

"I was going to do that anyway. The kids will be mine, Deron. Manny and I can take much better care of them than you can."

"Nobody can take better care of my own damn kids than I can," he says vehemently. "Ya know what, just get out now. I can't stand to look at you anymore. I'll pick up the baby from Hannah's."

I stand there, unsure of what my next move should be. "Get the hell out," he shouts.

I grab my purse and head out the door, dialing Manny's number as I go. I feel exhilarated and scared at the same time. I let the phone ring five or six times, but I don't get an answer. No big deal. I'll just go over there. He'll be excited to see me and even more excited to hear that I told Deron that it's over.

I take an expensive cab ride to the Upper West Side and smile my way to Manny's front door. I don't have a key yet, so I knock. And knock. And knock. God, he has to be home. I don't know where else to go. I'm dialing his number on my cell again when the door flies open.

"Dee Dee," he says, sounding confused. "What's up? You didn't call."

"Oh, I called, Manny," I say, walking past him and into the foyer. "You just haven't been answering. As he closes the door, I take a closer look at him. He looks like he just woke up. And it's only six.

"So, I'm glad you came," he says unconvincingly.

"Are you?" I go over to him and give him a hug. I rub my face along his and breathe in deeply. And that's all it takes for me to know. "Who is she?"

"Who is who?" he asks.

"Don't play with me, Manny! I can smell pussy all over your fucking face!"

"Lower your voice," he says anxiously.

"Lower my . . . Manny, I don't give a damn who hears me! Do you realize that I just told my husband that I was having an affair with you? That we're in love and I was leaving him? And the whole time you're eating some heffa's nasty-ass pussy!"

"I didn't tell you to do that. I didn't tell you to tell him. Not yet. I wasn't ready."

I can feel my face turning red the more he talks. I can feel the anger rising inside me. I hate him. He's doing it all over again. Everything that he did before, it's like a fucking flashback. But I can't stress myself because I don't want to hurt the baby.

"Manny, you disgust me. I gave up everything for you."

"Manuel, why are you keeping me waiting?" a voice from upstairs yells out.

"Stay up there, Consuela," Manny yells back. But it's too late. She's already walking down the steps. All nineteen years of her. Dressed in an emerald-green silk robe that barely covers her thighs.

"Oh, I didn't know you had company," she says sweetly.

"Me either," I say. "So this is it, Manny? This is how we're going to end?" I say, gesturing toward his new lover. "It was all a lie?"

"Dee Dee, just leave, please," Manny says. He opens the door. And when he does that he answers my question at the same time.

I hail a cab and tell the driver to just drive. I don't know where to go. I think about calling Lia, but she warned me about this. She told me over and over. All of my friends did. But I didn't listen. The last place I want to go is back home, but what choice do I have? Deron will just have to deal with me until I figure out my next move.

When I get back to my house, no one is there. He must have taken Deidre and gone to his mother's house. I suppose it's better this way. I don't think I could face him right now. I take a warm shower and lie down in my bed, maybe for the last time. I try to fall asleep, but all I can think about is how stupid I was to fall for Manny's lies all over again. I had someone who loved me. I had it all. My life was beginning to be what I always dreamed about. And I threw it all away. For what?

I wake up to Deron standing over me. I'm startled for a minute because he's just standing there, quiet. I sit up slowly, squinting and rubbing my eyes.

"You came back," he says. "I didn't think you would."

"I had to," I say. I look at the alarm clock. It's one in the morning. "How long have you been standing there?"

"Not long. I left Deidre with Hannah and went out. How long have you been sleeping?"

"Not long enough. Hey, about earlier—"

"There's nothing I want to say or hear about earlier," he says.

"Understandable, but realistically we have to talk about it. I really need to tell you exactly what happened and why." And I really need to tell him that I take it all back. And maybe he'll take *me* back.

"Not tonight. I'll be on the couch." As he walks out of the room I feel my heart being ripped to pieces. I don't really expect him to forget what I said. But it wasn't the truth. I know now that what I felt for Manny was nothing more than the product of his scheming ways. It wasn't real. It wasn't love. Love is in the next room, sleeping on my couch.

Chapter 19

Lia

I'm somewhat apprehensive about going to work today. I'm supposed to call Rick Roman and get an update about my sister, and either way it goes I'm going to feel stressed. At the office I'm greeted by Rhonda and a fresh cup of coffee when I arrive. I immediately shut the door and take a deep breath. Here it goes. I dial the agency's number and almost lose my mind when I'm put on hold for five minutes. Finally Mr. Roman picks up.

"Ms. Wells, good to hear from you. I've got good news."

"Really?"

"Of course. You just happened to pick the top private investigator in the city of New York."

"Lucky me," I say, trying not to sound too sarcastic.

"Anyway, as I was saying, I've got good news, as well

as some bad. I'll tell you the good news first. We found your sister."

"Are you kidding me? You really found her?"

"We really did. Her name now is Maya-Lin Underwood, previously Maya-Lin Martin. She's married to Jonathan Underwood, Dr. Jonathan Underwood, that is. She has one-year-old twin sons, David and Aaron."

"Oh my God. This is so strange. You're telling me about family members that I didn't even know existed."

"And you know what else is strange? This is the bad news I was telling you about."

"What?" I ask, with a sinking feeling in my stomach.

"She's been living in Fort Lee, New Jersey, for the past two years. I'd say probably twenty minutes away from you at the most."

"That's the bad news?"

"Yes! All this time she was right under your nose. You've probably passed her on the street a hundred times."

"You're right. I probably have."

"I can have everything faxed to your office whenever you like. I have her home address, phone numbers, license plates, everything."

"You can send it now. Thank you so much."

"That's my job, Ms. Wells. I'll have my secretary send it right over. Good luck."

A few minutes later I'm reading over all the information I receive from Mr. Roman. I find out that Maya-Lin graduated from Rutgers University and, get this, went to law school in Texas. We're both lawyers! That's too crazy. I continue to flip through the pages until I come to a newspaper clipping of her wedding announcement to Jonathan. There's a picture of her, one of those professional photographs. She looks so much like me I almost fall back in my chair. The hair, the eyes, the nose, the smile. It's all me.

Mr. and Mrs. Ralph Martin of New Brunswick, New Jersey, proudly announce the engagement of their daughter, Maya-Lin Martin, to Dr. Jonathan Underwood, son of Dr. and Mrs. Nathaniel Underwood of Houston, Texas. A New Year's Eve wedding is planned to be held at the Hilton Hotel in Houston.

Well, at least one of my father's daughters did the whole marriage thing. She seems like she has the perfect life. Do I really want to disrupt that? Then again, I'm family. And I've come this far. I pick up the phone and start pressing the numbers to her home. My heart is about to beat out of my chest. But I don't have much time to think about it because someone has answered the phone.

"Hello?" a woman says.

"Uh, may I speak to Maya-Lin?" My throat is dry and my hands are shaking.

"May I ask who's calling?"

"This is Lia Wells."

"Lia Wells?"

"Yes."

"Well, I'm Maya-Lin, but I don't think I know a Lia Wells. Is this a business call?"

Okay, here's the moment of truth.

"Maya-Lin, I know you don't know me, but if you give me a minute to explain I think you'll understand why I'm calling."

"Fine. Go on."

"Please don't get upset. I'm not sure how much you already know. Um, when my father was stationed in Taiwan about twenty-five years ago, he met a woman named June, who he had an affair with." I stop to steady my breathing. I hope she doesn't hang up. "As a result of their relationship, they had a child. A daughter."

"June is my mother," she says softly.

"I know. And my father, Samuel Wells, is your biological father too."

"You're my sister?"

"Yes. My father, our father, passed away a little while ago. He told me all he knew about you. His dying wish was for me to find you." I hear her start to cry on the other end. I'm starting to tear up myself.

"They never told me. Even when I turned eighteen my parents didn't tell me."

"I'm sure they had their reasons. Listen, I'm not trying to freak you out or mess up anything you have going on in your life. I just wanted to do this for my dad. And myself too."

"This is incredible. I really don't know what to say," she says.

"I don't expect anything from you."

"I know, I just . . ." Her voice fades.

"Listen, we can talk later. You don't have to take all this in one sitting. I know it's overwhelming."

"Lia, right? Where do you live?"

"I live in Manhattan."

"Oh my God! I live twenty minutes away! I'm in the city all the time!"

"I know. I hired a PI to find you. He told me a lot about you."

"This really is unbelievable."

"Like I said, nothing has to happen today. I just wanted to—"

"I want to meet you, Lia. I have to," she says.

"I was hoping to meet you too." I really was, but this seems to be happening way too fast.

"Okay. Well, how about later this week?"

"How's Thursday?" I suggest.

"Sounds good. I should write down your number just in case. And I'd love it if you would come to my home and meet my family."

"I'd love it too."

"As soon as I hang up I'm calling my parents. The truth will set you free, you know?"

"No doubt about that," I say. After I give her my home and cell numbers, she promises to call tomorrow with any news she learns.

"Even though this is the most bizarre thing that's ever happened to me, it's probably one of the best things too," she says.

"Me too." I hang up the phone feeling a mixture of enthusiasm and curiosity. I just didn't think it would be that easy to make a connection with her. I try to imagine the tables being turned, and it was Maya-Lin who had called me, claiming to be my long-lost sister. In all honesty, I probably would have given her a hard time. I know that's bad, but I'm just really skeptical about people and their motives. Blame it on being a Capricorn.

After my conversation with Maya-Lin, the hours seem to go by extremely slowly. Finally around six I get myself ready to go home. I'm still a little shaken by what happened earlier, but overall I'm feeling good about it. I want to call my mother and tell her the news, but I'm not quite sure how she'll handle it. After all, Maya-Lin is the living proof that my father had been unfaithful.

I get home, change, and stretch out on my sofa. I see my machine blinking, but I don't feel like answering it right now. I am feeling myself starting to doze off when I hear a knock on my door. No one has been buzzed up, so I have a pretty good idea of who it is.

"Hello, Ty," I say when I see him standing on the other side of the door.

"How's it goin', Lia? Mind if I come in?"

"No. I don't really need that nap after all," I say with the usual sarcasm I have when I speak to him. He laughs it off and takes a seat on my couch.

"I didn't tell you before, but I like the way you have this set up," he says.

"Thanks. My friend Dee decorated for me."

"Maybe she can help me out with my place."

"Yeah, maybe."

"Wait, she's the one who was with that Yankees guy, right?"

"Yes. You saw the *Post*?"

"Rena told me what happened."

"Oh. So you two are still dating?" I ask as I pour a glass of wine. "By the way, would you like a drink?"

"No, thanks. And we were never dating. Rena's a cool person. I like her. But it's totally platonic."

"If you say so," I say, sitting down next to him. "So what made you come by anyway?"

"Haven't seen you around in a while. I was curious about what you were up to."

"But why? I'm sure you have other interests to keep you occupied," I say as I remember the night I heard the giggling woman at his house.

"Other interests as far as women go? Sorry to disappoint you but that's not true. I haven't really met anyone I could see myself getting serious with."

"That's too bad, Ty. New York is filled with beautiful women," I say, finishing off my wine.

"True, but I'm looking for a beautiful mind," he replies. "Hey, do you give good massages?" Here we go. I knew it was coming.

"No, I'm horrible at it," I tell him.

"Well, I'm actually pretty good. I can show you better than I can tell you."

"Okay. I could use a massage right about now." I lie down on my stomach and wait for him to begin. "What's the holdup, Ty?"

"I can't do this with your shirt on. It defeats the purpose."

I laugh on the inside at his weak attempts to get me naked. But I do want a massage and I think Ty deserves to be teased. He did try to get with my best friend, after all.

I sit up and pull my shirt over my head revealing my satiny purple bra. It's a push-up, so I know I'm looking more blessed than I really am. I resume my position on the couch and close my eyes. I soon feel Ty's masculine hands kneading into my shoulders and neck. He wasn't lying. This almost feels orgasmic.

"Your skin is really soft, Lia. Like silk or something," he says. As he continues to rub my back, I have to try hard not to let out any sounds of pleasure. I'm sure his head is big enough.

"This damn bra is getting in the way." And no more than two seconds later I feel him unhooking the clasp. A lot of nerve, right? But I decide not to fight it. I feel too relaxed. "How does it feel, Lia?" he asks me. His voice has taken a different tone. He says my name almost in lust. But before I can answer I feel his tongue on my lower back. Kissing me all the way up to my neck. He turns me over and I slide out of my bra. I don't know how it gets to this point, but I'm too caught up to care.

"I've wanted you since the first time I saw you," he says, his lips caressing my breasts. It feels as though everything is happening in slow motion. He takes off his shirt while I slide out of my shorts. He takes my hand and puts it inside his pants, wanting me to feel what I have coming to me. And damn, does it feel good!

"Tell me what you want," he says. By now he's gently pulling on my ears with his teeth. I grab his face with my hand and hold his chin in my palm as if he were a kid. I lick my lips and look him dead in the eye.

"I want you to *fuck* me." I put every emphasis I can on the word *fuck*. No time for sweet lovemaking today, y'all. And definitely no need to tell him twice. Ty gives me a little grin as if to say, *I knew you liked it rough* and then comes out of his jeans and boxers. His dick has to be at least a good ten inches. And Lord knows it's been a while for me. But I'm far from scared. I take his dick and guide it down to my pussy, thankful that I'm superwet so it slides in easily. And then it's all him after that. Ty uses all he has to fuck the hell out of me. I'm sure I'm going to be a little bruised in the morning. He takes me from behind and tugs at my hair. I get loud as hell, screaming, *"Do it, Daddy, take it! Fuck me, fuck me!"* So it's no surprise that someone knocks on my door, probably wanting me to shut up. I ignore it and tell Ty to keep going. But the knocking gets louder.

"Maintenance! Coming in!"

I lift my head off the couch as Buddy, one of the maintenance guys, walks in. Wait a minute . . . where's Ty?

"Oh, I'm sorry. I didn't think anyone was here," Buddy says.

"Uh, it's okay. I, uh . . ." I wipe the drool from my mouth and suddenly realize. It was a dream. A fucking dream. In every sense of the word. Damn it.

"You called yesterday about the water pressure in your shower. I'm just here to check it."

"That's fine. Go ahead," I say. I don't get it. A sex dream about Ty? Why? Better question: why was it so good? I try to push it all out of my mind and forget it ever happened. But how can I even look at him the same? I saw his ding-a-ling! One thing's for sure. Ty must really want me bad. You know what they say about sex dreams: either you or the person involved wants it to happen for real. And seriously . . . it's definitely not me.

Chapter 20

Rena

I just left the clinic and my stomach is turning. This is going to be the most nerve-racking week of my life. I've decided not to tell anyone anything until I know the results. I don't want anyone worrying needlessly. It's still hard to fathom what's happening to me. I'm the last person anyone would expect to be going through this. I could blame plenty of people for the situation that I'm in. Tak for being unfaithful. Lia for stabbing me in the back. And of course Lace for, well, for everything. But the fact of the matter is, I chose not to be safe and at least use a condom. So in the end, it all falls on me.

I don't feel like going home right now, so instead I walk up a block to the nearest Starbucks and order an iced latte and a huge chocolate chip cookie. I pick up a copy of the *New York Times* and skim through it while I sip on my drink. Soon after a somewhat attractive man approaches my table. He's a little stockier than I would usually go for, but he has the prettiest brown eyes.

"Mind if I sit with you?" he asks, already sitting down.

"I guess I don't," I say with a laugh.

"I'm sorry. If you're busy I'll find another table."

"No, really, it's fine. I'm Rena, by the way."

"Russell. Nice to meet you, Rena. I won't invade your space long. I'm just stopping by on my way to my fi-ancée's house. Meeting the parents for the first time."

"Wow. I know you must be nervous."

"Very. They're from the South, so I'm scared I'll come off too strong for them."

"I'm sure they'll like you. When is the wedding?"

"Next April. I'm more nervous about that," he says, taking a swig of his coffee.

"Why? Marriage is a wonderful thing. And you love her, right?"

"Absolutely. But it's for the rest of my life. And I'm a Sagittarius, Rena. We're horrible at the committed rela-tionship stuff. I'm serious. We get all weird and end up messing the whole thing up. We love our independence."

"Come on. That can't be true across the board," I say. "Are you scared you're going to cheat on her or something?"

"I don't know. I don't think so. She's the most amazing person I know. She's pretty and smart as hell. I know I'd be a total ass if I let her get away. That's why I proposed. But the thought of forever freaks me out."

"Look, she obviously wants to marry you. She must be aware of most of your major flaws, and guess what? She loves you still. Just relax. It'll work out."

"You have so much wisdom. And no offense, but I notice you're not wearing any rings. How is it you speak with such experience?"

I think about his question for a minute before I respond.

"I'm a Sagg too, Russell. I've felt everything you're feeling now. So you better hold on to your fiancée. We only get one perfect love in life."

He smiles and laughs. "Wow. It must be fate that I chose to sit at your table. You know what I was really going to say when I came over here in the beginning? I was going to ask you how you would feel about having sex with me right now, no strings."

"Are you serious?" I ask, shocked.

"Unfortunately yes. I was so scared about this whole thing. I thought I needed something like that to calm my nerves. But you've done that for me."

"That's really sad," I say.

"I know. And I apologize for the thought. But just out of curiosity, would you have said yes?"

"Just out of curiosity, would you still want to if I told you I was HIV-positive?" I ask. He looks at me blankly. But I can sense his fear.

"You are?" he asks me quietly.

"The point is, Russell, you don't know. And you didn't even think twice about it."

"Damn. You're right. I must seem like a total idiot to you."

"No, just careless. The truth is I'm not one hundred percent sure of my status. I just was tested today."

"Well, good luck with that, Rena. But I have a good feeling that you're perfectly healthy."

"And I have a good feeling everything is going to work out with your marriage, if you let it."

"Thanks. And it was really nice talking to you. I should go now and face the music."

"You'll be okay, Russell," I say.

He gets up and shakes my hand. "Do you believe in angels?"

"Of course," I say.

"Well, you may be mine. You saved my sanity and maybe my life all in one conversation."

I smile at him.

"Good luck," I say. As he leaves the coffeehouse, I reflect on what he said. Maybe I really am his angel. I think God puts people in your life at strategic times to either love you or teach you. You may not always accept the love or learn the lesson, but the opportunity is there nonetheless. Maybe I'm one of Russell's teachers. Just imagine if there had been another woman sitting at this table. He may have propositioned her, and she may have said yes. Then a chain of events would have transpired that potentially could have ruined his life. Like I always say, everything happens for a reason. Lace was put in my life to teach me and, believe me, I got the message. And Tak . . . he was brought into my life to love me. And I need to decide once and for all if I'm going to accept it.

When I get home a couple of hours later I still have some time before my neighbor brings Lion back. I whip up a quick lunch of grilled chicken, pasta, and garlic bread and invite Tak to come over. Luckily he's not busy and says he'll be over soon. I don't even know what I'm going to say to him. All I know is that it's not fair to him or to myself to continue to keep us in linger mode. Finding out that I could have a fatal disease really gives me a lot of perspective. Tak has been in my life for so long. He gave me the most beautiful gift in the world, my son. And even though he. didn't want to marry me for years that we were together, I never doubted his love. Just as I was telling Russell, you only get one that's perfect. The rest are just reminders of what you could have had. I don't want to look back ten years from now and say, "If only I would have . . ." That is, if I even have ten years.

When I hear the knocking on the door I yell for him to

come in. I'm just finishing putting the food on the plates when Tak walks up to me and kisses me on the cheek.

"Is that still allowed?" he asks.

"Don't be silly, Tak. Have a seat."

"I'm really surprised you asked me to come by."

"Why is that? We've had lunch together plenty of times."

"I know, Rena, but come on. You know why."

"I suppose."

"So what's up? You make me this food and invite me over for what? To finally say it's over for good?"

"No," I say. This is already difficult enough. I wish he wasn't being so snide.

"So what is it, then?"

"I want us to be together. For real. I want our relationship back."

"You do?"

"Yes. And I want you to put that gorgeous ring back on my finger."

"Rena, you realize what you're saying, right? You want to marry me?"

"More than anything in the world."

"Why did you change your mind? You told me you fell out of love with me."

I knew this part was coming. But I've been thinking about my answer. "Listen, Tak, I never 'fell' in love with you to begin with. People who say they've fallen in love are just running after the myth that being in love is a big bang with fireworks and butterflies and all of that other stereotypical fairy-tale nonsense. It's when you grow in love that it becomes official." I stop to see if he's following me. He still looks interested, so I continue. "Growing in love means your heart has made the other person a permanent light that will always shine inside you. It lasts forever." He's looking at me with a dreamy expression. I wait a few seconds for a response, but instead it takes a few minutes.

"You know I could listen to you for hours. You could be talking about toilet water and I'd still be fascinated."

I laugh at his comment and take a drink from my cup. "Tak, this isn't funny. Do you get what I'm saying to you? I could never fall out of love with you because you're within me. I'm trying to be serious."

He gets up and walks over to my chair.

"I know, I know. I'm sorry. I'll be serious now." He drops down to one knee.

"Wait, you don't have to do that again. I'm coming for you this time," I say as I pull him off the floor. "Tak, I want to be your wife," I say looking up into his eyes. "I'll never drag our love through the fire again."

He smiles and kisses me, for the first time in a long while. His hand starts to move up my skirt, but I push it away.

"What's wrong, Rena?"

"Lion will be back soon. We don't have time."

"Do you know how long it's been? I think we have time to do a little somethin'," he says, kissing my neck.

"Tak, not now. Later, I promise. I just don't want him to walk in on us . . . like before."

He grins and backs away. "You're right. Poor kid is already traumatized. But I'll be back later tonight. I gotta go get some clothes from my place."

"You're staying over tonight?" I ask, terrified of what that means.

"Of course. See you later, babe," he says as he walks out the door. I can't make love to him yet. Not until I know for sure what the prognosis is. But how can I keep putting him off? We just got engaged. And we haven't been together for at least a month. But that's not even my biggest concern. What if I do have it? What will it be like to tell my future husband that I'm HIV-positive? Will he even still want to marry me? I mean, God. I went and had sex with a guy just because Tak gave Lia a little kiss. I'm not excusing what he did, and we were broken up at the time I called Lace over. But it seems like what I did is far worse. And keeping it from him only adds to my guilt.

Chapter 21

Jas

After a crappy day at work I head home with nothing but rest on my mind. I've been drained for weeks. I wish I could just get away. I thought about going to South Carolina to see my parents and sisters, but I don't think that would help. Every time I speak to them I get a lecture on the evils of the big city. They think I'm going to rot away by living here. But maybe that's not so far from the truth.

Once I get home I take a long bath and pop a frozen pizza into the oven. While it's baking I sip on a beer and turn on the radio. I'm halfway listening when I hear a familiar voice. Oh my God, y'all. It's Asaji! I recognize the beat and I definitely remember his flow. This is crazy. He's finally doin' it. I wonder if he got signed. Wow. My baby is doin' big things! Well, my friend . . . my, uh . . . something. I grab my cell to call and congratulate him, but it rings before I get a chance. I look at the number and see it's Joelle.

"What's up, Joelle?" I answer.

"Hey, Jas. Are you busy?"

"No."

"Cool. So are you up for being painted today?"

"Well, I don't know. How long will it take?"

"We won't do it all in one day. But we can go for as long as you want."

I giggle a little at what she says because it sounds a little sexual. Or maybe my mind is just in the gutter right now.

"Okay. That'll work. Are you on your way now?" I ask.

"Yeah. I'll be there in about thirty minutes."

"Okay. Bye." Well, so much for rest. I eat a couple of slices of pizza and drink another beer before Joelle arrives. She has a four-foot canvas and a bag filled with paints and brushes.

"I hope you took a cab. 'Cause if not I know you had a hard time on the train," I say as I help her with her things.

"Neither. I drove. I had to park about a block up, though."

"Oh. I didn't know you had a car."

"Yeah. A '98 Beemer. The true love of my life."

"I feel you, girl," I say. She starts to set up everything quietly. It's kinda weird because I know Joelle is really talkative.

"Everything cool?" I ask her.

"Yeah. But, um, I really want to apologize for Terrence the other night. It was really inappropriate for him to say those things. You know, considering."

"It's no big deal. I can tell he likes to fuck with people."

"He does. But I just don't want you to feel uncomfortable around me, or coming to the meetings."

"Girl, please. I'm over it. So, how are we going to do this? Is there a certain pose or somethin'?"

"It's up to you. You can sit or lie down. It doesn't matter," she says.

"I want it to be sexy, you know?"

"Go nude, then," Joelle says with a chuckle. "I'm kidding."

"Wait now. That doesn't sound too bad. Can you make it so that you know I'm naked, but you can't really see anything?"

"Are you serious, Jas? I mean, I can do it if we set up the lights so that there's a shadow. But you still have to be totally naked."

"I don't have nothin' you haven't already seen," I say, taking off my shirt.

"How about a cute little bra and panties? That would be sexy too." Joelle sounds desperate to change my mind, but I like the nude portrait idea. And I totally trust her. I don't see what the big deal is.

"If you really don't want to paint me nude, then okay," I tell her.

"No. It's your picture. Your choice."

"Good. I want to do it on my bed," I say while I finish undressing. I go to my bedroom and lie on top of the black silk sheets. Joelle looks at me wide eyed.

"Huh?" she asks, surprised. I guess I'm not the only one with a dirty mind.

"The pose, silly! I can be on my side like this with an expression on my face like 'Shut up and kiss me' and then—" And then she does. Joelle presses her lips against mine without any warning. They're soft and taste like vanilla ice cream. But wait! What the hell is she doing? Just as I'm about to pull away, she does first.

"Jas. I'm sorry. Shit. That was a fucked-up thing to do." She looks like she wants to cry.

"Hell yeah, it was. Damn, Joelle. What is wrong with you? It's not like that with us. We're just cool."

"I know. I messed up. I'll just go." She walks out of my

bedroom, leaving me butt naked and dumbfounded on my bed. She shouldn't have kissed me, but I don't want this to be the end of our friendship. I throw on a robe and go after her.

"Joelle, wait a minute. This is stupid. It was a mistake and I can forget about it if you can. Besides, I really want my damn picture!"

She smiles at me, thankful that I'm not being an asshole about it. "Okay. But can I get a shot of something? Anything?"

"Sure. I got some Hen." I go to the kitchen and pour her a double shot of Hen on the rocks. "Don't get too tipsy. I don't want you screwin' up my painting," I say with a grin. "Or tryin' to screw me!" We both crack up. Joelle downs her drink in seconds and chews on a piece of ice.

"Can I be real with you, Jas? Really real?"

"Yeah. As long as it's you and not the liquor talking," I say with a smile. The two of us sit side by side on the sofa.

"I think you're beautiful. Really. You're gorgeous."

"Thanks. But I think maybe you drank that Hen too fast."

"No. I remember when we met at the meeting. I thought to myself, damn. I knew I could never even think about asking you out or anything, simply because of the circumstances."

"Joelle, the biggest circumstance is that I'm not gay."

"I know that now. And I respect it. But unfortunately I can't change these fucked-up emotions I have."

"It's my fault. I shouldn't be so fuckin' hot," I say. We laugh again for a long time. Joelle's green eyes are glistening and her long brown ponytail is shaking from the laughter. She almost looks beautiful herself. She stops when she realizes that I'm staring at her. All of a sudden I feel so close to her. I can feel the heat rising from her skin. Maybe it would be wrong to take advantage of her feelings for me just so I can settle this new curiosity. I've kissed a woman before. Even let her touch me a little. But I've never done it all. On the other hand, I know she likes me. And having sex with her would only lead her on. Then again, she's grown. And not having sex with her isn't going to make her like me any less. Sex aside, though, she's a really nice person. But what else? Thinking about all of this makes me wonder about who Joelle really is. . . .

"Jas. Snap out of it," she says, pushing my shoulder. "What's on your mind?"

"I don't know . . . you. What's your deal, Joelle? I mean, tell me something about yourself."

She looks at me with a twinge of surprise, but then she grins.

"Well, that's a broad question but . . ." She pauses for a few seconds before she finishes her thought. "I'm a survivor. First and foremost. And being a survivor has allowed me to overcome my rape, the discrimination I face as a black woman, and the hate I receive because I'm gay."

"That's awesome, Joelle." I'm so impressed by the strength in her words and in her voice. "Do you mind telling me about what happened when you were . . ." I don't know why I suddenly can't say the word.

She looks at me understandingly. "Of course I don't mind. Telling my story is a continual part of my healing process, you know?"

I nod my head as she begins.

"I was at a frat party with a few friends. I didn't really want to be there because you know how crazy those guys can get. But it was my friend's birthday and she really wanted to go. It was loud and crazy . . . everyone was drunk. I was a little tipsy . . . just to numb the annoyance I felt from the random guys trying to hook up with me. One of them was really persistent. He kept trying to touch me and I was getting pissed off, so I started looking for my friends to tell them I was leaving. He must have followed me upstairs. I was pushed into an empty room. I screamed and started hitting him, but he was a big guy. He just laughed . . . told me I needed to loosen up. As he came closer, I just knew. I felt myself being raped before it even happened." She stops and looks down at her hand. I didn't even notice that I had grabbed it while she was talking. Even though she doesn't seem to mind, I pull it away.

"Sorry about that," I say softly. But she takes my hand back.

"It's okay, Jas. Just . . . go with it." We sit in silence for a few minutes, hand in hand. My thoughts wander . . . trying to make sense of why I feel so comfortable with her.

"Thank you . . . for sharing, I mean," I say. She smiles and squeezes my hand.

"Anytime," she says, before eyeing her art supplies. "So, should I get set up or do you want to . . ."

"Oh yeah . . . let's do it." We carry her supplies into my bedroom and after a few minutes we decide on a pose. Once we get started I can't focus and my thoughts turn to Asaji again. Between him and Joelle, I don't know how I should be feeling. What I do know is that I still miss him a lot. I meant to call him and tell him how proud I am that his music is finally getting airtime. Now that I think about it, he may be with someone else by now. What if I call and a female answers? How sick to my stomach would that make me?

"Jas! What happened to the shut-up-and-kiss-me look? You look more like shut-up-'cause-I'm-about-to-throw-up."

"My bad. Think we can finish later? I'm getting sleepy."

"Sure. Want me to come by tomorrow, same time?" she asks.

"Yeah, okay. See you tomorrow, then."

After she leaves I get my cell and call Asaji. I'm so happy to hear his voice when he answers.

"How you been, Jas?"

"Fine, I guess. I heard you on the radio today. Congrats."

"Thanks, Ma. It's been a long time comin', ya know?"

"Yeah."

"What's new with you?" he asks.

"Nothin' really."

"You seein' anybody?"

"No. Are you?"

"No one worth mentioning. A bunch of rah-rah chicks."

"I see." I want to ask if he's given the dick to any of these "rah-rah" chicks. But I don't have the nerve. "Well, I just called to tell you I'm proud of you. And don't forget me when you hit platinum status."

"Never that, Ma. I told you you're special."

"A'ight. Talk to you later," I say, and hang up. He didn't say that he misses me. He didn't mention anything about us. But I can't blame him. Everything is the way it is because of me. So if it just gets worse from here, I have no one to blame but myself.

Chapter 22

Dee Dee

In about half an hour I'll be meeting with Deron and his lawyer to discuss the divorce arrangement. Deron and I haven't spoken about our marriage since the day I told him about the affair. He doesn't know what happened with Manny and that I'm not seeing him anymore. He doesn't know that I'm having second thoughts about the divorce. Hell, I'm having third and fourth thoughts too.

As I sit in the office of Kaylin Harper, the attorney that Lia introduced me to, my stomach is doing all kinds of flips. I never expected to get to this point. And for what? I don't even know why I'm doing this.

"Is everything all right, Mrs. Smalls?" Kaylin asks. "Do you want a glass of water or anything?"

"No, thank you. I just want to get this over with."

"The marriage or the meeting?"

"The meeting. I mean, the marriage too," I say. He puts down the papers he was looking at and focuses on me.

"Mrs. Smalls, have you spoken with your husband at all about this decision?"

"Of course. I mean, it's something that we both want."

"And there's no room for reconciliation?"

"What are you, a divorce lawyer or a therapist?" I ask crossly.

"I've seen it happen a hundred times. A couple comes in here who hasn't really figured out what exactly they're doing. They just stop trying and stop communicating. Divorce is the easy way out."

"Excuse me, but there is nothing easy about breaking up my family and putting my daughter through a custody fight. If there were any other way . . ."

"But there is another way, Mrs. Smalls. The question is, will you take it?" I cannot believe that my lawyer is trying to talk me out of divorcing my husband. Is he for real?

"Mr. Harper, your two o'clock is here," Kaylin's secretary says as she peeks into the office. I stiffen when Deron walks into the room. He looks at me briefly before taking a seat across from me.

"Well, I suppose we should get started," Kaylin says. "This is not a difficult divorce. Mrs. Smalls is giving Mr. Smalls the house, the car, and fifty percent of the total liquid assets they have accumulated during the marriage. She just wants full custody of the children."

"Well, then this is more difficult than you think, Mr. Harper. My client is not willing to forfeit custody."

"Deron, you know you can see the kids whenever you want," I say.

"Please, Dee Dee," Kaylin says, reprimanding me. "This point is not up for negotiation."

"And on what grounds is your client filing for full

custody? Mr. Smalls has been an exemplary father," Deron's lawyer says.

"That's a matter to be discussed in court. Is that where this is headed?"

Deron and his lawyer speak in a whisper to each other for a minute. He glances at me with sad, tired eyes. He looks like he's ready to be finished . . . finished with the arguing, the tears, the deception. He looks like he's ready to surrender.

"My client has decided not to contend the custody petition."

What? I thought for sure Deron would fight me on this. He even said . . .

"Well, I'll get the final draft of the divorce papers drawn and have them faxed to your office," Kaylin tells Deron's lawyer.

And that's it. In a matter of minutes my marriage is over. And if you ask me why, I can't even tell you. Okay, who am I kidding? I can tell you. I cheated on my husband, simple as that. I destroyed his trust in me. I broke his heart. I'm the only one to blame in this situation.

I leave Kaylin's office and hail a cab. After I get inside and shut the door of the car, Deron runs up and knocks on the window.

"Can I ride with you?" he asks.

"Sure."

He gets inside and gives the driver directions. We sit in silence for a good ten minutes.

"That seemed simple enough," he says finally.

"Yeah, simple. Hey, um . . . why didn't you fight for custody?"

"That's like asking me why I didn't fight the divorce period. I love you, Dee Dee. Anything that's going to make it easier for you to live, I'm going to do it. Or in this case, not do it."

"So you don't want to end this? Even after what I told you about Manny?"

He sighs and looks away. "My entire world fell apart when you told me you were seeing another man. I know I haven't been the best husband. I've been out of control and distant and unavailable. I've put you through it, Dee."

"Still, it was no excuse. I shouldn't have gone outside the marriage," I say.

"Oh, I know that. That was . . . there are no words for that. But if that's where I was taking us, I guess it was just a matter of time."

"So, then, that's it?" I don't know what I expect him to say or to do, I just feel like this can't be my ending.

"Yeah, this is it. We'll be signing the papers soon and you'll be moving in with—with him."

"About that—" I begin. But he cuts me off.

"Please, I don't want to hear the details. I just hope that you get from him what you couldn't get from me."

"But, Deron, you don't understand. Look, I haven't been completely honest."

"Again?" he asks sarcastically. Okay, I deserved that.

"Manny and I won't be living together."

"That's a relief. I was hoping you would take it slow because of the kids."

"When I say we won't be living together, I mean . . . ever. I'm not moving in with him."

"What? But I thought . . ."

"Listen, I'm not going to be with Manny. We aren't together. The whole thing was a huge mistake."

"You're telling me you're divorcing me over a 'huge mistake'? You're taking my kids away because of a 'huge mistake'?" His voice is louder and more aggressive. But he has every right to be angry.

"Deron, listen to me," I say, taking his hands into mine. "I don't want to get a divorce. I just felt like I had to go through with it. I mean, everything happened so fast. And then we were just sitting in that room with the lawyers . . . I didn't know what to do."

"Damn it, Dee Dee! What are you doing to me? You told me you were in love with someone else."

"I'm not," I say as the tears form in my eyes. "I lost my mind for a little while, but now I know. I know where my heart is, where my home is. With you." He recoils from my grasp.

"I don't know what you want me to do," he says while turning away from me.

"I want you to help me save our family." For me to have the audacity to say these words to him shocks even me. But for some reason I have total faith in Deron's love for me. He's always been the strong one. And I really need him to be strong right now . . . while I'm at my weakest.

"Could you stop the cab, please?" Deron asks the cabbie. The driver stops and Deron hands him a twenty and gets out of the car. "I can't do this right now, Dee Dee." He closes the door and starts walking up the block and out of my sight.

I don't expect Deron to be at the house when I get there. And he's not. Hours pass and he still doesn't walk through the front door. So I start packing. I'm going to stay with my parents until I get my finances back in order. And then I'll be living life as a single parent. A divorcee. A dumbass. But wait a minute. I don't want to be a single parent. I don't have to be a divorcee. And I refuse to be a dumbass. I'm fighting to get my life back. Deron may be angry now but he loves me. We will get through this. I don't give a damn what has to be done or said.

I pull all my clothes out of the suitcases and put them back into my closet. I'm going to be here when he gets home. This isn't the end. I'm going to do whatever it takes to get my husband back. I just hope he doesn't resist. . . .

Chapter 23

Lia

After that wet dream I had about Ty I feel funny every time I see him. It seems like before I rarely saw him around the building. Now I can't leave my house without running into him. Earlier today for example I bumped into him in the lobby. He said hi and I stuttered hello. I could feel myself eyeing his crotch even though I tried not to. I don't know what's wrong with me. I just keep having flashbacks of him pulling my hair. . . .

So it's no surprise that he happens to get in the elevator the same time as I do when I get home from work.

"Damn, Lia. I feel like I see you more than I see my own girlfriend," he says as the elevator doors close. Girlfriend? I thought he said he couldn't find anyone. Oh, wait. That was the dream.

"So you found someone? Good." Good for her if reality is anything like fantasy.

"I actually met her around the same time I met you. I wasn't going to pursue it at first, but after getting to know her I found out that she has a lot of what I'm looking for. It's only been a week or two that we've been exclusive. But so far so good. She's a model. You might have seen her in *Vogue*."

What, is he bragging now? Am I supposed to be impressed? "Nope. Don't read it. We're at your floor. See you later." I press the Close button when he steps out, and rub my temples. Talking to him just gave me the biggest headache.

I get to my place and order Chinese before changing into sweats. I mean, what was he thinking telling me about his damn girlfriend? Like I care. And how clichéd is it to want to date a model? He's such a follower. I'm sure she's one of those models that have that strange beauty. You know, the kind that you have to try to see. I don't care anyway. At least he won't be bothering me anymore.

After feasting on wontons and chicken fried rice I go through my clothes trying to find the perfect outfit to wear tomorrow. It'll be Thursday and I'm going to meet Maya-Lin face-to-face. We spoke one other time after that first conversation. She said that she confronted her parents and after a few moments of denial, they came clean. She said her mother knew my dad already had a wife and child so she didn't see the point of ever telling Maya-Lin the truth. She married a year after Maya-Lin was born and her father adopted her soon after. Up until my abrupt appearance into her life, they were one big happy family. But she's really excited about meeting me, although her mother is less thrilled. Speaking of mothers, I haven't exactly told mine everything yet. I plan to, but I just have to find the way to say it.

Three episodes of the *Golden Girls* later, I'm on the floor doing my own bootleg version of Pilates when my phone rings. I almost don't answer it, but I can't stand to hear that annoying-ass sound.

"Yes?"

"Lia. It's Ty." I tug at my skin to see if I'm really awake.

"Yes?" I repeat with more attitude. As usual he pays no attention to it.

"I made some of my famous honey barbecue wings and somehow I managed to make them even more perfect than before."

"The point, Ty?"

"I'd like you to try some. Come down. I made extra."

"Ask your girlfriend to be your test taster," I say dryly.

"She's out of town. Come on, Lia. I bet you'll fall in love."

I think about his offer for a minute and figure what the hell? "I'll be down in a minute."

I hang up and hop in the shower. I use my favorite rose petal body wash and exfoliator. Don't ask why because I don't know. But I damn sure smell good.

When Ty opens the door for me, the scent of wing sauce hits me like a ton of bricks.

"Come in. I have them set out on the table. Help yourself."

"These better be bangin', Ty."

"Trust me. Want a drink?"

"Give me whatever you're drinking," I say, licking sauce off my fingers.

"You don't want what I have. It's too strong for you." Is he still talking about the drink?

"Just give it to me," I say. Damn. Am I still talking about a drink? He mixes a few liquors and juices together and hands me the glass. "Hey, Ty. These wings are actually really good."

"Told you," he says. "Try not to eat the flats, though."

"But I only eat the flats," I say.

"So do I. How's your drink?"

"Good. What's in it?"

"A little bit of this. A little bit of that. As long as you like it, that's all that matters, right?"

"Okay, Ty. So, how would your girlfriend feel about you having another woman over, eating your famous wings and sipping on your special cocktail?"

"You're not another woman. You're my friend. She knows about you."

Well, he's told her about me. I wonder what he said. I want to ask but I don't want to seem too interested. I get up and finger through his DVD collection, just to distract myself.

"Want to watch something?" he asks.

"No, just being nosy." I stumble a little bit back to the couch. Except that I miss the couch and land on the floor. I laugh at myself as Ty comes over to help me up.

"I knew that drink would be too much for you. Why didn't you tell me you were a lightweight?"

"Hey, now. I'm no lightweight. I'll show you. Pour me another." I hold out my empty glass and grin.

"Hell no. You've had enough."

"Aw," I say, scooting closer to him. "Just a little, tiny bit?"

"Lia, you're drunk. I'm going to walk you back to your place." He grabs my hand and pulls me up. Maybe I am a little tipsy. I feel kind of . . . and Ty's looking kind of . . . I pull him back down on the couch with me.

"Don't you feel, you know . . ." I whisper in his ear before kissing it. But he doesn't look happy about it. He pulls away and looks at me like I'm crazy.

"Lia, back up. I told you I'm with someone."

"But you like me. I mean, you used to."

"I still do. But I'm not going to cheat on my girl," he tells me. "Besides, you're only acting this way because you drank too much. So come on, let's go."

Tomorrow, after I've slept and the liquor has worn off, I know I'm going to feel so, so stupid. But for now I follow him out and back to my place.

The next morning I wake up with only a slight headache. I flash back to last night and suddenly wish I could kick my own ass. I was such an idiot. I made myself look desperate and easy. What was I thinking? I just hope he understands that it wasn't the real me who came on to him. Either way I have to put it out of my mind for now. I'm meeting Maya-Lin this afternoon and that's all I can focus on. We decided to meet at one o'clock in Central Park. Originally she wanted me to go to her house in Jersey, but I thought that would be too much, too soon. After much debate I decide to wear a pair of khaki pants and a white button-up. I pin my hair up in a way that looks done, but not like I tried, and head out the door.

When I step off the elevator and into the lobby I see a tall, dark-skinned woman with wild, natural hair at the front desk. She has a couple of Louis Vuitton suitcases by her side. She has to be at least six feet. I don't even know why I'm paying so much attention to her. She just looks so . . . striking. I am continuing toward the doors when I hear her say with an English accent, "Yes, Tysean Jackson in apartment 510. And could I get someone to help with my bags? I'm staying for a few days and I have some things to carry up."

So this is Ty's model girlfriend. Eww. She's not even that cute. She looks around while the desk clerk calls up to Ty's place. She catches me staring at her, so I have to make up an excuse or else look like a weirdo.

"I love your hair," I say in a semifake way. She smiles and turns back around. Bitch didn't even say thank you. Ty sure did pick a winner. Well, whatever. I have business to tend to. I go outside and hail a cab. In less than an hour I'll be saying hello to my sister. I wonder how my life will change. What if we don't even get along? Well, I'll do my best for my father's sake.

When I get to the park it's about 12:15, so I take a little stroll to pass the time. There are a lot of people here today. It seems like everyone is walking his or her dog at the same time. I buy a cup of frozen lemonade from one of the vendors and take a seat on a bench to watch a tai chi class practice. I find myself getting a little caught up in their graceful movements. I'd describe it as watching the wind if it were visible. It's relaxing just to look at, so I can imagine it must be heaven to actually do. I make a mental note to look into it later. When the class breaks fifteen minutes later the students disperse and go their separate ways. Just as I'm about to get up and go wait for Maya-Lin, I see Eric. He's wiping his face with a towel and waving good-bye to the tai chi instructor. I don't believe I'm seeing him here. The last time we spoke he led me to think that he really wasn't interested. As ridiculous as that seems to me, it's hard to think otherwise. I don't understand, though. What was the problem? I take a deep breath and prepare myself to confront him. And if he tries something slick I got somethin' for him. I have to walk a little fast to reach him, but when I'm close enough I call his name. He stops and turns around.

"Hi, Eric," I say.

He gives me a half ass smile. "Hi."

Oh, so he's going to try to play me now?

"It's Lia. Remember we had lunch? We met at Janet's party."

"I remember, hon. How have you been?"

"Good, good. But, uh, I was just wondering what happened with us."

"What do you mean?" he asks, sounding slightly irritated.

"Look, it's obvious to me now that you're not interested. I'm just curious as to why."

"Why? I don't know, hon. We just didn't click."

"Maybe, but it's as if you never even gave it a chance." Wow, how is it that I can see all of this now? This whole time I was throwing myself at him and he's been treating me the same way I've been treating. . . . Ty. Hmm.

"The truth, hon," he says after a sigh, "is that I'm just not attracted to you."

"Fair enough," I say tightly.

"No offense but I'm just not into black women. I'm sorry." Not into black women? Did he really say that? So that's why he's been acting that way. All those little comments he's made and his total disregard of the fact that I was ready, willing, and able to be with him . . . and this is his answer to it all? Why not just tell me up front? Why did he have to be such a bastard? God, what an ignorant jerk! I mean, I don't care if he doesn't date black women, but he was rude and nasty to me the whole time. Wait a minute. Oh my God. Is that me? Am I Eric?

"Don't apologize. I'm the one who made the mistake. Well, I don't want to hold you up."

"Okay. It was nice seeing you again, Lisa." He turns and jogs off.

"It's Lia, you asshole," I yell after him. For Eric to say he's not attracted to black women is funny because growing up I wasn't accepted by a lot of black people. In school the black kids didn't claim me. They made fun of me because of my funny eyes and thought I was stuck-up because of my "white people" hair. I remember in third grade when I had my first crush. This really cute boy named Brandon sat next to me in reading class. He had the most adorable dimples. Anyway, one day I was writing him a note in class but I got caught. The teacher made me read it to everyone. The entire class was laughing at him because the chink girl liked him. They all used their fingers to make their eyes look slanted. Brandon wouldn't even look at me after that. Even worse, he asked to be moved to another seat. I cried about that for a week. The white kids weren't any better. All they saw was my skin color. Until I was about fifteen I was forced to walk that line between being black and not. Then all of a sudden it became cool to have a light-skinned girlfriend with long hair. But that's the only reason I think the boys even liked me, because I happened to be "in." But I wasn't going for it. I would rather have been known as the stuck-up chick who didn't go with black boys than the girl who had a boyfriend only because her hair never got nappy. No one would ever use me, not like that.

It's ten till one and I've made my way to the exact location we said we would meet. It'll be easy to spot her because I've seen her picture already from the newspaper clipping. She said she hadn't changed much since then, so I shouldn't have too much of a problem. I sit on the bench looking around, wondering if she'll be late or if she'll even show up. I cross and recross my legs a million times. I look at the picture of my father that I brought. I kiss it and smile.

"This is for you, Daddy."

Chapter 24

Jas

I'm in my bedroom on my bed trying to get back into the exact pose I was in the last time Joelle was over. And of course I'm not having any luck.

"Jas, I think your shoulder was more . . . you know, forward," she says from behind the canvas.

"This is as forward as I can get it without it hitting me in the mouth."

She shakes her head and rolls her eyes as she gets up to try to adjust me.

"Now just tilt your chin down a little," she says, moving my head. I can feel her cinnamon-scented breath in my face. She steps back for a second to see if the pose is right. "I think that's it."

"Thank God," I say.

"Hey, this was your idea. I wanted you to just sit in a chair, remember?"

"Joelle, kiss my ass," I tell her.

"Don't say it if you don't mean it," she says. "Now shut up and be still."

"I'm hungry. I'm craving fried chicken and candied yams."

"Jas! I can't do this if you don't focus."

"Okay, okay." I stare into space as Joelle paints away. She's concentrating so hard, like this really will be a great masterpiece. Uh-oh. I'm getting an itch. I know if I move, Joelle will bitch about it. Damn it, it's right in the middle of my back. I can't stand it.

"Joelle, come scratch my back. It's driving me crazy!"

"Wait a minute," she says.

"Come do it now before I scream!"

She sighs and comes over to me. "Where?"

"Right in the middle. Don't scratch too hard, though." She starts to do it and I instantly feel better. "Thank you," I say.

"No problem. Now can we get back to work please? We can probably finish by tomorrow if we don't have any more interruptions."

"Fine. But it's too quiet. Talk to me. Tell me a story."

"What kind of story this time?"

"I don't know. Tell me about the first time you had sex."

"With a guy or a girl?"

"Whichever was the best," I say.

"Okay, I was seventeen, she was twenty-one."

"An older woman? Sexy."

"Jas, it defeats the purpose if you're still talking and moving around."

"My bad. Go ahead."

"We had been dating for two weeks maybe. I was ready to do it, ya know? Even though she was the first girl I had gone out with, I already knew I was gay. But she considered me bi-curious so she didn't really want to get too involved. She wouldn't even let me kiss her. Well, one night we were at her apartment watching TV and she was putting on this lip gloss. I asked her to put a little on me, but she accidentally squeezed on too much. So I was sitting there with these greasy lips while she was laughing her ass off. And I just kissed her. It was totally unplanned and unexpected . . . and unbelievable." She stops talking and continues to paint.

"Okay . . . what next?" I ask.

"What, you want me to get into details? Jas, you know what happened next."

"But I want to hear the words. You scared to tell me or somethin'?"

"I just don't understand why you want to know so badly."

"It's just hard to imagine you in a sexual way," I say.

"Thanks a lot, sweetie," she says with sarcasm.

"Not like that. You just seem so nice and cute and wholesome."

"Well, I guess you'll never know."

"Says who?" I ask.

"Says you! You're not gay, remember?" At this point Joelle has stopped painting and is looking at me directly in my eyes. I can tell just by her expression that she's really into me. And here I am lying on my bed, naked as hell, asking her to talk about sex. I feel like a total tease. And a little turned on. "Look, Jas, I like you a lot. And it's taking all the self-control in the world for me not to jump on you right now. But you told me you didn't want to take it there. So let's just drop it."

"What if I don't want to drop it?" I sit up and get off the bed. My nipples are hard and staring Joelle in the face.

"Jas, cut it out," she begs. "You can get dressed and we can do this later."

"I want to do it now," I say seductively.

"Jas, I'm telling you, in about two seconds I'm going to be all over you."

"One, two," I say. Joelle gets in my face and kisses me aggressively, pushing me on the bed. Her fingers stroke my pussy before she slowly slides a couple of them inside me. I moan in delight as she gets as deep as she can. But then the pleasure is lost. All of a sudden it doesn't feel good anymore. I sit up and push her off me.

"What's wrong?" she asks breathlessly.

"I can't do this, Joelle. I'm sorry." I grab a T-shirt and throw it on.

"Did I do something wrong? Just tell me what you want," she says.

"It's not anything you did. I just wouldn't feel right taking advantage of you like this."

"You wouldn't be. I know exactly what I'm doing," she says.

"But you don't know what *I'm* doing. Look, Joelle, you're a great person. You're talented and caring and all of those things. And if I was into women, we could probably have something. But at this time in my life, I'm not. And really, I have feelings for someone else. So I'd just be using you if we had sex. Trust me, if you were anyone else I wouldn't give a damn. But I don't want to hurt you. I feel like we connected and I really want to keep that connection pure. I haven't had too many of those, you know?"

"All right. I understand. And I agree. Us, our friendship . . . it probably never was about sexuality. I think I knew that on some level, but I'm attracted to you and that part of me took over. So I guess we should probably stop trying to do this painting. I'm sorry, but seeing you naked every day is bad for my heart," she says with a smirk.

"I should have warned you. This body is known for

givin' people heart attacks." We laugh for a little bit before she packs up her stuff.

"At least keep what I've finished. The face is done and most of the body."

"Okay, thanks." I walk her to the door and give her a hug. "See you later," I say as she opens the door.

"Okay. And let this be the last time you try to seduce a lesbian, all right, Jas?" she says teasingly. She turns to walk out and bumps right into . . .

"Asaji?"

"Did I catch you at a bad time, Ma?" he asks, looking Joelle up and down.

"Um, bye, Jas," Joelle says nervously as she slides by Asaji.

"You didn't tell me you were coming over."

"So you made other plans to seduce a chick?"

"Hell no! Look, come in and I'll tell you what happened," I say.

"Nah, I'm good." He eyes my T-shirt. "Was she?"

"Asaji, come on now. We didn't do anything."

"Damn, I wanted you to be my fuckin' girl, Jas. I told you some real personal shit. And you dissed me. You don't fuckin call me for weeks, but the first time you think I may be gettin' some dough I suddenly hear your voice. And now you doin' females?"

"Asaji, it's not like that, I promise. Just come in and I'll tell you—"

"Nah, fuck that. I came over here thinkin' maybe we could start kickin' it again. But you too out there for me. I should have known this shit wouldn't work. I was tryin to do right by you, Jas. I was ready to be your man. You fucked up."

"Asaji, please just stop and listen to me. I love you. Don't do this." My eyes start to water. "Please."

"I can't do it, Ma. I tried but I can't do it." He turns to

leave but I grab his hand. He glares at me harshly, but I can still see the hurt in spite of his anger.

"I love you," I say again in a whisper. But he just shakes his head.

"It's over. I'm done," he says as he pulls his hand from mine and walks away. I close the door and curl up on the sofa, tears falling from my eyes. I think I really lost him this time. Whatever hope I had of getting back with Asaji is completely gone now. I'm just another broad. Guess I'm not so special anymore.

Chapter 25

Lia

"Maya-Lin, I'm over here!" I wave to the beautiful woman wearing black crop pants and a red backless blouse. She smiles and waves as she walks over.

"Lia! Oh my God, this is crazy!" She gives me a long hug and a bouquet of white roses. Crap, I didn't bring her anything.

"Let's walk and talk," I say. "You know, you look just like your picture. You're so pretty."

"Of course! I look like you! I don't even know where to begin. Tell me something about yourself. I don't care what it is. I know you said you're not married over the phone, but are you dating?" Wow, she really goes in for the kill.

"No, not at the moment."

"Are you kidding me? You are gorgeous, Lia. What type of guys do you like?"

"You know, the usual. Tall, fine, and rich." We giggle a little as I think about how this is what it feels like to have a sister.

"Well, you know I'm married. It's difficult sometimes. But I love Jonathan so much. And the twins! Lia, you have to meet them."

"I want to. What's Jonathan like?" I ask.

"First of all, he is superfine, girl. Chocolate complexion, pretty teeth and skin. Just fine."

"Oh, I didn't know if he was black or white or what."

"Black of course. I've never really dated outside my race," she says. "Why? Do you?" How funny will she look at me if I tell her I've *only* been dating outside my race?

"I date all kinds," I say. That sounds like a safe answer.

"Oh, okay. Want to sit for a while? These shoes were only made for looking cute." We sit on a bench and chitchat about random things in life . . . our college days, fashion, childhood. But then she brings up my love life again.

"So come on, seriously. There has to be someone," she says excitedly.

"Well," I start out hesitantly, "I did like this one guy, but turns out he's a jerk. And now, well, there's this other guy in my building, his name is Ty. He's attractive, smart, and just a good person."

"And you're not dating him?"

"No. I mean, we're just neighbors. We're not dating. He has a girlfriend."

"I see," she says with a hint of suspiciousness in her voice. "Funny you bring his name up, though . . . since you're 'just neighbors' and all."

"Just throwing you a bone," I say with a laugh. We talk a little more about men before she brings up the one man that brought us together. My father.

"So, tell me about him," she says. "My mother didn't really . . ."

"It's really a shame that you didn't get to know him. He was a great father. All he cared about was making sure me and my mother had everything we wanted and needed. He loved us so much. He loved you too, Maya-Lin. He was always thinking of you." I take his photograph out of my bag. "Here he is at Christmas of last year."

She studies the picture for a long time. I know it must be hard for her to grasp the fact that the man in the photo is part of the reason she's here today.

"I have his chin, and smile," she says, trying not to cry. "I love my dad, you know? He's raised and loved me since I was a baby. I wouldn't trade him for anything. But I still feel a connection to this man that I'm looking at now. I can't explain it. I just feel like he's a part of me."

"He is. And so am I. Maya-Lin, I don't want to cause any strife for you. But ever since I found out I had a little sister I've been dying to find you."

"I'm glad you did, Lia. So what was your first impression of me? Am I all that you expected?"

"I didn't expect you to look so much like me," I say.

"I know! And the funny thing is that I was going to wear khaki and white, but my son spilled milk on me at the last minute."

"See, that would have been too much," I say with a chuckle. "So, where do we go from here? I don't want to overwhelm you with too much information in one day."

"I really would like for you to meet my family. Please don't think I'm being too pushy. But you're my sister, and even though I just found you, I've missed having you in my life. I don't want to waste any more time."

"I don't either. I don't have much family for you to meet, but I've been fortunate enough to have wonderful friends who I know want to meet you," I say.

"What about that guy in your building? Ty? Can I meet him too?"

"Why would you want to? I'm not with him or anything."

"I know. But you like him."

"Trust me, I do not like Ty. He's just someone who I had lunch with and hung out with once or twice. He's not my type."

"Lia, when you started talking about him your whole tone changed. Are you telling me that you don't have any feelings for him?"

I look away for a moment. Maya-Lin hasn't known me a day and yet she's trying to read me like a book. Of course I don't have feelings for Ty. I can barely even stand to be around him. I admit, I may be attracted to him physically . . . but just a little bit. But other than that, there's nothing there.

"Sorry to disappoint you, Maya-Lin, but I don't see Ty in that way. He's just a friend, if that."

She stares at me with a *yeah, right* look on her face but drops the subject.

"Okay. Whatever you say," she says.

"You probably should be heading back to Jersey. I don't want to hold you up."

"You're right. But I want you to call me tonight so we can set up when you're coming over."

"I will."

We stand and hug one more time. She tries to hand me the picture of my dad, but I push it away. "Keep it. He'd want you to."

"Thanks. Well, I'll talk to you later," she says.

"Drive safely." We walk away in separate directions. I still can't believe that was my sister. My actual flesh and blood. It still hasn't completely sunk in yet. But I'm sure it will soon.

When I get home I have a message on my machine. I hope

it's not my mother because I don't want to have to lie to her about where I've been. But it's not. Even worse, it's Ty.

"Lia, what's up? It's Ty. I'm calling to invite you out for drinks with Simone and me and some other people to celebrate my new promotion. It's in the neighborhood. That bar called Fire a few blocks down. We'll probably be out there around eight. Hope you make it."

Well, this is just great. And I take it Simone is his woman. He wants me to hang out with him and his stank-ass girlfriend? What exactly is he trying to prove? But if I don't go I'll look like I'm bitter and jealous. Which I am totally not. It is for his promotion, though. And he has been nice to me since day one. I guess a drink or two wouldn't hurt. I glance at my watch and see that's it's six o'clock. Okay. I'll go. It can't be that bad. I raid my closet looking for just the right thing to wear. I decide on my favorite little black dress. It shows just enough of everything. After hopping in the shower and brushing my hair, I get dressed, spray on a little Chanel, and head out the door.

I've passed by Fire a million times but have never actually gone in. It's a pretty cool place. I might bring Jas and Rena here one night. I spot Ty surrounded by about five other people at a table in the corner. He sees me and waves me over. Well, here we go. I walk over and he stands to greet me.

"I didn't think you'd come," he says. "Lia, this is my girlfriend, Simone, and my colleagues Hasaan, Kathryn, and Vick. Everyone, this is my neighbor, Lia." They all smile and say hello, except for Simone, who just nods her head. Bitch. "Have a seat, Lia. Want me to order something for you?"

"I wish I could get one of those drinks you made last night," I say, taking a quick glance at Simone to see if I get a reaction. Ty laughs.

"I bet," he says. He turns to Simone. "Baby, I made Lia

one of those drinks you showed me how to make. She was on her ass." Everyone joins in on the laugh.

"Not everyone can handle it," Simone says haughtily. Double bitch. The waiter comes over and I order a cosmo.

"So what do you do, Lia? Are you a model like, Simone?" Vick asks.

"Oh no. I'm an attorney," I say confidently.

"Beauty and brains. I'm feelin' it," he says, looking at me as if I were his last meal.

"Vick, leave the woman alone," says Kathryn. "You'll have to excuse him, Lia. He hasn't been the same since I broke his heart," she says with a smile. Everyone at the table laughs at Vick.

"You two used to date?" I ask.

"They were married," says Ty. "And divorced all in the same month."

"That's crazy," I say.

"We're still dating, though. That's the really crazy part," says Vick.

"Have you been married before, Lia? Or do you want to be one day?" asks Hasaan.

"Maybe. But the right one hasn't crossed my path yet," I reply.

"Don't be so sure," says Hasaan. "My wife and I lived next door to each other for three years before we realized we were meant for each other. We've been married for five years now."

"Yeah, Maria is good for you, Saani," says Ty. "Lia, his wife is the sweetest person. She has to be to put up with this one," he says, gesturing toward Hasaan.

"Don't tease him, Ty," Simone says as she slides closer to him. "You can be quite difficult yourself." She kisses his cheek softly as the others chuckle along. Watching the two of them together is sickening. I can't take it.

"Excuse me while I go to the ladies' room," I say, standing up.

"I'll go with you," Kathryn says.

Once we get to the restroom I reapply my lipstick and brush my hair.

"You don't like her, do you?" Kathryn asks me.

"Who? Simone? I just met her."

"Girl, you don't have to front with me. I don't like the bitch either. I don't know why Ty is even seeing her. She's a jerk."

"I don't know. I haven't known her long enough," I say. Even though I totally agree with Kathryn, I don't want to say so. I don't want to sound like a hater.

"Well, I can't stand her," she says. "Oh, Ty, I can't wait until we go to the Hamptons next month. Oh, Ty, you better call me every day when you move back to Chicago," Kathryn says with a fake English accent and a laugh. "Give me a break."

"Ty's moving back to Chicago?" I ask, not sure I heard her correctly.

"Oh, that's what his promotion was about. One of the VPs resigned and they offered Ty his position. He's leaving in two weeks. I thought you knew."

"Well, I knew half of it," I say. Why didn't he tell me he was going back?

"Wait a minute. Do you like him?"

"Ty? No, I don't like him. Why is everyone saying that?"

"It's just the expression on your face when I said he was moving. You looked kind of hurt."

"I'm not hurt, I just . . . I just didn't know. That's all."

She looks at me and grins. "Okay, then. Are you ready to go back out?"

I nod my head and follow her back to the table.

"We're going to order some dessert. Would you ladies care for anything?" asks Vick. "We're all getting cheesecake."

"Sounds good to me," says Kathryn.

"What about you, Lia?" asks Ty. I look at him and try to imagine what it will be like in a couple of weeks when I don't see him anymore. No more accidental bumps in the elevator. No more flowers sent to my office just because, or get-well packages at my door. He won't be calling me over to have wings and to just hang out. He'll be gone. And I'll never know what's it's like to kiss him, or make love to him, or just lie in bed holding him. And I'll never hear him say, "I love you, Lia."

"Lia, is that a yes to the cheesecake?" he asks with a smile, shaking me from my thoughts.

"Actually, I think I'd prefer chocolate," I say. We call the waiter over and place our orders. I look up at Simone and she's whispering and giggling into Ty's ear. I glance over at Kathryn and she's rolling her eyes. "You know, I think I should take mine to go. I have a busy morning tomorrow," I tell them. I stand and collect my things and tell the waiter to put my cake in a box.

"It was great meeting you, Lia," Kathryn says.

"Yeah, it was," say Vick and Hasaan.

"Too bad you can't stay," Simone says with a fake-ass smile.

"I'll walk you out," Ty says. I get my cake and we head for the door.

"Congratulations on your promotion. I'm sure you deserve it," I say when we get to the entrance of the bar.

"That means a lot coming from you. I know you're hard to impress."

"Yeah, uh . . . you didn't mention the part about going back to Chicago."

"Oh, I'm sorry. I must have forgotten."

"Is Simone going with you?" I ask.

"She has her own life here. We're still going to date, but I don't think a long-distance relationship will work, you know?"

"Right. Well, I better go. See you later, Ty."

"Is something wrong, Lia?"

Yeah, something's wrong. Extremely wrong. "No, why do you ask?"

"You just seem . . . I don't know. But look, I'm really glad that I met you. I'm sure we'll run into each other again one of these days."

"Me too. But hey, congrats again." My heart is beating fiercely. He gives me a quick kiss on the cheek.

"Thanks for coming," he says before returning to his friends.

When I get home I remember that I was supposed to call Maya-Lin. I hope it's not too late in the evening.

"Hello?"

"Hey, it's Lia. Sorry I didn't call earlier."

"It's no problem. Did you have a date or something?"

"No. I met Ty and his girl and some of his friends at a bar. He got a promotion so they were celebrating."

"Well, that's nice."

"He's moving back to Chicago in two weeks," I say.

"Oh. Well, did you tell him?"

"Tell him what?"

"How you feel! Lia, stop the games. Did you hear your-self when you said he was leaving New York? It's pitiful!"

"What, I should just say don't go because I think I might be falling in love with you?" And as I'm saying the words I know that it's true. You know how everyone has that one moment where it all makes sense? You can see your life so clearly and you understand why things are the way they are. You can flash back to each significant incidence and know exactly what it all means and where it was trying to take you. It's more than an epiphany. It flips your whole world upside down. And it's at that one moment when you know what you need to do. It's just a matter of doing it. Every little thing that Ty has said and done up until this point has been building up in my mind and, more importantly, in my heart. I don't dislike Simone because she's rude or beautiful or has that annoying accent. I dislike her because she's taking my place by being with Ty!

"Yes, Lia. At least if he knows how you feel he can make an informed decision. With all the facts. He may still go to Chicago and he may still date that woman, but you don't want to spend your life wondering if he was the one."

I listen carefully to her words and I think about how much time has been wasted because I've been so blind to reality.

"I know," I say with a sigh. "But he has a girlfriend now. . . ."

"Jonathan was dating someone when I met him. So we were just friends for a long time. But once I realized that I was falling for him I told him. Turns out it wasn't that serious with the girl so we decided to try it out. I'd hate to think what would have happened if I didn't tell him how I felt."

"Weren't you scared that he'd reject you?" I ask her.

"Terrified. But that's just pride. You have to do what you have to do."

"Yeah. I guess I have to." We talk a little more about the next time we'll meet and how she wants me to come to Jersey this Sunday. Then she puts Jonathan on the phone to say hello. We end the conversation and I get in my bed, wondering how I can ever tell Ty how I feel. God, I wish I hadn't been such a stank-ass to him this whole time. He might laugh in my face. Well, I only have two weeks to figure something out. But it's going to be hard with Simone in the picture. This is too much. I don't know if I can go through with it. I definitely have to call Rena to get some advice. Maybe Jas too. But I know they are going to trip when I tell them. Sigh. It's been so long since I've felt this way. I hope it's all worth it.

Chapter 26

Rena

Ever since Tak and I got back together he's practically moved in. He's here when I wake up and here when I go to sleep. And under any other circumstances, I wouldn't have any complaints. It's just that it's so much harder trying to come up with excuses not to have sex. I think he's getting suspicious. He hasn't come out and said anything, but he knows something is up. I can tell by the way he looks at me when I tell him I'm tired or don't feel well. But today is the day that it's all over. The clinic should be calling me at some point to let me know the results either way. I'm feeling extremely antsy, so it's no surprise that Tak comments on my demeanor.

"Rena, what's up with you today? Why are you acting so funny?"

"What are you talking about, Tak? I'm okay," I lie.

"You just seem, I don't know . . . different. Is there anything you want to talk about? Anything on your mind?"

"No. I told you I'm fine. Hey, are you still taking Lion to the museum today? He's been talking about it all week."

"Yeah, we're leaving in a couple of hours. What do you have planned for the day?"

"Nothing really. I'll probably run a few errands but that's it," I say.

"So, you think maybe later we can spend a little time together?" he asks with sex in his voice.

"Tak, we always spend time together. You're here morning and night."

"Well, damn, Rena, we are engaged. We just got back together. Are you tired of me already?" His tone is a mixture of hurt and frustration.

"No, I'm not tired of you. I just—" The telephone ringing interrupts me. I lose my breath for a minute, sure that it's someone from the clinic, and go to answer it. The voice on the other end is the one I've been dreading, yet waiting for.

"Ms. Redding, this is Dr. Holland from the clinic. Would it be possible for you to come in today to discuss your results?"

"I thought you could just tell me," I say, shaking.

"I'm sorry but our policy is to have each patient come in for the consultation."

"Okay, then. I'll be there in an hour." As I hang up the phone I force myself not to get emotional. After all, I don't know what they're going say. It could be excellent news. It could be . . .

"What was that all about?" Tak asks.

"Oh, someone from the college reminding me that I need to drop off some paperwork today. I'm about to go there now. I'll see you and Lion later, okay?" I give Tak a kiss on the cheek and yell good-bye to my son, who is taking a bath.

I wouldn't mind going to the clinic if it didn't have that smell. That antiseptic, impersonal stench. It's almost like they refuse to let you feel comfortable. I go to the front desk and sign in. The receptionist directs me to the waiting area and I take a seat next to a young woman holding a baby. She smiles at me while trying to wipe her baby's runny nose.

"She's had this same cold for two weeks," she says.

"Aw. I'm sorry to hear that. Have they told you anything?"

"Not really. Just a bunch of nothing."

"How old is she?" I ask.

"Ebony is thirteen months today," she says proudly. "The same day her mommy turns seventeen."

As she says the words her age becomes more apparent to me. I can see the softness of her face, the innocence that should be there but is long lost. I can only imagine the circumstances that led this young girl down the path of becoming a mother at such a young stage in her life.

"Well, happy birthday to both of you."

The receptionist calls my name and I wish the young mother and her child well before I'm escorted to Dr. Holland's office. When I enter she's seated behind her desk looking through a folder.

"Have a seat, Ms. Redding. I'm glad you could make it today."

"I had no choice," I reply. She nods her head and continues to look at the papers in front of her. I can't help but think she's taking her time on purpose. I wonder if it's harder to tell someone they're dying, or harder to have it said to you.

"Okay, I'll get straight to the point, then. We did the blood test and your results are negative for HIV," she states.

I shout inside my head. The feeling I have right now is

indescribable. I really feel like I've been given another chance.

"Thank God. Okay, well, I guess that's it. Thank you, Doctor," I say as I rise from the chair.

"But, Ms. Redding, your test came back positive for pregnancy."

"What? That can't be right. I haven't missed a period."

"Ms. Redding, your menstrual cycle shouldn't be your number-one indicator of pregnancy. You may have had one since you conceived, but I assure you that you won't have another for about eight months or so."

"Are you sure? I haven't felt any different. I've been pregnant before. I was very sick."

"Your body may react in varied ways for each pregnancy. Trust me, Ms. Redding. As sure as we know that you're HIV-negative, we know that you're pregnant. I wanted you to come in to see if you'd like to set up prenatal care with us or if you already have an obstetrician in mind."

The more she speaks, the more foreign she sounds. If I'm pregnant, that means I'm carrying Lace's baby. A man whose last name I don't even know. A man who's not my fiancé.

"Uh, I have an ob-gyn, thank you."

"Well, I recommend that you make an appointment soon so that we can ensure that your baby will get the proper care."

"I will."

"Okay, then, and, Ms. Redding, if this isn't good news for you I can provide you with information on alternatives."

"No, that's fine. I know my options."

"Well, if that's it, then you can sign out at the front desk."

Even though I received the information I came to get, I feel less knowledgeable leaving the clinic than I did going in. I don't have to tell Tak that I'm HIV-positive, but I have to tell him that I'm carrying another man's child. I probably have a better chance of holding on to my relationship if I were dying as opposed to this. And what about Lace? Do I tell him? Will he care? Will he want to be a part of this baby's life? As I walk down the subway steps, I wonder if it would just be better not to go through with the pregnancy. At least I can keep my family together and not drag Lace into a situation he most likely doesn't want. But what kind of toll will ending the life of my own child have on me? I can't imagine not having Lion in my life. I don't even know who I was before I had him. And now I have another chance to have that same feeling all over again. To be loved and depended on by one more person. It scares me to think about what will happen if I keep this baby. And it scares me to think about what will happen if I don't.

When I get home Tak and Lion are still gone. I use this alone time to meditate. I light some incense and sit on the floor. I try to focus on my body. I'm trying to feel a connection to the life growing inside me. I want to gain some insight on how I should handle this situation. Just as I'm slipping into a trance Lion comes running up to me.

"Mommy, we saw the dinosaurs and the monsters from a million years ago," he exclaims excitedly.

"Lion, go tape the new posters you got to your wall. You can tell Mommy about the rest later," Tak tells him. Lion grabs the posters from his father's hand and hurries to his room. "So, I see you were trying to meditate before we came in. Are you stressed? Can I help?" He kisses my lips and squeezes my ass. The last thing I want to do right now is have sex. Sex is how I got to this point. But I also haven't been close to Tak in a long time. I miss his touch and his sexual intensity.

"What about Lion?"

"He's fine. You just have to be quiet," he says jokingly. He leads me into my bedroom and locks the door. As he starts undressing me, I can't stop thinking about this baby I'm carrying. There's no way I can have Lace's child and expect to stay with Tak. He loves me, but being pregnant with someone else's kid during our engagement will not work. Unless he doesn't know it's someone else's kid. Wait. I could never do that. I don't even know why I'm thinking that way. But in that one moment I see my life without Tak and without his love. I can't take that risk. I can't . . .

"Baby, you seem distracted," Tak says. "You want to, right?"

"Yes. I do." I lie on the bed and let him tease my body with his tender kisses. "This is going to be so special," I whisper as I close my eyes.

Chapter 27

Jas

I've been moping around my house for the past few days, thinking about Asaji and how I managed to fuck things up all over again. What is wrong with me? Why can't I ever get my shit together? Sigh. I don't want to think that I'm destined to be alone, but it sure does look that way. I go into the bathroom and look at my reflection. But I don't just see Jas. I see a lover. I see a survivor. I see a fighter. And it all clicks. At that one moment I see all that I am. I don't have to settle. I don't have to spend my life thinking about being with the man I love. I can just be with him. I remember what the pastor said about having the control and I really believe it. I know Asaji loves me. And the only thing that's been keeping us apart is me.

After I get dressed I hop on the train and begin my ride to Harlem. Whatever Asaji is doing will have to wait until

I've said what I have to say. I'm finally going to tell him the truth about everything. When I get to the studio an instant feeling of nostalgia comes over me. Being here reminds me of the days when I was first started thinking Asaji was the one. I guess I've come full circle. I go inside and walk up the raggedy stairs to the studio. I expect to see Asaji, maybe Lace and a few other guys sittin' around, smokin' maybe. But instead I see a chick. She's sitting with her legs crossed, chewing on bubble gum. She looks up at me and shakes her head.

"Asaji told me to tell all the other girls that the part is taken."

"I don't know what the hell you're talkin' about," I say.

"For the hook. A lot of chicks been comin' up in here wantin' to sing the hook on his song, but it's already taken by me."

"Okay, sweetie, but I'm not here for that. Where is he?" This little girl is about to be put in her damn place.

"I don't know you to be tellin' you all that. You can wait outside if you want," she says, dismissing me. Oh, hell, nah. Shit ain't goin' down like this.

"Look, tell me where the hell Asaji is. I'm not some fuckin' groupie, I'm his damn girl."

She looks at me like I've lost my mind.

"You is not Asaji's girlfriend. And if he is your man"—she smirks—"he wasn't last night."

I don't know what comes over me, but the next thing I know I'm at her neck, chokin' her out. She's gasping, tryin' to push me off. I let go and shove her down on the floor. I feel someone jerk my arm. It's Asaji.

"Jas, what the hell is wrong with you?" He helps the battered girl off her ass and asks her if she's okay. She nods her head but tells him it's not worth it to do the hook if she has to put up with crazy-ass bitches. She stomps out and slams the door.

"Go ahead and run after your fuck buddy."

"Don't give me that shit, Jas. Damn, what did you do that for? I needed her vocals for my track. Why the fuck did you come over here anyway?"

"Did you have sex with her, Asaji? Just tell me that."

"It's none of your business Jas. Just like that broad you—"

"That broad I what? I didn't do anything with her. You wanna know who she is, Asaji? She's the fuckin' leader of my rape survivors' meeting. That night you came over I was actin' stupid with her, but I didn't have sex with her. I couldn't."

"What are you doing goin' to a rape survivors' meeting?" he asks, anger rising in his voice. "Did some punk-ass nigga violate you? Why didn't you tell me? Who the hell is he? I'll fuckin' kill him, Jas." His willingness to protect me and the fact that he cares so much gives me some hope that maybe all is not lost.

"It happened years ago. Back when I was in high school. But I've been struggling with it since then."

"I'm sorry."

"It's not your fault. Don't apologize. But I have to tell you the truth. When you first told me you wanted to be with me, I really wanted to. But I was scared. At the time, I was . . ." I don't think I can finish the words. It's embarrassing for me to tell him that I was basically having sex for money.

"What is it, Ma?"

"When you were telling me how special I was and so different from all the other girls you meet, you didn't know the whole story. And I didn't want to get into anything without coming clean."

"Come clean, then. I'm listening."

"Okay. Well, for a long time I was, um . . . using men to get my bills paid, go shopping, everything."

"What do you mean using them? What did you do?"

"I had sex with them," I say as fast as I can. I look down at the floor because I'm too ashamed to look him in the eye.

"Why did you feel like you had to do that? I don't understand."

"I'm just beginning to understand myself. It goes deeper than just wanting money. I guess doin' that made me feel powerful. Like I had what they wanted. I was getting revenge on the guy that raped me by treating men as nothing else but dollar signs. I know it sounds crazy, but I was scared. I didn't know how else to handle it." I'm waiting for him to cuss me out or throw me out or call me a ho.

"Do you still do that?" he asks after a long pause.

"No. I've stopped. I'm going to heal in other ways. Look, I understand if this is too much for you. It is some crazy shit."

"There you go thinkin' I can't handle somethin' again. When you gonna learn, Ma?" He hugs me tightly. "None of that shit changes my opinion about you." He kisses my forehead.

This is one of the greatest days of my life. I feel so clean now after telling him the truth about everything.

"So, do you still want me to be your girl?" I ask.

"You know I do, Ma. I love you. I want you in my corner, ya know?"

"Yeah," I say, smiling. "I love you too." But I squirm out of his embrace as I remember the little heffa who just left the studio. "Did you have sex with that girl?"

"What does that have to do with anything?"

"I need to know. I won't be mad."

"You can't be mad."

"I know. Just tell me, please," I beg. I don't know why I want to know so badly. Either way he answers will make me feel like crap.

"Look, Jas. I don't know why you think I would all of a

sudden do somethin' with a silly broad after I waited all this damn time in the first place. Hell nah, I didn't have sex with her. Give me some damn credit."

"I'm sorry. It's just that she said—"

"She kissed me. She tried to give it to me, but I wasn't havin' it. It was strictly business with her. Until now. You scared her away."

"Sorry again," I say. "You can find someone else, right?"

"Yeah, I have someone else in mind. But it'll have to wait till I get back," he says.

"Where you goin'?" I ask.

"Doin' a little promotional thing. I, uh . . . I'll be gone for a few months."

"What? A few months? Why didn't you tell me?"

"I'm tellin' you now. It's no big deal anyway. I'll be back by Christmas."

"So you're cool being away from me for all that time? We just got together, Asaji."

"We'll talk every day. We'll be a'ight."

"You promise?" I ask. This is true irony or poetic justice or whatever you call it. As soon as I get my man he has to leave.

"No doubt. So, you got any plans later?"

"No. Why, what's up?"

"I was thinkin' I could stay over my girl's place tonight." He grins at me shyly. Oh, hell yeah!

"No doubt," I say smiling. After locking up we walk out of the studio, hand in hand, and head to the subway. At one point I thought I'd never make it to this place. It seemed like there were so many obstacles in my way. But I should have known that Asaji was different. I don't really think about things as being meant to be. I think they just happen and sometimes they're good and sometimes they're shitty. But you deal with it the best way you can. I don't know if what I have with Asaji will last. He may go on the road and meet someone else or I may get too lonely while I wait. But at this very second I know I love him. And as long as I feel this way I'm going to try and hold on to him.

"What you thinkin' 'bout, Ma?" he asks me as we wait for the train.

"How you better not cheat on me with some groupie while you're gone," I say with a smirk.

"Come on now, Jas. I don't even get down like that. How dumb would I look cheatin' on the finest girl in the world? You the only groupie I need anyway."

"Asaji, I am not your groupie." I know he's just playin' with me, but I need to set the record straight . . . just in case.

"Yeah, right. As soon as you heard ya boy on the radio you called my phone."

"Just to be polite and tell you I was happy for you. Besides, I don't need to be a damn groupie. I'm wifey, right?"

"As long as you act right," he says, laughing. I playfully shove him just before he pulls me close. "On a serious note, Ma. I'm trying to do this for real. Forever. You cool with that?"

"I'm cool with it," I say just as the train pulls up. Jasmine Lewis . . . the girl who just might get her happy ending.

Chapter 28

Lia

"I think he's wet, Maya-Lin," I say, holding up the squirming baby. I'm over at Maya-Lin's house with her family. Well, my family too. Everyone has been very welcoming, even June, her mother. And Jonathan is just as delicious as Maya-Lin described him to be. But right now it looks like David may need to be changed. I love him already, but I'm not touching anyone's diaper.

"Lia, you are the prissiest person I know," she says as she takes him out of my hands. "Sure you don't want to do it? It'll be good practice."

"I don't need to practice. As long as I know how to hand a wet baby off to someone else I'll be okay."

"Well, come with me anyway. I have to talk to you about something."

I follow her back to the nursery, where she begins to strip David of his filthy diaper.

"So, have you thought about what you're going to do about Ty?"

I knew this question would come up sooner or later. The truth is it's all I have been thinking about. "Not yet. I'm beginning to have second thoughts anyway."

"Girl, don't even start. You have maybe five days at the most. Don't blow it or you'll regret it forever."

She's right. I know it. All I've been doing is imagining Ty and me having the type of life my sister has. Beautiful home, adorable kids. I want to at least give it a chance. I owe it to myself.

"How do I even bring it up, though? I don't want to sound like an idiot."

"As long as you speak from your heart, that won't happen," she says as she finishes taping on David's new diaper. "How about we get a man's perspective? Let's ask Jonathan," she says, handing the baby back to me.

"Hell no! It's too embarrassing."

"Okay, now you sound like an idiot. Jonathan! Baby, come here for a minute," she yells through the hallway.

"You need something?" he asks her a few seconds later.

"Baby, if a woman secretly had feelings for you and you were about to move hundreds of miles away, would you want her to tell you?"

"Of course. I may decide to stay," he says.

"See, Lia?" Maya-Lin says to me. "Okay, how should she tell you?"

"Personally, I prefer the straightforward approach. Just sit me down, look me in my eyes, and tell me."

"What if she had been kind of a jerk to you the whole time you knew her?" I ask sheepishly.

"Well, I'd definitely want to know. So I could laugh at her and leave anyway."

"Jonathan, be serious," Maya-Lin says. "Bottom line, Lia, you have to do it."

"Yeah, Lia. I was just kidding. You should tell him the truth," says Jonathan. The truth. Everyone keeps saying that. You want to know the truth? I'm scared as hell that I've screwed up things with Ty for good.

The next day I give Jas a call to get one last opinion about Ty. I would normally ask Rena, but she used to hang out with him so she may be biased. And lately it seems like Jas has been more settled and mature. Whatever she suggests I'll probably do.

"Lia, what's up?" she asks cheerfully when she answers.

"Nothing. You sound happy."

"Asaji and I are back together. This time it's going to work."

"That's great, Jas. He's seems right for you."

"He is. And you know what else is great? The sex!"

"Oh my God! You finally took his virginity?" I ask, intrigued.

"Yes, girl. And let me tell you. He put it down! He was kinda shy at first, but after a few minutes it was on! And his tongue game is ridiculous. If I never have sex with any other man I'll be all right."

"Yeah. But that's because you love him."

"You're right. I do. Oh, did you talk to Rena?"

"No. Why?"

"She thinks she's pregnant. She and Tak are gonna have another baby."

"Wow. That's good. I didn't even know they were back together."

"Yep. Engaged too. Don't mention it, though, because she hasn't told him yet," she says.

"I won't. But about why I called . . . remember Ty? The guy from my building?"

"Yeah. What about him?"

"He's moving back to Chicago in a few days."

"Oh. Well, I know you're happy. He won't bug you anymore."

"No, Jas. This isn't a good thing. I, uh, I kinda have feelings for him and . . ."

"Shut up," she says a little too loudly. "You know he's black, right?"

"Yeah, smart-ass. Anyway, I don't want him to go. I want to be with him and see where it can go."

"Lia, it's too late for all that. The man's leaving."

"So I shouldn't tell him how I feel?" I ask, regretting that I called her in the first place.

"Tell him. But only because you need to do it for yourself. Don't expect anything."

"Right. You're right. I shouldn't expect him to just pass up a great career move for me."

"Asaji is going out of town until December. I damn sure don't want him to leave me, but I wouldn't ask him to stay. I know it's important to him. We'll be okay because he and I are supposed to happen. If you and Ty are supposed to happen, then you don't need to worry." Wow. My little Jasmine is all grown up. When did she make the transition from ho-ish little girl to sophisticated adult?

"Well, the damn tables sure have turned," I say, chuckling. "Anyway, I better go. I'll talk to you later, Jas." After we hang up I decide to go downstairs to Ty's place and just get it over with. I mean, the worst that can happen is that he doesn't feel the same. I really have nothing to lose . . . except a small chunk of my pride.

Once I get in front of his door I take a deep breath and knock. Here goes nothin'.

"Oh, Lia. How are you doing, dear?" Okay, correction, *this* is the worst that could happen.

"Hi, Simone. I, uh, just came by to, um . . ."

"Well, Tysean isn't in at the moment. You're welcome to

wait for him if you like." She opens the door wider and ushers me in. The last thing I want to do is chat it up with the enemy.

"You know, maybe I'll just come back later," I say with uncertainty in my voice. This whole scenario is just too weird.

"Don't be silly. He should be back any time now," she says, that damn English accent rolling off her tongue. "Would you like a beverage?"

"No, thank you." I sit on the couch and look around uncomfortably. I'll never be able to talk to Ty with her here.

"You'll have to excuse the mess as well as the lack of furnishings. We've been doing a lot of packing."

"I understand. Are you flying out with him?" I ask, nervous about her answer.

"No. I have a fashion show in Paris in two days. But I'll be here to see him to the airport."

"That's nice," I say. I notice Simone eyeing me, like she's trying to figure me out.

"Lia, Tysean told me that the two of you are just friends. But he also said that in the beginning he wanted to be more but you turned him down. May I ask why that is, if it's not too personal?"

Great. A heart-to-heart with Simone. Just what I need.

"Well, at the time I just wasn't interested in dating anyone exclusively," I lie. "Ty's a great guy. I just wasn't ready."

"But you're ready now, are you not?" Her tone has turned from inquisitive to interrogatory.

"What?" I ask, a little shocked at the way she just came at me.

"Listen, I'm no idiot, Lia. I can tell you're interested in Tysean. But rest assured that he's not interested in you."

"Simone, you are out of your mind. And I don't appreciate you talking to me like that," I say, trying to keep my cool.

"I just want you to be clear, darling. I'm going to be in Tysean's life for a long time. And after Friday, you won't be."

"Hey, baby. Lia, what's up? What are you doing over here?" Ty walks in just as I'm about to go to Simone's ass. She gets up and kisses him on the cheek.

"Lia just stopped by to speak to you and I told her she could wait," Simone says, glaring at me.

"Really? What did you need to talk about?" he asks, looking at me with those beautiful brown eyes.

"It can wait. You have company, so I'll come by later."

"You sure? Simone won't mind, right, baby?"

"Of course not. I have few telephone calls to make anyway. I'll just go into the bedroom."

"No, really. It's not important," I say as I walk to the door.

"Okay. See you later, then," he says.

"Good-bye, dear," says Simone. What, is Ty blind or something? Why can't he see what a monster Simone is? She may be tall and flawless, but she has such a fake personality. Men are so naive. But what if she's right? He's obviously with her because he likes her . . . or more. What makes me think I can just step in and change all that? Then again he did say he wasn't planning on maintaining a serious relationship with her after he leaves. . . . I don't know. But I will know the next time I see him.

The next few nights are restless for me. I toss and turn, completely worried about what's going to be the outcome of my confession to Ty. When Friday finally arrives I wake up early, take a bath, and make a mimosa. I need a little something to steady myself. After an hour or two of stalling, I finally go downstairs to see him. When I get there the door is open and a cleaning crew is inside. Oh no. Don't tell me I'm too late.

"Excuse me but what time did you guys get here?" I ask one of the men steaming the carpet.

"About eight thirty," he says. I look at my watch. It's ten o'clock. Shit. He's been gone for at least an hour and a half. He could be in Chicago by now. I didn't even find out what time his flight is or which airport he's leaving from. God, why didn't I just say what I had to say when I had the chance? Now I may never see him again. I get on the elevator with teary eyes and head back to my condo. When the doors open at my floor I run right into . . . Ty.

"Lia, I was just at your door. I wanted to say good-bye before I fly out. Hey, were you crying?"

"I thought you left. I was just downstairs. I thought I was too late." I know I'm rambling but I can't help it. My mind is racing and my heart is going just as fast.

"What's wrong? Why are you upset?" he asks.

"Ty, I need to tell you something. And I have to get it all out, so don't say anything, okay?" He nods his head.

"I know I haven't been the nicest person since you've moved here. Actually, I've been a bitch to you. And you've been nothing but sweet from the beginning."

"Lia, no need to apologize. It's water under the bridge."

"Listen, no interruptions, remember? Um, I'm just going to come out and say it." I stop for a minute to make sure this is really what I want to do. I don't want to confuse his life or anything. Maybe I should just cut my losses and let him go.

"Lia?" I must have zoned for a minute.

"Sorry. Okay, um, I am going to miss you so much, Ty. When I found out you were leaving I felt bad . . . really bad. And I realized that I felt that way because—" His cell phone rings.

"Sorry," he says as he presses IGNORE. "It's Simone. I'll call her back." Hearing Simone's name is all it takes to give me that something extra I need to get through this.

"Ty, I think I'm falling in love with you. And I know it's

crazy and out of the blue, but really it's not. Because you're everything I ever wanted in a man. And if I hadn't been so stupid before I would have realized this a long time ago." I stop for a second to see if he wants to say something, but he just continues to look at me. Is this good or bad? "Um, and I know it's unfair to tell you this when you have a girlfriend and when you're on your way out of town. But I had to get it off my chest." Okay, this time I really do need a response, a question, a comment . . . anything.

"Damn, Lia. I don't even know what to say."

"I don't expect anything. I just wanted you to know."

"I'm going to Chicago in a few hours. I barely have enough time to take all this in."

"I'm sorry. Maybe I shouldn't have told you. Um, have a nice trip, Ty." I step past him and walk down the hall. Well, I tried and I failed. Maybe he's not the one after all.

"Lia, wait a minute," he calls out after me. I turn around slowly, not wanting to keep subjecting myself to the realization that this is the last time I'm going to see him.

"Yes?" I reply.

"We probably would have been good together."

"I know."

"I wish you would have seen what I saw that first day," he says, brushing a few stray hairs from my face.

"Too little, too late, I guess," I say, a tear rolling down my cheek.

"It's never too late." He lifts my chin and kisses me deeply. I close my eyes as I get lost in the rapturous feeling of his lips on mine. When he pulls away he smiles. "Do you know how long I've wanted to do that?"

"Do you know how badly I want you do it again?" I ask. He obliges and takes me on a whirlwind ride one more time. It's even better than in my dreams.

"I have to get to the airport," he says, looking at his watch.

"I know. Want me to ride with you?"

"Simone is meeting me there. It wouldn't be right."

"Oh," I say, looking at the floor.

"What am I going to do with you, Lia? You have my mind spinning right now."

"What does that mean? Ty, I need to know if I have a chance with you. Or if you're going to stay with Simone."

"I told you, Simone and I will still hang out, but it won't be serious as long as it's long distance."

"So the same goes for me too, I suppose," I say. He doesn't say anything for a while.

"I'll call you when I get settled, Lia." He hugs me and says bye right before he gets on the elevator.

I feel like I broke even on the whole ordeal. Maybe he didn't cancel his trip or ask me to come with him. Maybe he didn't say he'd leave Simone alone for good or tell me that he loves me too. But he kissed me. And I felt something. I don't know what the future holds for Ty and me. But at least now I know there's a possibility for one.

Chapter 29

Dee Dee

He never came back: It's been about a month since the day we left the meeting with the lawyers and Deron never returned to the house. I called his job. I even called his mother's house, knowing that I'd get cursed out by every woman in his family. No one will tell me anything. I understand he needs time. I understand that what happened was tragic to our marriage. But does he understand that I love him? And does he understand that I'm willing to do anything to make it work? I just wish he would stop running away from me.

At about noon I put Deidre in bed for a nap and stretch out on the couch to get a little rest myself. I'm feeling myself drifting into a comfortable sleep when the phone rings loudly. I lazily reach over to the coffee table and grab the cordless phone.

"Hello," I say with my eyes closed.

"Dee Dee, turn on the TV. Channel five!" Lia says. "Hurry up!"

"Okay, hold on." I sit up and use the remote control to turn to the channel. I can't believe what I'm seeing. It looks like . . .

"Can you believe Manny is married now?" Lia asks with a tone of disgust, interrupting my thoughts. "The man only recently was trying to get with you! Oh, damn! Dee, do you think he was dating you both at the same time? Because if he wasn't, then he married her after only knowing the little hooch for a few weeks!"

I hear Lia talking but I'm only half listening. Manny is on the screen with his new bride, talking about how they're so excited to start a life together. The reporter asks him if he realizes how many hearts he's broken by taking himself off the market so suddenly. He chuckles before he replies. "I hope all my fans are happy for me because I finally found the one who will make me happy for the rest of my life. My beautiful bride, *mi estrella*." I turn the TV off and tell Lia I'll call her later. Well, if I didn't know it before I definitely know it now. Manny never loved me. He never wanted to be with me. It was such a huge joke that he even came back into my life. Well, that chapter of my life is undoubtedly closed forever.

I lie back down, unsure if I'll be able to capture the sleep that I was about to fall into before. And after a few minutes I'm sure that I can't. I get up and check on Deidre right before I hear someone open the front door. It's Deron. He's here. He's finally come home.

"Deron," I say softly as he walks into the living room. He looks at me like he wasn't expecting anyone to be home. He looks the same, but different. His features and his clothes haven't changed . . . but his eyes look rested. His vibe seems calm.

"Hi, Dee Dee," he says. There's no hint of anger, animosity, or resentment in his voice. He sounds very much at peace.

"I missed you," I say as I go to hug him. He holds me tightly and kisses the top of my head.

"I missed you too. Is my baby sleeping?"

"Yes, I just put her down. Come and sit. Let's talk. I mean, it's been a month. You didn't call. No one would tell me where you were," I say, trying to sound more relieved than angry.

"No one really knew. I had to get my thoughts together. I had to figure out what direction I needed to take. I'm sorry I didn't call. I feel bad about that. But talking to you would have clouded my head even more. You understand, don't you?" He looks at me as I take everything in.

Sure, I understand. But it still hurts. "What matters now is that you're back and we can move on with our lives. We have a family to raise and a marriage to repair."

"But, Dee, you didn't even ask me what I've been thinking about. You didn't ask what I decided to do."

"What do you mean? I didn't think there was any doubt. I mean, you needed time to heal, but you came back and now we can be a family again," I say pointedly.

"Baby, listen to me," he says slowly. "I came back because I have a daughter and another child on the way and I need to be here for them. But as far as our marriage—"

"Deron . . ." I say while my eyes begin to tear. "Please don't do this."

"As far as our marriage goes," he continues strongly, "it's over."

His words echo in my head. *It's over. It's over*. And it's all I hear. *It's over*. The impact those three syllables have is nerve-racking. I can't even think. I can't even speak. Why should I? What could I say to counteract what has just been said to me?

"Dee Dee," Deron continues while touching my hand, "I tried. I want you to know that I tried to reconcile with the fact that you cheated on me, lied to me, wanted to leave me, and take my kids. I tried to deal with it. I promise you I did." I can hear his voice choking up. He covers his face with his hands for a few seconds. "But after all of that I realize that we don't have a marriage anymore. We have a relationship that used to be monogamous and committed. We have a relationship with kids and a house . . . but we don't have a marriage."

"I'll do anything, Deron. We can go to counseling . . . anything," I plead. But I know from the expression on his face that it's in vain. I have lost the battle and war.

"I'm sorry I'm not strong enough to go through this with you," he says sincerely.

"You shouldn't have to be," I say. "You shouldn't have to deal with this." And I believe that. He's a good man and he doesn't deserve to have to pick up my broken pieces.

"I love you, Dee. I will always love you," he says. He kisses my cheek and gets up from the couch. "I'm going to pack a few things and go to my brother's house until I can find another place in my budget. I'd like to see Deidre on the weekends—"

"Yes, that's . . . that's fine," I say. The tone of the conversation has instantly gone from intimate to just cordial. It's breaking my heart. And I have to play along.

"And I'd still like to take you to your doctor's appointments, unless you'd rather I not."

"Of course I want you there."

"And . . . we should probably call the lawyers. We have to discuss arrangements again and sign—"

"I know," I say, cutting him off. "I know. Just . . . give me a few days."

"Sure. That's fine," he says. Silence speaks as he goes into the bedroom to pack his clothes and I stand alone, wondering how I'll get through this when I feel like I can't really express how I feel.

"Deron," I say after walking into the bedroom. "I want to scream. And I want to yell and throw anything I can get into my hands. I want to curse you and me and Manny and everything that has anything to do with this moment that I'm in. But I have to remember my condition and the baby and stay calm."

"That's true, Dee. Don't stress yourself."

"However," I say firmly. "I just want you to know that we may sign these papers, and you may move out, but I will always fight for you. I will not give up."

He looks at me intently for a few seconds and sighs.

"I have, though," he says, zipping up his suitcase. "I have." He walks past me and goes into the baby's room to kiss her good-bye.

"I'm not giving up," I say again as he opens the front door. He looks at me and says good-bye before walking out of my house and my marriage. The truth is, I don't have any master plan or secret weapon to get him back. I'm relying on the fact that he loves me and deep down he wants this thing to work. I'm not crazy, I'm just hopeful. Hopeful even though my life just said bye and walked out my front door.

Chapter 30

Jas

I miss Asaji so much. I never really knew what it was like to be in love before him. And now I'm experiencing this whole new feeling of longing. It's so shitty it's not even funny. Yeah, he calls me almost every day, but so what? He's not here, next to me. Sigh.

The good news is that before he left, he made me promise to work on my music every day. And I've really been sticking to it. I've got a few really hot pieces that I'm excited about and I can't wait for him to hear. I'm actually at his studio now with a couple of his friends, listening to them record.

"Yo, Jas, you wanna battle?" Tony, one of Asaji's boys, asks jokingly.

"Don't you know I'll embarrass you?" I shoot back with a grin. Everyone gets a few laughs in, but Tony persists.

"Okay, Lil' Kim. What you got?"

"What? I can't rhyme," I say. "I was just playin'."

"Come on, yo. It's all in fun. You can't be the girl of a soon-to-be big-time rapper and not have picked up a few skills. Here, I'll give a beat." He starts pounding on the table with his hands and fists. "Come on, you got this," he says. I can't believe I'm about to play myself by trying to rap, but whatever. It'll give me something to laugh about later.

> "You really put me on the spot
> but it's okay 'cause I'm that hot.
> Don't really freestyle,
> but I got style.
> Don't really rhyme like that
> but I'm fine like that.
> Lips, hips, finger tips
> I'm a dime like that."

Everyone is cracking up. It's funny, yeah, but I feel stupid as hell.

"Yo, that's kinda a'ight for your first time," Tony says in between laughs.

"Shut up," I say. I feel my phone vibrating and go into the next room to answer it. It's my baby!

"What's up, Jas?" he says when I answer.

"Baby, I was just in there tryin' to rap. It was not pretty."

"Are you serious?" he asks, trying to hold back a laugh.

"Yeah. I was a mess. I don't even wanna talk about it. I'm sure Tony will tell you."

"Oh, Tony is there? I know he was rollin'."

"Baby, it's not funny," I say with a fake pout.

"I'm sorry, baby. But anyway, did you do any writing today?"

"Yes," I say with a sigh. "Is that the only reason you called? To see if I did my homework?"

"Nah, I wanna ask a question."

"Go ahead."

"Do you miss me?" he asks.

"Hell yeah, I miss you. I don't think I can take this much longer."

"Well, come see me."

"Are you for real, Asaji? Aren't you busy doing promo stuff?"

"I can make time. I want to see you even if it's just for a few days. Bring one of your friends or somethin'."

"Okay, I mean of course I'll come see you. You really think I'd say no?"

"Not really," he says. I can tell he's smiling.

"You are so cocky."

"No, I just know what's up. We're in Detroit now, but we'll be in Chicago tomorrow for about a week. You think you can manage to make it?"

"Yeah, definitely. I'm gonna try to book a flight tonight. Maybe I can fly out tomorrow."

"Cool. So, what color panties are you wearing?" he asks slyly.

"Boy, get off my phone," I say, grinning.

"I love you, Jas."

"I love you too." Oh my God, I haven't seen him in, like, a month. And I didn't really think I'd see him for another month. But fuck that. I'm 'bout to see my baby! I'm 'bout to see my baby! I go back into the main room and tell the guys I'm sorry I can't be their court jester anymore, but I gotta go. As I leave the studio and walk the few blocks to the train, I dial Lia's number on my cell and hope it doesn't go to voice mail. She's the only other person I know who could benefit from going to Chicago. After she told me what happened with Ty, I felt bad. I mean, she finally realized that she had feelings for the man, but it was kind of too late. She says that they talk on the regular, but it's hard to try to develop something when they're in two totally different regions of the country. This trip could be a nice little reminder of what she could have.

"Hello?"

"Lia, I'm going to see Asaji. Come with me."

"What, Jas? Hell no. I'm not in the mood for a trip."

"Please, Lia. Just for a few days," I beg. "He'll be busy some of the time and I need someone to hang out with."

"No! I have a lot I need to take care of and I don't have time to follow you around the country while you run after Asaji's ass. No."

Really, I didn't want to have to use this as ammunition, but she's leaving me with no choice.

"Chicago," I say.

"What?" she snaps.

But I can tell she's interested. "Chicago. That's where I'm going."

"Asaji is in Chicago? But—"

"Right. Do I even need to say anything else?" I get quiet for a few seconds as she digests what has the potential to become a very good situation.

"But I can't just pop up at his doorstep. We didn't make any plans to see each other yet. I'd look crazy."

"Damn, Lia, haven't you learned anything? You don't want to be caught up in a what-if, do you? You don't want to think 'what if I would have gone to see Ty instead of staying in New York tryin to be a hard ass?' You want to see him. Make it happen." I get to the subway entrance and wait for a reply. "I'm going to lose my signal in a second. What's it gonna be?" She sighs and I almost think she's going to say no. But then . . .

"I'll book two flights," she says finally. Yes!

"Girl, you came through! I'll call you when I get home."

I walk down the steps on the subway and start mentally packing my bags, trying to decide what I need to take. Thank God it's the weekend so I don't need to call my job. I'm sure those fuckers would have given me a hard time.

When I arrive home I get everything together and call Lia to get the details. She tells me that the plane leaves at nine tonight and we'll get to Chicago at about eleven thirty. But it will only be ten thirty there, right? I don't know, these time zone changes always confuse me. After hopping in the shower and putting on a pair of blue Juicy sweatpants that make my booty look just that, and a matching hoodie, I grab my two suitcases and go outside to hail a cab to La Guardia. I start to think about the last time I saw Asaji, the last time we kissed, the last time we made love . . . God, I miss him so much!

When I get to the airport and finish going through all the security bullshit, I call Lia to find out where she is. She says her cab just dropped her off outside and she'll be on her way in shortly. I find the gate where I'm supposed to wait and take a seat, watching all the travelers rush by. I text-messaged Asaji earlier to let him know I was definitely coming and to make sure he's cleared his schedule. No shows at any clubs, no passing out fliers on the street. Tonight is my night. Thirty minutes later I see Lia walking toward me. She's wearing Seven Jeans, a white button-up shirt, and a caramel-colored blazer. Her chocolate-brown Balenciaga bag and round-toe boots match perfectly . . . of course.

"Did they find a switchblade in your bag or something?" I ask when she gets close. "Why did it take so long?"

"The woman in front of me couldn't speak English, so they had to find someone who speaks German. But anyway, don't you look cute with your tight-ass pants on? I know someone is getting some sex tonight," she says, elbowing me.

"Maybe," I say shyly.

"Girl, whatever. I was talking about me anyway," she giggles.

"Oh, that's right! You and Ty never . . . What if it's lame?"

"Please don't say that. That would be such a waste."

"You could teach him," I say with a grin. "Okay, Ty. Now you flex your back and try to get as deep as you can. And when you hear me moan like this, that means you hit the right spot."

"Stop," she says, pushing me in my shoulder. "I don't want to talk about it. Ty knows how to work it, I know."

"How?"

"I had a dream."

"Okay, MLK . . . you stay in your dream all you want. But holla at me when you know what's up in real life."

"Anyway," she says, disregarding me. "I know one thing. I will feel really stupid if I go to his house and he's like 'what the hell are you doing here?'"

"What? He wouldn't say that. He's into you, Lia. If he lived in New York you guys would have it on and poppin'."

"Yeah, I mean I think so. But, Jas, I told him I was falling for him a while back."

"Only a month ago, Lia. Let's get some perspective here."

"Okay, a month. But he hasn't said anything like that to me. I mean, I really think he's the one. I don't even want to date anyone else because I have this gut feeling that I'm supposed to be with him."

"Well, that's good enough for me. And it should be good enough for you. Not like it matters anyway. We are on our way to the Chi and you will see him. End of story." Jeez, sometimes I feel like my friends are just clueless . . . like I have to show them how to live.

After hearing our flight called over the intercom, we

line up to board the plane. Once on board, we get settled and I pull out my silver iPod. I scroll through all the songs until I get to the *Stripped* album by Christina Aguilera. I don't care what nobody says . . . that lil' skinny-ass white girl can sing her ass off.

A couple of hours later after we've landed and gotten all of our luggage, I call Asaji to get his hotel info. After I get sent to voice mail twice, he finally picks up.

"What's up, baby?"

"What's up is that I got your voice mail, like you weren't expectin' me to call," I say, frustrated.

"My b. But yo, I was on the phone with this dude who was tellin' me that Twista heard me on the radio today and he wants me to come to a studio session tonight. Maybe lay a few tracks."

"Baby, I just flew in . . . for you!"

"Jas, you gotta understand. Shit like this don't just happen to everybody. This is a chance to show a veteran in the game what I got. You need to be behind me on this."

"So when are you gonna be done?" I ask, knowing that there's no way I can change his mind.

"I don't know, baby. I mean, I'll try not to be all night. I'll call you."

I can feel tears forming in my eyes, but I shake it off. I don't want Lia to think anything is wrong. "Okay. Just tell me where the hotel is. Leave a key at the desk."

"Comfort Inn on E. Ohio Street. I'm in room 212. And, Jas, I'll make it up to you."

"Yes, you will," I say right before I hang up. I walk over to Lia, who's a few feet away, checking herself out in her mirror.

"Is everything okay?" she asks.

"Yeah. We just have to get a cab and go to the hotel."

"Where is he staying?" she asks suspiciously. I know

Lia is not going to want to stay at any hotel unless Marriott, Hilton, or Omni is in the name.

"Comfort Inn," I say quickly.

"The what? Hell no, Jas. Look, I've been skimming through this brochure and there's a Doubletree five minutes away. I'll just go check in there and you go spend time with your man. I'll call you in the morning."

"I can't spend time with him because he's not going to be there," I say, the tears finally falling the way they wanted to.

"What's wrong, Jas? What do you mean?"

"He's going to the studio. He'll probably be there all night," I say while wiping me eyes.

"That little bastard. This whole trip was his idea. Well, you can join me at the Doubletree tonight and we'll go kick his ass tomorrow."

"Okay," I say with smile. "Ya know, I'm sure there's a bar or something around here. . . ."

"Can we at least get settled before you start talking about getting drunk? Come on, we need to get a cab."

After checking into the hotel and getting to our room, I wash my face and finger-comb my hair a little bit. I really want to go out somewhere to distract myself from the fact that my boyfriend stood me up. But I can tell Lia's not tryin' to hear it. She's already changed into shorts and a T-shirt.

"So, no bar tonight?" I ask, plopping down on the bed beside her.

"Girl, I'm sorry but I am so tired. Plus, I can't have myself looking like I've been out all night when I see Ty tomorrow."

"Yeah, that's true," I say. This really sucks. I came all the way out here to Chicago, which, don't get me wrong, is a nice city . . . but it's definitely not New York, and I definitely didn't come here to have a slumber party with Lia.

"Hey, you realize that this is just a taste of what it will be like when Asaji becomes a big-time rapper, right? You won't always be able to see him when you want, or even if you make plans to." And she's right. He'll always be busy. Always out of town. Always putting me second to his first love. Is that the type of life I want? Can I deal with that? My vibrating phone interrupts my thoughts.

"Jas, where are you? How come you're not at the room?" It's Asaji, sounding upset.

"I'm with Lia. I thought you would be gone all night."

"I left. I felt like shit doin' that to you, so I left to come see you. But you ain't even here!"

"I can come now," I say, standing up and putting my shoes on.

"Nah, you don't know this city like that to be out at night by yaself. We'll get up tomorrow."

Fuck! Why me? "Fine. I'll call you when I wake up." This is bullshit. First he tells me he can't see me tonight, and then he tells me he can, but he doesn't want me to come over. God, he makes me sick. I glance over at Lia, who is knocked out, and decide that the best thing for me to do is just go to sleep too. So far this trip has been a disaster. And tomorrow he better make it all up to me.

Chapter 31

Lia

When I wake up in the morning, Jas is still asleep in the next bed. I almost don't want to get up either because this bed is so damn comfortable. But I know I need to because today I'm going to Ty's place, ready or not. After my shower I get dressed and shake Jas on her arm. It's about eleven.

"Jas," I whisper. "I'm going to get brunch from that little diner next door. Do you want me to bring something up?"

She opens her eyes a little and shakes her head. "Girl, I get up at noon on Saturdays, okay? You better get out of my face talkin' about some damn brunch. Bye."

"Okay, stankie. But I'm going to Ty's right after. So I may not be back for a while." She immediately sits up . . . like I knew she would.

"Well, let me make sure you doin' it right," she says. "Stand back; let me see what you have on." She examines my cream-colored, long-sleeved, V-neck sweater and matching scarf and my too-tight True Religion jeans. "Okay, you pass. Now get the hell out and call me when it all goes down."

"I will. Bye, girl."

I get outside the hotel and my entire appetite just disappears. I'm so nervous about seeing Ty that I can't even eat. I decide just to go ahead and go to his house and whatever happens, happens. I pull out my BlackBerry to look at his address one more time even though I know it by heart. I get the guy in front of the hotel to get a cab for me and I give the driver the address. At this point I just have to suck everything up and hope for the best. A million and one scenarios play and replay in my head as I sit in the backseat of the taxi and gaze out of the window. My favorite one is where he opens the door and smiles because he was just thinking about me. Then he invites me in and tells me that he's in love with me, he just didn't know how to say it. And of course he rips my clothes off and we make all kinds of love in his bed, on the table, on the floor . . .

The driver slows down and stops in front of a tall condominium building. I give him some cash and get out of the car, half expecting myself to get right back in. But I don't. Instead I go inside after the doorman lets me in, and take a deep breath. I'm almost there. There's no turning back. I take out my compact and make sure everything looks the way it should and make my way to the elevators. I think about calling Jas, but I need less of a pep talk and more like Pepto-Bismol because my stomach is a mess right now. *Damn it, Lia, get it together!* It's not that big of a deal. It's just a little visit to a little friend and that's all. *Relax*. And I almost do relax . . . until I hear it. That voice . . .

"Lia? Pardon me, but is your name Lia?" the excruciatingly painful-to-hear voice asks as I turn around to face . . .

"Simone," I say through clenched teeth. Unbelievable. I'd rather see the fucking devil himself than this bitch.

"Oh my, it is you," she says, disappointment oozing off every word. "You're here for Tysean?"

"Yes, I'm here to see Ty. It doesn't have anything to do with you, however. So if you'll excuse me," I say, turning back to the elevator to press the Up button.

"This is bloody ridiculous," she says, sounding upset. "How dare he invite us both here to see him on the same weekend!" The elevator opens and shuts without me getting on it.

"He invited you?" I ask, making sure I heard her right. I can feel my heart breaking into pieces.

"Of course. He rang me earlier in the week and asked if I could come since he couldn't get away. Did he give you the same story?"

. "Uh, I . . ." I have no idea how to respond. I mean, what do I say? No, he didn't invite me . . . he doesn't even know I'm here!

"Bloody ridiculous," Simone says again while pulling out her cell phone. "I'm calling that bastard right now to tell him to go to hell."

"Wait, Simone," I say. Okay, she wins. It's obvious now that Ty wants her and not me. I shouldn't get in the way. I mean, he wants her here. He asked her to come. I have no right to screw it up for them.

"What's the problem?" she asks with a perplexed expression on her near-flawless face. "Oh, of course! We should confront him together. Come on, let's go up," she says, grabbing my wrist.

"No, listen to me. I'm going to leave now. Just forget you saw me here, go up and see Ty, and just . . ." I'm struggling to say the words. "Just forget you saw me. This never happened and Ty is upstairs now waiting on you and only you, okay?" I turn and walk away before I completely break down. It's over. It's really, truly over. God, I'm such an idiot! I could have had him. He wanted me . . . I had so many chances. I blew it. Tears fall from my eyes and I have to bite my lip to keep from sobbing.

I ask the doorman to hail a cab for me while I stand inside. The Windy City is definitely living up to its name today. I know I should call Jas to give her all the pathetic details, but I really don't want to talk to anyone right now. I see my cab outside, so I walk quickly to the car to get out of the fierce wind.

"Where're you headed?" the driver asks.

"The Doubletree by the—" My cell starts ringing loudly before I can finish and I answer it before I even look to see who it is . . . I already know it's Jas. "The airport, I'm sorry," I say to the driver. "Hello," I say as the car starts to move.

"Lia, where are you?" Oh my God! It's Ty.

"I'm—I'm in the cab. I just left—"

"What are you doing? Come back!"

"Stop the car, please," I say to the driver. "This is fine, thank you." I open the door before he even comes to a complete stop and hand him a five-dollar bill. "Ty," I say, turning my attention back to the phone, realizing that I don't know what to say.

"Lia, are you crazy?"

"Because Simone . . ." I'm walking as fast as I can back to his building. When I get inside I see him standing in the lobby. I hang up the phone and go over to him. He's just as good looking as the last time I saw him. He has on jeans, a button-up, and a smile . . . like he's actually happy to see me.

"Because Simone what?" he asks.

"She was here. You asked her to come see you and here I am just popping up out of nowhere. I felt like an idiot."

But even if I did then, talking to him now, having him this close to me makes me feel a little better. "Where is she anyway?"

"Gone," he says simply.

"What do you mean? I just saw her. . . ."

"She wasn't going to stay long. I had to tell her I couldn't see her anymore."

"What?" I ask, trying not to smile . . . yet.

"She has been talking about getting serious, and truthfully, I couldn't see myself being with her on that level. So I figured it was better to just end it now before it got any deeper."

"How deep was it anyway?" I ask.

"For me, not very. For her, I could tell she wanted more. It was best to just end it. She's a beautiful woman but just not right for me. And besides, I like the direction you and I have been going lately. . . ."

Come on, Ty. Keep it coming. "What direction is that?"

"The direction that brought you here to see me."

"So what are you saying?" I don't want to jump to any conclusions. I need him to spell it out.

"I've always been scared to try the long-distance relationship thing. But with you, I think it's worth it to give it a shot." He takes my hand. "I want to be with you, Lia. No one else."

Wow . . . it happened. Everything I've wanted for a long time has finally happened.

"That's what I want too. I just want to be with you," I say as I hug him.

"Do you think we can actually do this, Lia? Are you ready for this?"

"Oh, hell yes," I say, grinning. "You don't know how long I've been ready."

"When is your flight out?"

"Tomorrow," I answer.

"Well, stay with me tonight, then." He kisses me and I can feel the heat between my legs. This man is no joke.

"Okay, but I need to call Jas. She came here with me and I need to make sure she's okay."

"I'll be upstairs. Come up when you're ready. Are you hungry? Did you eat yet?"

"I'm starving," I say.

"I'll order a pizza, then. Sound good?"

"Perfect. I heard Chicago has pretty good pizza. Can't beat New York but . . ."

"What? You'll see," he says with a smile as he gets on the elevator. Yes, I will see, I say to myself while dialing Jas's number. I'm gonna see exactly what Chicago has to offer!

"Hello?"

"Jas, it's me."

"I know. How'd it go? Are you with him?"

"Girl, I can't tell you everything now, but yes, I'm with him and yes, I love you for making me take this trip."

"That's good," she says. But there's no enthusiasm in her voice. Something is wrong.

"Jas, are you all right?"

"Yeah, man. It's just that Asaji . . ."

"Oh Lord. What did he do now?"

"He's been in this studio all day. I've been here too, but we haven't really gotten much time alone."

"I'm sorry, girl. But think of it this way . . . your man is trying to get paid, okay? He's doing this for him, but also for you. You know it will pay off, right?"

"It better. Hold on a sec, Lia," she says. I can hear her talking in the background; then a guy picks up.

"Hello, Lia?"

"Is this Asaji?" I ask.

"Yeah. Yo, I'm gonna take care of ya girl right now, a'ight? We're leavin' the studio and I'm takin' her out and you probably won't see her for the rest of the evening, a'ight?"

"Okay," I say, laughing. "Remind her that our flight leaves at three p.m., so meet me at the hotel around one or one thirty."

"A'ight, Ma. Peace."

Well, at least now I know Jas isn't sitting around somewhere still pissed off. Not that it would have ruined my mood . . . because guess what? I'm about to go upstairs and fuck the shit out of Ty. He'll be so hooked on what I got that he'll curse the day he ever met Simone. I'm so gonna put it on him. After riding the elevator to the eighth floor, I get to his door and knock, knowing that everything I want is on the other side. My dad must be up in heaven making sure they treat me right down here, because I really feel like God came through for me on this one. There's always the chance that Ty and I won't make it, but you better believe I'm going to fight to keep this one.

Chapter 32

Dee Dee

One year later

"Deidre, baby! Come eat lunch," I yell as I put the applesauce back in the refrigerator. She comes running into the kitchen with a huge grin on her face. "Were you in there making a mess?" I ask as I pick her up and kiss her cheeks.

"No, Mommy," she says sweetly. Yeah, right. She has body lotion all over her hands and clothes. I am going into my bedroom to work damage control when the phone rings.

"Hello," I say.

"Dee Dee." It's Deron.

My heart skips a beat. It's been one full year since the divorce. One year of my life that's thankfully over. It's been a hard transition, but it gets easier day by day. He knows

I'm still in love with him, and he still loves me. But the trust . . . it's gone. And I understand, but it still hurts. Deeply. He was there when Deron Jr. was born, and he takes excellent care of the kids. But he can't take care of my heart.

"Deron! I miss you. What's going on?"

"Book signings and tours. And they're talking about turning my book into a feature film. My agent is in a meeting now."

"I don't know what to say. That's great."

"Yeah. How's my baby girl and DJ?"

"They're both fine. They miss you too. When are you coming over?"

"I'll be there to see them soon. Next week."

"Oh. I was hoping that maybe you'd be able to come with me to the engagement party. I left you a message. . . ."

"Yeah, well, I don't think I'll be able to make it. Send her my best, though."

"I will." I get quiet for a few seconds. I can feel that he's about to end the conversation and I don't know how to hold on. I guess that's why we're not together now.

"Um, have the checks been enough? I put another one in the mail yesterday."

"We're fine with money, Deron."

"Good. Okay, well, I just called to check in. I should go," he says.

No . . . you always go. This time stay. Please. "Hey, I love you."

"I know, Dee. Bye."

Unfortunately, most of our conversations end up like this. There's still a part of me that believes that even though we are divorced, it's not over. There is a reason that he hasn't dated anyone else, and it's not just because of work. So many things are going on, but at the same time, so little.

The next evening after I put the kids to bed I grab the prerelease, unedited version of Deron's latest novel from my nightstand. I've been reading it almost nonstop since it arrived in the mail earlier today. He's so talented it scares me sometimes. I am munching on some Oreos and turning the pages when someone knocks on the door. It's a little late, so I'm surprised anyone would be coming by.

"Who is it?" I ask through the door.

"Me." And he doesn't have to say another syllable. I open the door to see Deron standing there with an overnight bag.

"I thought you were coming next week," I say, trying to hold in my excitement.

"I miss my kids," he says. I know he didn't come here for me, but he came here. It's something.

"They're sleeping."

"Oh. Did I interrupt something?"

"No. I was just reading your book. Deron, it's so good."

"Thanks."

There goes that loud, intrusive silence again.

"How long are you staying?" I ask as I take his bag from his hand.

He gives it to me hesitantly. "Only a few days. I should really get a hotel—"

"No! I mean, it's fine. You can sleep here. I don't mind." Silence again.

"I had a long drive. I think I'm going to turn in now," he says.

"Okay. Good night." This is the epitome of the word *estranged*. We can be two feet away from each other or miles away and it's the same damn feeling. I start reading again and don't even realize how an hour passes. I'm so wrapped up in the book that I jump when I hear Deron's voice.

"Dee, you think you'll be reading for much longer? I can tell you how it ends," he says with a grin.

"Don't do it," I say. "But I don't know, why do you ask?"

"Just wondering when you'll be coming to bed."

And this time the silence isn't deafening. It's soothing and calm. Like the eye of the storm. But is the worst really over? Is he really reaching out to me?

"You want me to come to bed with you?"

He shrugs his shoulders. I put the book down and go over to him. "Do you want me to come to bed with you?" I ask again.

"Yes. I think I do." He puts his arm around my waist and squeezes me tightly. The first hug in over a year. And now it's time for the first kiss. I look at him for a split second before closing my eyes and putting my lips on his. I half expect him to pull away, but he doesn't. He kisses me back. Over and over. When I finally pull away, it's like . . . everything that has happened between us has been re-placed by what just happened now. I almost don't want to speak for fear of ruining the moment.

"Dee, this doesn't mean—" he starts, but I stop him.

"Shh, I know. I'm not your wife anymore. You're not my husband. But can't we just have this one night?"

He nods his head and leads me into the bedroom, where we make love for hours. It's slow and soft, just how I like it. When we finally finish, he lies next to me for a few minutes before getting up.

"What's wrong, Deron? Where are you going?"

He looks at me with heavy eyes. "A hotel. I'll be back in the morning to see the kids."

"But, Deron, we just . . . You don't have to go." I'm beg-ging for him to stay all over again.

"Dee, I made a mistake. We made a mistake. God, I know in my heart that this is over. I don't want to get back to-gether, okay? I'm sorry." He walks out of the bedroom and I hear the front door slam shut a few seconds after. I cry softly, but intensely. He finally set me free. This entire year I've been holding on to shreds of optimism that he gave me about this relationship, thinking that there was a chance. While all along there wasn't. I can move on, once and for all. How to move on, is another question. But at least I know that I gave my all to make everything right again . . . but as it turns out, it would never have been enough. I can be at peace with that . . . because I can never give more than what I have.

Chapter 33

Rena

"Tak, it's your turn," I say groggily as I pull the covers over my head. It's three in the morning and the baby is wailing again.

"Okay, baby. One minute," he says. But I know he doesn't mean it.

"Now, Tak, before she wakes up Lion."

He then gets out of bed and walks over to her crib.

"Shh, Sahara," he says quietly while he rocks her in his arms. I try to fall asleep again, but I know it won't happen right away. I lie in bed, waiting for Tak to calm Sahara down so he can come hold me. A few minutes later she's sleeping again and Tak is back in bed. He cuddles up to me and squeezes me tightly.

"Even though she's a loud one she's the most beautiful gift you've ever given me," he says softly in my ear. All these months later I still hate when he says things like that. I may have reconciled with the fact that Sahara's not his biological daughter, but it still hurts to carry this huge lie. I made the decision to tell Tak that I was pregnant with his child not for myself, but for everyone else who would be affected. Lace, who I haven't spoken to since that day he called me and said that I should be tested, most likely did not want to be a father. He and I are not together, and I'm sure he has many other interests that he would like to focus on. If I had told Tak the truth, it would have devastated our entire family. I couldn't do that to my son or my daughter. I believe everyone's life is better this way. I gave her the name Sahara so that she would have something besides DNA from her father. Since that's the name Lace gave to me when we first met, I decided to give it to her. I'm the only one who knows about Sahara's paternity. I didn't even tell Lia or Jas. I'm not ashamed of what I've done; I just want to be sure that the truth never comes out.

"Rena, wake up, baby," Tak whispers in my ear. I open my eyes and glance at my clock. It's twelve already? I never sleep that late.

"I don't know why I slept for so many hours. I'm usually up by nine," I say as I stumble out of bed.

"Relax, Rena. You had a long night."

"I know the kids are up. Did they eat yet?"

"We're going out to lunch today. Get dressed. We're all waiting on you."

"Out to lunch? That's sweet of you, Tak," I say. I try to give him a kiss, but he pushes me back.

"Nothing sweet about that breath, baby," he says, grinning. I give him a playful slap on the arm and go to the bathroom to get ready. Half an hour later we're on our way to Midtown to eat at one of my favorite restaurants, Houston's.

"Lion, could you wipe your sister's mouth please? She's spitting up again." Ever since Sahara was born Lion has really taken on the role of big brother. He's very protective of her already. Once we get to the restaurant and settled into our seats, our waiter comes to take our drink orders and we start to look over the menu.

"So, Rena, are we sticking to the Valentine's Day wedding? I think we've changed it fifty times."

"Yes. Valentine's Day. Unless you want something different," I reply.

"No, I just need to know something final so my family can get their travel plans arranged." Actually, Tak and I are already married. We just didn't have a wedding. A few months after I told him I was pregnant we went down to the courthouse and made it official. But we still wanted to have a ceremony for our families and friends.

"Am I still the best man?" Lion asks his father.

"You're the best man I know," Tak says.

"Is Sahara gonna be old enough to be anything?" Lion asks, looking at his little sister.

"No, but she'll be watching her big brother," I say. "Speaking of weddings, Tak, don't forget we're going to the engagement party tomorrow."

"Oh yeah. It's still a trip that she's getting married."

"He's good for her and she's so happy. I'm proud of her," I say. After we order and our food arrives, we talk a little more about the wedding and school and moving into a house next year.

"Can we get a basketball hoop at the new house?" Lion asks between bites of his french fries.

"Sure we can, sweetie," I say.

"Hey, I'm going to the restroom," Tak says. "You need to go too, Lion?"

"Yeah." As the two of them leave the table I take Sahara out of the high chair and sit her on my lap.

"Rena?" Someone calls my name from behind. I turn

around and see Lace walking toward me with another guy. "Rena! It's been, like, what? A year?"

Lace stops abuptly and looks down at the baby I'm holding, studying her eyes, her nose, her mouth. His eyes widen before he looks at me again. "She's very beautiful," he says finally.

"Thank you, Lace," I say nervously. "How have you been?"

"Great. Um, Rena, this is Desmond, my friend." Desmond sucks his teeth at Lace. "I mean my boyfriend."

"Nice to meet you, Desmond."

"Likewise," he says, still looking at Lace with a glare.

"I guess a lot has changed since the last time we spoke," Lace says.

"I guess so." Tak and Lion return to the table as I finish my words. "Tak, this is Lace, an old friend of mine, and his friend Desmond."

"How's it goin'?" Tak says, shaking their hands. "This is our son, Lion, and you already met Sahara."

"Sahara. Like the desert," Lace says. He looks at me intently. I can tell that everything is beginning to register in his mind. He looks troubled, yet grateful at the same time.

"We should get to our table, Lace," Desmond says.

"Yeah. It was nice seeing you, Rena . . . and meeting your family."

"It was good to see you too," I say, my heart beating fervently.

"How do you know him?" Tak asks me as the couple walks away.

"Uh, we met at the poetry spot a long time ago."

"Oh. He's gay?"

"Yeah, looks that way," I say, taking a long sip of my lemonade.

"What's gay mean?" asks Lion.

"We'll talk about it later, sweetie," I say. "Are you guys ready to go?"

"Yeah. You guys can go to the car while I pay the bill."

I get the kids and have started walking out when Lace runs up to me and grabs my arm.

"I just need to know, Serena," he says desperately. I don't want to answer him. He already knows in his heart. "You don't even have to say the words," he pleads. I look down at my daughter and nod my head. I know I'm taking a big risk by telling him that Sahara is his daughter. But I just couldn't look him in the eye and say no when it's so obvious to him that she is.

Later that evening Tak and I are watching TV together; he's massaging my feet. I'm halfway falling asleep when . . .

"Were you ever involved with Lace?"

"Involved?"

"Yeah. Did you date him or something?"

I don't know where this is coming from, but I don't plan to let it get too far.

"No. We were just friends," I say shortly.

"It's just that he looked at you like . . . the two of you had some sort of connection. He was talking to you with words, but more so with his eyes."

"Tak, you're reading way too much into it. We just hadn't seen each other in a long time."

"And he seemed really interested in Sahara—"

"Oh my God, stop! Just drop it, Tak," I say, pulling my feet away from him and sitting up. My hands are shaking, so I put them under my lap.

"Relax, baby. Don't get so uptight about it."

"I'm not uptight. I just don't get why you're bringing him up."

"He came off as a little odd, that's all."

"Well, that's just his personality."

"Okay, damn," he says. I was really getting annoyed

with Tak's curiosity with Lace. The longer he keeps Lace in the back of his mind, the more uncomfortable it makes me feel.

"I'm going to bed," he says a few minutes later. I continue to sit in front of the television, still uneasy about Tak's concern with Lace. Is he suddenly getting suspicious? Or has he always had doubts? Or maybe it's neither and I'm blowing it all out of proportion.

I turn off the TV and join Tak in bed. He immediately turns over and wraps his strong arms around me.

"You know, Rena, I love you no matter what. I don't have any regrets. I hope you don't either."

"Regrets?"

"Yeah. Don't second-guess yourself," he says.

I'm a little confused because I don't know where all this is coming from. "Okay. I won't."

He kisses my neck before dozing off. And it's true. I don't have any regrets. I'll never know if Tak was referring to Sahara, because neither of us will ever mention it. She is his baby girl . . . always. And I don't regret having her, or choosing him to be her father. I don't regret doing what was necessary to keep my family together. Life is a series of decisions and outcomes. Everything is a means to an end. Problems only occur when we overanalyze the stuff in between. No . . . I don't have any regrets.

Chapter 34

Jas

"What about this one, Miss. Lewis?"

"You can put it right over there, next to the window," I say, pointing. The delivery guys are setting up the new furniture I ordered last week. I'm still waiting for the decorator to get here so we can start discussing plans for the dining room. Even though I just moved in a month ago, this place really feels like home. After Asaji got signed to Def Jam on a twenty-million-dollar contract, everything started happening so fast. His first CD is already platinum and it's only been out for two months. Our lives have been going nonstop since then. First he bought us this beautiful home and told me to do whatever I want with it. Then he bought me my first car, a brand-new pecan-colored Jag. But hard as it is to believe, money hasn't changed anything about who he is or who I am. I mean, yeah, we have nicer things but I still hang out with the same people, party at the same clubs . . . and Asaji is as laid-back as ever. As for myself, I sold some of my work to a few different artists. A couple of them are up and coming and have said that my sound is pretty dope and fresh so they really wanted to make their debut with my music behind them. Speaking of Asaji, I need to call him to tell him what time we have to leave for the party tonight.

"Hey, baby. Are you busy?"

"Nah, just meeting with the accountant. Is something wrong?" he asks.

"No, everything is fine."

"Did the furniture get there yet?"

"Yes. It looks so good. You're gonna like it."

"I know. My baby has excellent taste."

"Yeah, I do. It's going to look really nice once we get the walls painted that burnt-orange color that I love. But you're getting me off track, Asaji. I was calling to tell you that we should probably be at the hotel around six."

"But the party's not even until seven thirty."

"Well, don't you think *we* should at least get there a little early?"

"Yeah, I guess. A'ight, baby. Could you pick up something for me to wear if you don't find anything in the closet?"

"Okay. Done," I say.

"I'll be home at about five. Love you."

"Love you, baby."

Asaji's not really into the whole engagement party idea, but he's going along with it for me. I don't get to see my girls as much as I'd like because everyone is extra busy these days, so tonight will really be special for all of us.

I go upstairs and rummage through Asaji's closet looking for something suave, but not too dressy. Once I figure out what I want him to wear, I pick out my outfit. I have this gorgeous cocoa-colored dress by Carolina Herrera but no shoes to go with it. I have, like, three hundred pairs of shoes, but one more won't hurt.

When I'm on my way to Fifth Avenue my cell rings. It's an 803 number . . . that's South Carolina. But I don't recognize it.

"Hello?"

"Jasmine?"

"Yes. Who is this?"

"Rod . . . from high school," the voice replies. You gotta be fuckin' kidding me. What are the chances of this guy calling me?

"Roderick?" I ask, just to be sure this isn't some glitch in the matrix.

"Yeah. Your mom gave me your number. I hope you don't mind. I hear you're dating that rapper now?"

I almost hang up. I mean, what could he possibly have to say to me after all these years? Is this some kind of mind trip? I can feel my fingertips reaching for the End Call button on my phone, but I stop myself. I have no reason to run anymore.

"What do you want?" I ask semiharshly.

"I just wanted to check up on you. It's been a long time," he says, totally blasé. Check up on me? Why is he speaking like nothing happened? Did he fuckin' forget?

"Rod, I don't understand what you're calling me for."

"Look, I know we had one messed-up night, Jasmine. But damn, why can't you get over it? We were kids," he says flippantly.

"One messed-up night? Get over it? Nigga, you raped me!" I stop walking and notice people around me looking at me funny. But I don't care. I have to let this loser know the truth. "You used me and hurt me and stole something that I can't get back. But you didn't break me, Rod. I need you to know that. You didn't break me."

"You're crazy. Ain't nobody raped your ass. I did not rape you!"

I've often dreamed about the opportunity to confront Rod in person about what he did. To tell him that even though he's a perverted bastard, I'm okay. And I was going to make him admit what he did and apologize to me. But now I realize that I don't need that. He can remain in denial about it for the rest of his life. I really am okay. My life is wonderful. And the more he blows it off, the stronger I'll become.

"Roderick, it was good to hear from you. Hope your life is everything you deserve it to be . . . and that's not much. I have to go now. Lose my number." I exhale deeply as I hang up. I feel like I have complete closure now. The rape was the one loose end of my life that needed to be tied. And now it has been. Maybe it didn't happen the way I imagined, but it happened. God allowed Roderick to call me because he knew I was ready to face it once and for all. And ya know what, I was ready.

After an hour or two of shopping and finding just the right heels, I start making my way back home. Asaji's already there and dressed when I walk in the door.

"Damn, baby, I thought I was gonna have to pin you down and force you to wear that," I say, putting down my bags.

"Nah, it's cool. I like it. And I love this dress you're gonna put on. You tryin' to be a showstopper tonight or somethin'?"

"Hardly. But these shoes may do it. Check these out, baby," I say, pulling the shoes out of the box. "Exclusives right here."

"Whoa, Jas. Now, those are hot. Is that feathers around the ankle?"

"Yep," I say, sliding one onto my foot.

"How 'bout we skip the party and me, you, and the shoes kick it here in the bedroom instead?"

"Just the shoes?" I ask seductively.

"You don't need on nothin' else," he replies.

"Asaji, you know we can't do that. And I need to start getting ready, so back it up." I push him off me and go into the bathroom to get dressed.

When 6:15 rolls around, Asaji and I are walking into the Waldorf. I run into Gina, the party coordinator, and ask her if any of the girls have arrived yet.

"No, we're still setting up. Why'd you come so early?" Gina asks, looking over her clipboard.

"Thought maybe you'd need some help or something," I say.

"Oh no, we're fine. We have it all under control. You guys just need to enjoy yourselves. There's champagne if you like."

"We'll wait, thanks," I tell her.

Asaji pokes me with his elbow. "I told you, baby. We're here too damn early."

"It's not a big deal. Tell me what happened with the accountant."

"Not much. Went over a few numbers. If the negotiating goes right I may be doing that Adidas endorsement."

"Okay, good. You wear Adidas, don't you?"

"I have a couple pairs," he says.

"I hope you get it. That'll be some nice money."

"What you worried 'bout money for? We're good for a long time without this sneaker thing."

"I know, I'm not worried. But the more exposure you get, the better for your career," I say just as I see Rena and Tak.

"Jas, you look so pretty." Rena approaches us with Tak by her side. She has on a gorgeous, ocean-blue dress.

"Thank you, so do you. Damn, it's been weeks since we've seen each other. How's the baby?"

"Fine. Getting so big so fast. Hello, Asaji."

"Hi, Rena," Asaji says. "Tak, you wanna grab a beer, man?"

"Yeah, man. Jas, you're looking good," Tak says as the two of them walk off.

"Is Lia here yet?"

"Hell no. And she is the main one always bitchin' about being on time," I say. "What'd you and Tak get her?"

"Some African artwork."

"Nice. I didn't know what to get her, so I just put a couple thousand on a gift card for Nordstrom. Is that tacky?"

"No. I'm sure she'll put it to use," Rena says.

"Do you know exactly when she's moving to Chicago for good?"

"I think by the beginning of next year . . . January, I want to say."

"It'll be weird not having her in New York. Lia practically is New York. And now she's moving away to play wifey."

"All of us are playing wifey now, though. You and Asaji may not be married . . . yet. But you guys live as husband and wife. I'm just glad everything worked out for her and Ty."

As I hear Rena speak I realize that everything worked out for all of us. Last year was rough. Very rough. I almost lost my sanity. But I gained so much at the same time. I know I've grown. I found true love. I followed my heart instead of my wallet and ended with more than I could ever need. And I came to understand myself in a way that I didn't know I could. And now here I am at the engagement party of one of my closest friends, who is marrying a man she wouldn't even look twice at a year ago. Just goes to show you that life and love will happen with or without you. You can either let it fly by you or grab a seat and go along for the ride. And from now on, I'm ridin'.

Chapter 35

Lia

Why am I running late to my own engagement party? Because when I got out of the shower Ty was standing there, ready to throw me on the bed and make me scream his name. And he did. So now we're about forty minutes late and I know everyone is wondering what the hell is going on.

"Lia, hurry up," he says while looking in the mirror at his outfit, an expertly tailored, smoke-colored Ralph Lauren suit.

"Don't try to rush me now. You weren't worried about me getting dressed when you had my legs in the air," I say while I apply my mascara. He laughs.

"You're right. Take your time," he says, grinning.

A little while later we're at the hotel and Gina comes

running over to me looking a little bit angry. Okay, very angry.

"I've been calling and calling. Some people were getting impatient," she says with her hand on her Donna Karan–clad hip.

"Yeah, like us." I turn around and see Jas and Rena.

"Give me a hug, punk," says Jas.

"Where's Dee?" I ask. They look at me, then each other. Uh-oh.

"You know she wanted to be here, but she called me last night after Deron stopped by," Rena says.

"Oh . . . what happened?" I ask nervously.

"She's really going through it. She and the kids are at her parents' house on Long Island. She said she's not feeling well at all and looks like hell from crying all night. She didn't want you to be distracted from your night by worrying about her. She's sorry she couldn't make it."

"Damn, I wish she would have called me. I feel bad for not being there for her," I say, feeling a little guilty about my engagement when my friend is dealing with divorce.

"She knew you had this to do today and she didn't want to get you sidetracked. She's not selfish like me, 'cause I would have called your ass and had you on the phone with me all night," Jas says. "But as it turns out you're late anyway."

"Lia, your mother is so upset with you," Rena says.

"I bet she is. But it's not my fault, I promise," I say, glancing at Ty.

"How're you doing?" Ty says as he hugs my two friends.

"It's great to see you again, Ty. Even though you're taking my best friend away from me," Jas says.

"Okay, this is really cute, but we have to announce that you two have finally arrived. Come on," Gina says, leading us into the reception room. Once we walk in and everyone notices us, they stand and give us a round of applause. I spot Maya-Lin and Jonathan, my mother, and some of my associates from work. It's kind of surreal to be here right now. After my little trip to Chicago and we decided to be exclusive, we actually took things kind of slow. But our trips back and forth to see each other started occurring more and more often. It's like we couldn't get enough of each other. To make a long story short, he proposed to me on one of his New York visits after we saw *The Color Purple* on Broadway. He took me to get after-theater drinks and dessert and there was a three-and-a-half-carat princess-cut diamond ring in the whipped cream on my cheesecake. I can't even describe how I felt at that moment. It was so right. Everything about it was perfect. The timing, the ring, his words . . . it was all so right. Anyway, we decided that I would move to Chicago. At first everyone thought I was crazy to leave my career at Virgin. But the truth is, I've accomplished all that I want to in my field. I've obtained the success that I worked for so many years . . . to the point of rejecting other successes that I want as well. I passed up the chance to have a family before because of my commitment to my job. This time my heart is calling the shots.

"Okay, before we bring out the food I need you to say a few words to the guests. You know, just a little something," Gina tells me in a rushed tone. She's a great party planner, but if she gives me one more damn order . . .

"Hello, everyone," I say as the noise dies down. "Ty and I would just like to thank all of you for joining us this evening to celebrate our engagement announcement. We really love and appreciate all of you. And I just want to give a special thank-you to my mother, my sister, and of course my best friends, Rena and Jas. I hope you all enjoy yourselves."

The servers start bringing in the food and Ty and I take a seat at our table after I go and say hello to my mother and Maya-Lin and her husband.

"So, Lia, are you really ready to let this man take you off to Chicago and turn you into a Mrs. Cleaver?" Jas asks with a smirk on her face.

"I think that's your new name, sweetie," I reply. "But yeah, I am ready to be a wife and a mother soon. I guess I just reached that point."

"I knew it would happen. I mean, I knew Ty would be the one," Rena says matter-of-factly.

"Oh, really? How so?" Ty asks.

"Because you couldn't shut up about her," she says. "I remember you went on and on."

"Like you did with Tak, right?" he says. We all get a few laughs in before the Cornish hens are brought to the table.

"You think you're going to miss New York, Lia?" Jas asks.

"Of course. After living here it's, like, where else can you go?"

"I know. But Tak and I will probably move to Long Island next year," Rena says.

"What? All my babies are leavin' me," Jas says in a whiny voice.

"I'm sure you and Asaji will be out of the city at some point too, Jas."

"I doubt it, right, baby?" Jas says, looking at her man. "I love our new place. I don't want to leave any time soon."

"I feel you, Jas," I say. And I really do. She's living the life of her dreams. All she wanted was a rich man to take care of her forever. Well, now she has that. And the bonus is that he is completely in love with her. It's not about sex or lies or pretenses. It's about Jas and who she is. He sees who she is and loves her because of it. Jas has turned into this beautiful, mature woman and I can finally see what has been hiding behind that sexually out-of-control girl. Rena, who has always been who I considered the most stable, has come full circle with Tak. They went through a lot, and I know she had to go on her own journey to come back to where she wanted to be all along. Now she has another adorable child to make her family complete. And me, I've had my eyes opened . . . wide. I guess we all had that one moment where our life flashes in front of us and it's either put up or shut up, do or die, and get your shit together. A lot of times people don't want to accept responsibility for what happens in their lives. But hopefully you learn how to do that before it's too late.

The next few months involve Ty flying back and forth between New York and Chicago and me trying to take care of some loose ends before I finally resign from my position at Virgin. But tonight is the last night the girls and I are going to have together for who knows how long, so nothing else has my attention. When I get to our spot I decide to wait for them outside. I look around at all the hustle and bustle and feel the brisk air, and take it all in. I breathe in the city and the life that it possesses. Soon I will not be living here anymore, but NYC will always be home.

"Hey, Lia," Jas says as she gives me a hug. "This feels funny, right? The last time we'll hang out like this for a while."

"I know. I was just absorbing the moment. Let's go in and wait for Rena and Dee. It's cold out here."

We go inside and sit at a table next to the stage. I take off my black leather jacket and hang it on the back of my seat. Jas lays her white faux-rabbit-fur coat on the seat next to her.

"We've had so many good times here, ya know," she says after ordering a double shot of brandy.

"Yeah, we have," I say. "But you're talking like we'll never see each other again. I'll be back for Rena's wedding in February. And Ty and I are getting married in the spring. It'll be like we still live in the same city."

"Except that we won't. I know you guys are probably sick of me goin' on about it, but other than the three of you

I don't have any real friends. And you've been tight with me since I moved to New York."

"I did decountrify your ass, didn't I?" I say teasingly. "Introduced you to Jimmy and Manolo."

She laughs. "See what I mean? What am I gonna do when you leave?" Just as she finishes talking, Rena and Dee Dee walk over and take a seat.

"Sorry, but Sahara spit up all over me and I had to change," she says while she flags down a waiter. She looks very pretty in all black. Her dreadlocks are pinned up in an intricate bun.

"That's so funny. DJ did the same thing. Except his came out the back and front," Dee says with a laugh while fixing the collar of her champagne-colored blouse.

"This is what you're leaving me for, Lia. A life of baby puke and poop," Jas says, sucking her teeth.

"Jas, you probably won't even notice I'm gone. You have all these things happening with Asaji. You'll stay busy."

"Yeah, Asaji is a full-time job," she says, sipping her drink.

"Any man is a full-time job," says Rena. We all laugh in agreement.

"Okay, serious question," I begin, leaning into the table like I'm about to drop a bomb. "Are you happy?" I look at the expressions of my friends after I ask the question and see different things on each of their faces.

"Well, yeah, I am," Jas says. "I look back at who I was and everything that's happened. How can I not be happy? My boyfriend is a fuckin' millionaire. I'm in love. My whole identity has changed. Happy doesn't begin to describe how I feel."

"Wow. That's good, Jas," I say genuinely. "What about you, Dee?"

"Am I happy? I'm better, I can say that. I'm my own person. I'm learning more about myself as each day passes, and the more I learn, the more I like. Yeah, the divorce was a struggle, but it has helped me grow and given me so much to be thankful for so that one day I can say that I'm happy."

"Damn. If a divorce can do all that for you, then just imagine what a marriage will do, Lia," Jas says. We all get a good laugh in before Rena answers the question.

"Happiness is a state of mind, not a state of being," she begins. Leave it to Rena to turn it into something too deep. "I'm not happy because of my circumstances, I'm happy because I'm choosing to embrace them. Even though it seems that my life is going well, I still have many issues I'm dealing with. There are things that could blow up in my face at any minute and send my life spinning into chaos."

"Damn, Rena. What the hell is going on with you?" I ask, looking at Dee and Jas to see if they're as confused as I am.

"The point is, none of it matters as long as I make the decision and the effort to maintain my happiness," she finishes.

"Preach on, sista," Jas says while laughing. "Okay, your turn, Lia."

I pause for a few seconds before I speak. "You know, for a long time I would never describe myself as being happy, ever. To me claiming to be happy meant there was no room for improvement. People would ask me, and I'd say that I was content, but never happy. The word *happy* was just putting it over the top."

"The point, Lia," Jas says with an exaggerated sigh as Dee and Rena giggle at her.

"Okay, ass," I say to her. "The point is that I had to reach a new understanding. Saying that I'm happy isn't saying that everything is perfect. It's saying that I have a reason to smile."

"Aw, Hallmark is hiring, ya know," Jas says. We all laugh while we finish our drinks.

"I should probably get home," Dee says. "Babysitters aren't charging five dollars an hour anymore, you know?"

"Yeah, me too," says Rena. "I promised Lion I'd read to him before he went to bed."

"Yeah, you guys should get home with those babies at the house. Well, I'm going to miss you guys," I say as I stand to hug them. "If you need anything you better let me know."

"I'm going to miss you too, Lia. You have a safe trip and keep Ty in line," Rena says.

"You know I will," I say. "And I'll see both of you in February for the wedding."

"Okay. Love you, Lia," Dee says as she and Rena start walking away from the table.

"Love you too, girl."

Once they leave the table it's just Jas and me. I look at my best girlfriend and smile as I think about all the drama of the past year and how she's been there through it all. I think about how she's grown so much and changed in ways that have made her so much more beautiful as a person. I can tell she's a little apprehensive about the next words that will come out of our mouths . . . she knows it will be good-bye. That's probably why she's looking around the bar, trying not to focus on the moment.

"You ready?" she asks after her eyes finally meet mine.

"Yeah. You know I'll call you as soon as I get there," I say, hoping she doesn't cry. Because I know if she will, I don't stand a chance.

"I know," she says, looking away again and glancing down at her French-manicured nails.

"And you'll meet all kinds of people. You have Asaji to take you to all the hot parties now," I continue. I'm convincing her, but also reminding myself that I'm not abandoning my girl.

"True. I'll be okay," she says softly.

"So much more than okay, Jas. You're my girl! You are so beautiful and just . . ." I stop because I can feel the tears coming and I really don't want to turn this into a show.

"Girl, please don't," Jas says with a smile while dabbing the corners of her eyes with her fingertips.

"I'm not, I'm not. But let me just say this last thing. I know I have Maya-Lin in my life now, but you have always been and will always be my baby sister."

"Believe me, I know," she says, this time not bothering to prevent the few tears falling down her cheek. We give each other a long hug before saying good-bye for the last time.

I get home and Ty is on the bed, the last piece of furniture in my house, looking over some paperwork.

"How was it?" he asks as I walk over to him, dropping my Hermes bag on the floor before I lie next to him. He looks so sexy even though he just has on a white T-shirt and sweatpants. Reminds me of the first time I saw him in the fitness room. God, I never would have thought for a second that I'd end up here. Life is funny like that. So is love.

"Nice. A little hard with Jas. But when it was all said and done, we were okay." I place my head on his strong shoulder and he puts his arm around me. "What if it doesn't work, Ty?" I ask. And I realize that it's so random for this to pop into my head, but the truth is, it scares me. I love Ty with everything in me. I know I want to be his wife. But what if? I could be wrong about the whole thing.

"What? Us?" he asks, a little confused.

"Yeah. We haven't lived together before, maybe a week at the most. What if it doesn't work?"

"Lia, we can handle each other. Don't worry about it," he says confidently before kissing me on the forehead. But is he too confident? I find it hard to believe that he's just a hundred percent sure about this move. I mean, he's a guy after all. They're supposed to get cold feet.

"Are you sure? You don't have any doubts?"

"Nope. No doubts. Don't get me wrong, baby. I have thought about all the possibilities. I know that there could be many different endings to our story. But this is what I want to do. And I know it's what you want too."

"You're right. I do," I say, thankful that he said what he just said.

"Save that for the wedding," he says, chuckling. He pushes his papers aside and holds me close. "I love you so much, Lia."

"I love you too, Ty."

And I can really say I'm happy. Finally. From now on.